Robert Cok
Chasing I

If thou of fortune
be bereft,
And of thine earthly stores
hath left,
Two loaves, sell one, and with the
Buy hyacinths to feed the soul.

Chasing Dragons
1507892578

"On the bank of the river he saw a tall tree: from roots
To crown one half was aflame and the other green with leaves."
'Peredur' (p.243)

PART I

Prologue

A storm has shattered the sky not so long ago, its purple clouds are still visible in the distance. The ground is a maze of puddles trying desperately to evaporate in the already waterlogged climate, it's a lively state of affairs. If you look closely you can see it, an almost invisible waft of over-humidified air just above the ground. It's quite pretty really. It swirls, infinitesimally thin, light as any vapour, revelling in the dance as a breeze from a running foot spills the air to the side. It's very rude, but then someone must be in a hurry. No-one likes to be outside when it's like this.

Chapter One

The humidity had been building for days, the tropical nature of which had brought all manner of weathers. In the past week alone there had been morning mists, followed closely by torrential downpours and scorching heat. This recent renting of the sky however was particularly brutal and had been expected to break the tail of the suffersome heat. Lightning had flashed in great sheets across the Earths' roof, and rain had thrashed the ground for fully nine hours.

For a while the precipitation had drowned the stagnant day. But just as quickly as it had left the damp pressure had returned, once again forcing the city to its knees. The lightning had instantly dispelled the static in the air however and the sultry atmosphere would now have a battle on its hands if it wanted to stay for much longer. Of course with summers like this, who could predict the way the climate would swing.

A street light flickers in the haze of dusk, the buzz of electricity seeming to people the heavy air with excitement as the humid heat of the day slowly turns to the suffocating heat of the night. A few misguided moths flutter in a futile way around the lights' head as if they're waiting for something, the bright fluorescence providing nourishment for their alien bodies. The light gives a final flicker before falling to the temptations of sleep.

Men will arrive in a few days and then the struggle will begin once more, but for now a gentle sombreness transcends.

Heat pushes the focus down, sliding slowly across the body of the streetlight until it reaches the grass at the bottom. What used to be grass. Now there's nothing left but coarse, broken twigs. It's quite disheartening. Once fresh and new green shoots grew here, now broken glass lies in its dried and thorny shadow, water collecting in the upturned basins.

In the darkness that surrounds this place the buzz of blue fire can still be heard, rattling through transistors and capacitors. Speedily, hungrily it makes its way. Coursing, rushing, always taking the path of least resistance. Nothing can stop the flow of energy! Finally it reaches the streetlight, and realising that there's nothing there rushes on, heedless of its wasted journey. Sparks cascade along copper wiring. The searing heat contained within makes the heat of the night pale in comparison. Finally, an outlet is found, a release, a way to freedom, a vent for the pent up energy.

Click.

Charlie fumbled nervously with the light switch, and gave the door behind him a sharp shove to slam it. A single bulb swung gently on its cable, a calm juxtaposition to Charlie's obvious excitement. Energetically he threw himself onto the floor, his jeans rucking up at the legs as he skidded onto the wood. There wasn't much in this room, he didn't need much just the various paraphernalia of his habit. Grinning the young man fished a clump of cling-film from the side of his trainer and emptied its meagre contents onto the flat surface of a world atlas. On the outside the bag was damp with sweat from his sodden socks but the contents inside were wonderfully hard and dry. It cracks, breaks, large chunks coming off.

Charlie's brow furrowed in concentration as he chopped, the sandy coloured drug before him breaking easily into powder under his knife. Soon a good portion of China was obscured, although Charlie was far too excited to consider the significance of this. Why hadn't he got more? He knew it wouldn't be long before he needed another hit. Even *dumbers* would do at a push. It wouldn't scratch the itch in *quite* the same way but it would certainly help. *Anything* to numb the painful existence that he currently occupied. Not that it was *that* bad. But if he couldn't get scag then he needed *something* to take his mind from his nightmares. To keep the wolves at bay. A life in habit can give you a *lot* of nightmares.

Tying a tourniquet tightly around his arm Charlie started to cook up. Heat rose onto metal. The narcotic danced in the bubbles as the water in the spoon boiled, slowly dissolving into a delicious opium rich solution. A substitution for his own imposed reality but all that he had all the same. Charlie put his lighter down, the metal spoon now hot in his hand and carefully he dipped the point of a fresh needle into the solution. Pulling back the plunger, he watched as the rough liquid was sucked invitingly into the hypodermic.

He holds the needle up to his eye and gives it a few taps to rid the fluid of any air bubbles and he places the syringe onto the floorboards beside his crossed legs. Anticipation frothing inside him he begins to smack his forearm, urging the ruined veins to come to the surface, willing them to let him desecrate them just one more time.

For a second Charlie gazed at his feet, his eyes slightly crazed against the dark wood of the floor.

"Just one more time." He said to himself quietly, and pleasure flowered through his body. Slowly he lay back, and watched as the world enveloped him.

At that same moment, Richard Cochrum was looking at his car. It was the same car he drove every day, except for one big difference, his car didn't have a wheel clamp on it.

"Dammit! Five goddamn minutes late and they clamp you!"

It had already been a bad day, and looked very much like it was going to continue along that track.

The answer phone beeped as he walked through the door to his apartment, his wallet lighter and his face dour. It was a nice apartment, tastefully decorated with a deep leather sofa and forest green on the walls. It was open plan and light but somehow didn't quite match with Cochrum. He pressed the button on the machine and turned to the sideboard to pour himself a drink.

"You have one new message. First new message:..." Cochrum waited for the machine to beep and in the meantime sloshed another healthy amount into his glass. He didn't even add ice this time, no one ever called him unless it was about work. He downed the liquor in one and listened. He knew he should've left his mobile on!

"Cochrum! If you value your job..." The voice pulled itself together, "...check into the office *now* lad." It was Sergeant Morris, for some reason the guy had always had an eye out for him. "That brown-nose Marks has taken the shout, and much as you're a bastard I'd rather you got a promotion than him. Now get your arse in gear!" There was a tone and the message was done. Cochrum was already pulling his jacket back on. He knew exactly what Morris was talking about, he'd been working this case for months now and still hadn't quite caught a break. *Everyone* was on his back... why couldn't they just cut him some slack, it wasn't as if the truth was just leaping out here. It was messed up from the start.

"Ok lads here's the surgeon, now get the hell out," three men in green run at full pelt to an ambulance, it's stood in a rank but the back doors are open and the engine is humming loudly. Two men clamber quickly into the back, one of them is carrying a

5

large green shoulder bag. The other man runs to the front. The doors slam, sirens wail.

"Eddie." Introduces the surgeon proffering a hand.

"Dan." Replies the paramedic, "That's John in the front... Hey, how far John?"

"Not far now mate, nearly there," The radio crackles over the siren, wailing fills the street, "Come in base, Tango-Niner on route to site, confirm circumstances, over."

There is silence over the radio and then... "Circumstances are as read John, you sure you guys are okay for this, you'll be the first on site."

"Don't worry Angela," replied the driver, "we're all good." He hung up the receiver and quickly pulled up on the curb. The ambulance jolted slightly as it came to a halt and the back doors flew open. Dan and Richard struggled out, each carrying a case. John was already at the door and the window, looking to see if anyone could be seen.

"There's blood on the window Dan,"

"Hello?"

"Hello, it's the ambulance service"

"Out of the way!" The door crashes in. The walls are red. The surgeon steps forward, the floor is wet, he lifts his foot...

When the paramedics had arrived at the first scene there had been no doubt in their minds that there was something more

6

sinister going on. The brutality of the killings aside there were far too many other factors and things just hadn't added up. There was so much to consider in fact that finding any kind of evidence within the mountains of material they came back with was... the mind trails off. That in itself was the problem.

When Cochrum arrived at the site there was already a healthy swarm of police milling around.

"All right Marks, what have you got so far?" he addressed a tall man in a dark brown suit, he was talking quietly to a subordinate officer and noticeably winced as he heard Cochrum speaking. Bringing himself quickly to his full height Marks turned around. His eyes flicked over Cochrum with obvious distaste and his lip curled up slightly at the side. An involuntary tick that Cochrum was sure he wasn't even conscious of. There was *tooth*. It was quite amusing.

"Not much different." Marks said eventually, careful to leave the silence just a few moments too long. His voice was full and rich and his mouth twitched slightly at the end of the sentence. "She was about twenty-ish with blonde hair. As far as we can tell from the bits we've found anyway." Cochrum grinned broadly, enjoying his peer's discomfiture and turned his head to watch the house. So this was how it was going to go was it, well if he had to work a bit in order to stay in the loop then so be it, this had been Marks shout after all and technically Cochrum was off-duty. But he

7

was still heading the investigation… well, for the time being, and he was there. Which counted for a lot in his own personal book. Unfortunately those a little further up the hierarchy were beginning to get a little impatient and Cochrum was aware that he was slowly being pushed to the side. Answers were needed and he wasn't providing them fast enough. The body count kept rising and he hoped that this time he might find that little bit extra that he needed. Cochrum was getting desperate. And worse than that his vanity and his pride were getting bruised.

The house was fairly unremarkable: a mess of a front yard, wheelie bin, white plastic front door, the kind that looks neat but is still moderately inexpensive.

"She had her jaw torn clean off." Marks broke the silence, "The right arm's been ripped off as well, we think that happened when she was thrown against the wall. There's a big splash of blood next to the door leading to the kitchen, we've got forensics on spatter analysis. Oh, and when you go in watch out for the…" He gestured, "You'll see what I mean."

"Thanks." Replied Cochrum, still staring at the house, "Don't let me keep you. I've got the investigation from here as you know but the scene is yours of course." He paused and grinned, "Oh, erm… I'm sure the Chief wants as little community exposure as possible. You know the procedure I'm sure."

Marks looked at him, his eyes hiding nothing of his loathing as he stalked off into the mess of blue uniforms and yellow tape. It was his shout but Cochrum was senior, for the time being.

Sure enough, as Cochrum walked into the house his eye was drawn indefatigably to the gore that seemed to cover every surface. How could a body contain so much? He gagged and leant heavily against the wall. It didn't matter how many you saw, you could never get used to it. The smell, the blood, the lifeless bits of flesh carelessly strewn around the room. It was just so brutal. It was primal and primitive and it scared him shitless.

Chapter Two

Charlie sat in his bedroom, the only other room in the tiny flat apart from the lounge, and scraped cack out from under his fingernails. He'd made himself a nice cup of tea and was now waiting for it to take effect.

It had been about half an hour now and the focus around Charlie's fields of perception had already started to blur. He felt the familiar knot in the top of his stomach and revelled in this small part of the experience. He pushed his mind a bit, just a bit, just to see. This was the best part, when you were aware but still unaware, and even perhaps more aware all at the same time. He looked at the wallpaper and as he did so, slowly ever so slowly he found his vision slipping out of focus. It was strange, he always thought it was strange at these times, times when things became unfocused, because as they did the world seemed to make so much more sense. The wall was a sea now, a mass of swarming insects, they dripped uncomfortably. He knew that all it was in reality was that horrible cheap stuff with the chipped wood in it to make it bumpy, but for the next eight hours he could guarantee it would be the most life changing sight he had ever seen. He sat staring silently at the wall opposite, and allowed his mind to unravel.

"He says his name's Phil sir." A short pudgy officer was addressing Marks as Cochrum walked over. He had been all around the house. Same thing as usual, no sign of a forced entry, the first mash of gore was as always nowhere near the entrance. It was as if someone had just *let the thing in*. It had then set to work on the girl and escaped through the window. Why the hell it didn't ever leave the way it had come he had no idea, especially as there would have to be some sort of handler he supposed, but the glass was always broken from the *inside*.

Phil stood to one side, a rangy twenty something year old with hollowed out eyes and a scrawny frame. He was mumbling disconcertingly to himself and was clearly 'hepped up' on something that he shouldn't be. Wasn't that what the kids said? Marks walked over.

"So Phil, what are you doing hanging round in the cupboard under the stairs?" he grinned, "Bit dusty in there?"

The scrawny kid said nothing. He was shaking all over and kept tugging on one ear. "I don't think we're gonna get much out of this one tonight," said Marks addressing the constable wearily. "Take him to the hospital an' let him sleep off whatever he's taken. We'll interview him in the morning."

"You're clutching." said Cochrum after a lengthy pause, "I can see it in your face." He smiled, "You think that kid really did all this?" He left the sentence hanging in the air and he turned briskly and strode away into the breeze.

Marks glowered at him as he walked away, in his gut he knew it was the right thing. Stupid really to rely on gut instinct.

11

And the red tape certainly wouldn't like it, but a perfectly justifiable course of action. Not that he needed to justify his actions to Cochrum in any way, not at this point, not until the chief told him otherwise.

Charlie rolled on the floor, feeling the camber that his mind was providing, and pushed his brain to the very limit. He stared into a corner, it was dark, he didn't like that and he screamed. That wasn't nice either and he looked away, childishly pushing his jaw shut with the ball of his hand. He didn't want to see that anymore and as he turned away his eyes fell on a small sheet of paper by his foot. He watched it for a while to see what it would do, then he picked it up and ran his tongue all over it, revelling in the sensations.

The Lycerin suffused his body causing the electrical impulses in his brain to skip synapses and the serotonin in his pituitary gland to bubble with corruption. Suddenly his trip took on a whole new life.

Chapter Three

Stories flood through our childhood. They swamp us and surround us, and everything in them develops a life of its own within our minds. This is how we learn and stay safe in our early years. As we grow older however, the world takes on a new dimension and for the first time we can see that the stories already had a life, one based in fact. Phil knew this, he knew all about stories, he knew all about the way they teach us lessons, teach us how to be safe. Sometimes he would watch the stories, he would see them pull together from nothing, amalgamate from the detritus of his room and he would realise where everything fitted, why the stories were there. He understood so deeply that by his very nature there existed the inevitability of the attack at the house. At least he suspected, and it saddened his heart deeply. Stories surrounded and encapsulated Phil. He'd seen his story unfold, had watched it weeks before when he'd left. It was paranoia certainly, but aside from that he felt compelled, as though the sky itself would swallow him if he didn't comply. Whether it was the *Annwn* he couldn't tell. Whether the celestial bodies felt his part in the world he had no idea but he did know that it had felt dark and that he was inexorably drawn up in it. That it would be his end and the end of many and that it was down to his hand. In some manner. Phil knew many things, not as many as some but still many. There was a darkness coming and it was because of him.

The middle-aged man that now sat at a large wooden desk in a dark and isolated room also knew these things. Most of them. He'd done his part, he'd shown the oracle his path, but he feared that what he once thought a two sided deal had been painfully misconstrued on his part. He was deep in concentration, his mind stretching itself to gaze out through decrepit eyes. He like so many others also owned the haggard and necrotic look that that was trademark in these parts. He turned the page in the big leather bound book he was reading. It was red, not in the normal sense of red but the lustrous red that shows time and wears it well. He made a small note in the margin. The pen that he was holding was almost out of ink and made a satisfying scratchy noise on the paper. His handwriting was spidery, spindly, like the doodle of a small child pretending that they could write rather than that of a grown man. He read the commentary back to himself quietly and pushed his shoulders further into the spine of his chair. His hands automatically found their way to the back of his head, his fingers combing through his hair as they went and he heaved a heavy sigh as his elbows sagged. His eyes bloodshot and half closed, he allowed his mind to go out of focus and watched the tales that began to unfold in the semi-blurred darkness. From the primitive confessions of the subconscious they all swam into view. Stories in their purest sense, not pinned down on paper, not made comfortable with age but the stories that stand behind. The creatures that lie at the root, that scream in the night as they are nailed to the page.

It was during these times that he saw what was real and what wasn't, it was during these times that the truth of the world showed itself.

The mans eyes flick back and just for a moment he thinks he sees a flicker of movement in the corner. With a turn of speed that's entirely unexpected considering his gaunt appearance he quickly grabs an iron horseshoe hidden under a pile of papers and hurls it as hard as he can. The metal clangs off the wall and rebounds onto a patch of floor a few meters from the man's feet. He peers into the shadows and smiles to himself nonchalantly before sitting back down, apparently satisfied.

"You won't get me that easily!" he flinches slightly, his ears listening for the silent scream of his tormentor. Perhaps it would be best not to be so blasé in future, after all you never knew when they would find you next. The man shivers visibly and huddles deeper into his chair. The room seems colder now, so much colder. Steadily, his lower lip now quivering he picks up his book again and turns to the very back page. It's covered over and over in the same single word, each scribing of which with it own imminent importance. The word is his name, and each writing of it has been a reminder. The middle aged man picks up his pen and finding a relatively clear space carefully scratches with his spidery hand...

Chapter Four

Charlie lay on his side, his hand outstretched a little way in front of his face along the floor. He'd been lying like this for some time now, quite still. He stared intently, his eyes focussing on something just beyond the reasoning of his mind. Softly he giggled to himself and a trickle of saliva rolled down his cheek following a path created by the reams of vomit that he had so recently ejected. Charlie sat up quickly, he was suddenly panicked, suddenly terrified and frantically tried to wipe the drool from the side of his face. His hand slapped to his cheek over and over and he hardly noticed the tears burning his eyes until too late. His face turned pale, all colour washing from it and his eyes traced down to the moisture on his arm. *His* arm. It was covered in a myriad of scales, tiny in themselves but outlined in the most brilliant of greens. The slowly drying skin on his scant muscle seemed to glow in effervescence, undulating to its own inner rhythm.

"It's funny how it doesn't stay in one place! And there's always more of it, there's never the same amount!" he said, calmly resting his arm back down.

It didn't matter that there was no one there to hear, Charlie only vaguely knew that these were his words, they didn't sound like his after all. They sounded slow, deep, like when the batteries in a Walkman are running low but you keep on listening to the music. He slumped against the wall behind him and his gaze travelled once more up to his hand. This wasn't *his* hand, it seemed too far away, miles away, but it was so close as well. It looked like someone was lying under him and putting *their* hand up through his legs.

As Charlie's eyes unfocussed, as he stared into... whatever. He watched... and as he did the metacarpals under his skin began very slowly to ripple, ever so gradually rising and falling, moving up and down and along like little slugs just under the surface. He felt the warmth as they moved into his veins. The coolness left behind as they travelled. He tried to track their progress around his body, excited by the movement this produced but as soon as they got to his elbow they were instantly absorbed into his circulatory system, vanishing disappointingly from his sight. All the same, by now a new set had started the same journey and his eyes moved excitedly to watch them instead. These ones were moving much faster than the last set, and his inability to track them accurately made him frown in frustration. He ran his fingers along the furrows of his brow, feeling the changes in texture as he wiggled his eyebrows. Slowly a large grin spread across Charlie's face and he resolutely settled back down, watching in fascination as the metacarpal slugs sank into warm oblivion inside him. He could feel them, mimicking the steadily increasing pulse that was coming from his heart. *Thump thump, thump thump, thump thump.* He imagined the outline of his veins and arteries, the small clusters of

17

capillaries that were his kidneys, atrophied with abuse, the swelling of his heart in the centre of it all. Towards all of this travelled the little metacarpal slugs, steadily moving around, stepping one by one into his largest muscle, and with each one the beat grew faster, faster, faster. His hands were numb now but strangely not at the same time. He felt dizzy, sick and he had pins and needles all over his body. Finally, twitching he slumped to the side, his muscles no longer able to support his weight, the blood moving so fast around his body that oxygen had no time to unload before it was carted off again.

"Police, we have a warrant to search these premises!"
The door crashed open and blue uniforms poured through the gap. The night detective quickly took in the scene. The pool of vomit on the floor, Charlie slumped up against the wall his head lolling unnaturally, the various paraphernalia lying on the uncarpeted floor. Shit! Bloody neighbours, why can't they just let the stupid bastards shoot-up in peace instead of calling *him* out in the middle of the night. So what if she knew what he was doing, let the sod kill himself. Now he had to sort all *this* out.

"Someone call for an ambulance!" He said, his voice filled with authority. "Someone call an ambulance *now*!"

Charlie felt his body convulse one more time and he slumped forward, the slugs were racing now, not even letting the previous ones enter his body before they coursed out of his hand. Pins and needles ran their way down his fingers, tingling uncomfortably as his blood pressure increased. Charlie's eyes unfocused, and the electrical pulses in his brain piled up against the synapse that could end his life. He started to fit, and his mind finally lost its last grip on his body.

There are valleys in this place, deep and beautiful, they plunge and glide for miles and miles. Pull back, there is an age here despite the relative time of existence. Time is relative. Pull back further, leather, deep luxurious leather. Taught, soft and uncaloused, a sacrifice of skin.

The book contained truths, pored over and added to as the millennia passed. That it had somehow come into the possession of those who knew, those who understood was fortunate to say the least. But as it had the text had grown, pages glued and spliced, the spine broken and widened so many times. The book contained knowledge, understanding, but also past the tales that it held, past the stories and the fables there was fact. There was truth. There was darkness. It was a key to potential, although to whose the man called Goeth didn't know. He'd thought that it was the boy Phil, had felt the lines of the book, those sometimes twisted sigils telling him that the boy must be exposed, that he had a part to play. To him the darkness had passed, and with it had gone the cloud shadowing reality.

Goeth sat in the dark now, cradling the night-testament in his arms, wishing, willing it not to be true for the thousandth time.

19

He rocked back and forth, his knees brought up tight to his body, the tears dribbling pathetically from his eyes. He still remembered though, he still had his identity and that was important. He needed to hang onto that, that and everything he had learnt, but if he couldn't still be him, be a person then what was the point. Roughly he smudged a grubby wrist across his cheek, replacing tears with grime. He didn't want to do it any more, but it was so frightening, he didn't want to die this way. Paranoia gripped his soul, he knew that, he was constantly terrified. He could go through rehab, get help, become the man that he knew he was under all the Lycerin and Ambrosia. But that would mean he would forget it all, the creatures that hunted him in the corners, and then they would get him, he would have no way to protect himself because he wouldn't know anymore. That was why he had to keep going.

He dried his eyes once more and placed the leather bound book on the floor beside him. Shakily he reached into his pocket and took out some skins and his pouch. A smoke, just a smoke, that would calm him a bit, and if he made it... enough, if he packed it out, maybe on it's own it would show him. Deep in his soul though he knew that it wouldn't be enough, there would still be that small amount of *rationality* telling him that some things just weren't real, that they couldn't exist.

Letting his mind go blank he concentrated on the task anyway. He crumbled a fair amount into the skin and gave it a light covering of tobacco. Then, tearing a small piece of thin card from

20

an empty cereal packet he made a roach and began to roll. The tobacco mingled with the drug and tightened as his fingers moved. He licked the gum and burnt the end off near the roach so that it didn't duck-arse and placing the cylinder between his lips he shakily sparked up. He inhaled deeply, holding the first few puffs, then settled back as the drug started to take effect. Immediately he felt it relaxing his tense muscles and he stared at the cherry for a moment before taking another huge drag. He *wasn't* going to let them get him. Not yet anyway, he would speak with *Ap Nudd*, although time was surely short. Countermeasures would need to be put in place. Protection would be required. The essence of the cycle demanded attention, the tick of the clock would remain intact.

Chapter Five

Darkness flashed through Charlie's mind. The mind that was Charlie, although not alone, but a small, almost irrelevant stone in the great whirl of existence that defies. Defies his transcendence to death. He is prevented, bereft of faculty and set adrift upon the streams of Ellysia. That *otherworld* a symposium of sound and past glories. Down Charlie sinks, further the delusion, the expulsion of his person. See through the twisted torment of mortality that surrounds something much... but not to name, as such.

The Earth lies, frozen in space. It hangs, no sun to light it but it glows with its own captive iridescence. Great tears and cracks stretch across its side, and in the mirror of the oceans tidal-waves lie still and angry at our satellites crushing blow. The moon that holds forever smashing into continental landmass. A tectonic apocalypse saved only by the effort of the world itself. That squeezes time like a cloth and wrings out every last drop. This it gives to the people, the ones left behind. To live. Survive. But its action has crushed each and every dimension. All time exists now, all time for the people, and the Earth left a shell of crushed pasts. All this to stop... But for the time being darkness remains subjugated.

The wolf has seen the boy before, has tracked him through the wood, the demon still not quite willing even now. The boy grows weaker by the day, his fictitious grasp on reality blurred and distant in the wavering truth. The wolf has taken him before but each time when the pain leaves he must begin again. And as Charlie sinks further into his drug-baked tumult the wolf stalks just a little closer. If the key is not given willingly then the door must be broken. And yet the *other* body, the wolf, would still have to find its own hammer. The boy Charlie watched, submerged in a viscous water. His mind was repugnant at the very images it was showing itself, and yet still, a creature, a half decayed putrid conglomeration of the living and the unalive slowly dragged a broken nail across his body. He stared in agony, the breath stolen from him literally as his chest split open and his lungs were carved from where they lay. He felt the flesh of his oesophagus, of his tendons and arteries being severed, the searing pain causing him to gulp in great mouthfuls of fluid, paralysed by the yellowing eyes of the monster. But there was nowhere for even the fluid to go. In panic he fought to breathe, his back arching with the effort. The wolf steps closer on the bank, and in the distance a familiar sound, just on the very edge of hearing, the sound of a human voice.

"Fifty milligrams of adrenaline... Pads! Give me two hundred and thirty volts. Okay, everybody clear please. Shocking!"

Phil looked up from where he was lying. He felt like shit, the methadone they had given him had barely taken the edge off and already he needed another hit. He gave a quick glance out of the window into the hallway. One of the police guards gave him a stern look and he slowly turned back, resting his head on the pillow again.

They didn't seem to be in any rush to interview him; he guessed they were still going over the scene or something. His mind was calmer now, more collected, if such a thing could exist inside Phil's head. He was losing his sight, his gift of understanding was slipping from him as his dislocation from the perceived rational world waned. Shit he needed a hit. His memory flashed momentarily: *It drags its claws across her stomach, severing and tearing muscle and skin. Worms of intestine fold out and it curls its fingers to grip them. She screams as it pulls, her mouth spurting blood in an elegant jet toward the ceiling.* And then the relief he'd felt for her when she finally fell still! He blinked once or twice to dislodge the image from his head. He had to get another hit soon. Anything would do, just to take the corners off reality a bit, anything to send him back into his head. It was a scary place the real world, a place that he had turned away from a long time ago in favour of the safety inside his mind. He craved that safety more than anything now. He could feel ideas and notions in the back of his brain that had been so easy to feel not so long ago, but now everything was so sharp and solid that he couldn't even begin to conceive of how to get to them.

There was a snort from the bed next to him and Charlie sat up with a start.

"Wha...?"

Phil turned and for the first time gave his roommate proper consideration. He smiled toothily but said nothing.

"Who the hell are you?" said one.

"Phil!" replied the other.

"Yeah, right, whatever." He smacks his lips, they're dry, "Why am I in a hospital?" Charlie glanced out into the corridor. "And why are there police in the corridor?"

Phil considered his reply, he smirked quietly before speaking, "Took too much didn't you." He gestured to the door, "An' the police are outside the door 'cause apparently your neighbour busted you." Phil paused for a moment. There was no reason for complete honesty was there? But even so there was an affinity between them. A feeling, not quite dark but certainly with the warmth that accompanies the dark. It was like a cloud in his mind...

Phil's mind changes track... a partial truth would suffice for now. But there was a debt that he owed to a dear man who had shown him his destiny, albeit a dark destiny, and unknown to Phil at the behest of a greater power. And with that revelation the addict had both fled *and* vowed that his mentor would not be alone in the months to come. There was much to arrange before he could destroy himself, and even then the essence of space might never be the same again. Others needed to be prepared, before it was too late. Finally he spoke. "I got arrested last night as well, different reasons though." The addict sniffed, as if testing the air. "There's some big investigation goin' on an' they didn't wanna waste too many pigs, so we got chucked in the same room!"

Charlie stared blankly at Phil while he waited for all of this to sink in. Eventually he relaxed a little and leant slowly back onto the uncomfortable hospital bed.

"My neighbour really got me busted?" he asked.

"Sounds like it!" replied Phil, relieved at the change in atmosphere.

"Fucking bitch!" said Charlie.

Blood dries slowly on a saturated carpet, seeping in deep, staining the wood of the floorboards. Such a waste, the carpet, the floorboards. Good interior design is hard to come by.

The wind whips quietly around Conardly Terrace, and the small group of people still hoping to find something new at number forty nine pull the zips of their jackets up just that little bit higher. Black and yellow police tape flutters in the breeze across the doorway and a man in a white overall stops on the front step. He unbuttons his overall and reaches decisively into its recesses, coming out almost at once with a packet of cigarettes. He lights one and inhales deeply, breathing out the blue smoke into the fresh morning air.

"Okay lads," he calls back into the house, "I think that's about it, lets get back to the station an' get all this crap filed."

Chapter Six

Morning came early, daylight streaming in through the thinly blinded windows. Phil blinked in the light and turned on his side, turning to his roommate and taking in Charlie's appearance. He had about three days of stubble and a bony, drawn face, pale apart from around the eyes where burst capillaries gave him a slightly crazed look. It was just like looking into a mirror, or would have been except that it had been a very long time since Phil had looked into a mirror. He had skinny arms, and Phil noticed they were scarred deeply around the insides of the elbows. He could easily recognise the signs of collapsing veins. Charlie caught Phil's eye, "What?" he said.

"You'd better be careful." replied Phil shortly.

"It's nothing, they'll be fine." Charlie snapped, annoyed at the attention.

"No, they won't!" said Phil quietly. Charlie didn't answer, he could feel his body dying. Could feel the push to take it further. There was something in him that turned his mind, as if with each desecration a door would open into a darker place. A place that Charlie *wasn't sure* he *didn't* want to enter. Phil stared ahead of himself, thinking quietly. There was something in the back of his brain, niggling away at him like a splinter but he just couldn't reach it. Eventually he broke the silence.

"You wanna hit?"

"I've got nothing mate." Said Charlie bluntly, "There's nothing I can do for you."

"Right, yeah," replied Phil.

"Yeah, so there's no point asking again."

Phil picked up his tone, he was losing his audience. "Okay, that's not really my problem you see." He paused and lowered his voice a little further. "I can get the shit, I just can't get *at* it." He turned and stared momentarily out of the window. He could feel Charlie's eyes on him, leave it *just* long enough. "Alright, here's the deal. I'll share with you, but only if you can distract those two out there for long enough for me to get to it. It'll only take a few minutes." He paused, *almost* a look of earnest crossing his eyes.

Charlie stared hard at Phil, his eyes sharp and unblinking. For a moment he sat thinking to himself. Then, still looking at Phil out of the corner of his eye Charlie raised his hand to his face, he paused for a second and then gently eased his fingers between his lips. All of a sudden he gagged, his knuckles scratching on his teeth and a jet of bile erupted from his gullet. He winced as his stomach convulsed, there was nothing left, he'd thrown it all up last night. Eyes watering, he forced his hand further into his mouth, as far as he thought he could.

"Good lad." said Phil quietly, then making sure he could be heard yelled at the top of his voice:

"*What the hell!*"

Phil smirked broadly at Charlie and gave a conspiratorial wink, glancing quickly through the window to the corridor. The two guards were struggling to organise themselves, batons unsheathed and ready. As they came running through the door one of them turned conscientiously and called to a nurse who immediately came running.

"Get me to the goddamn toilet!" spluttered Charlie and he threw the cardboard bowl the nurse had given him to the floor. He flashed Phil a quick grin before a fresh wave of bile belched it's way from his stomach.

As Phil had hoped, the panic was such that neither guard thought to stay behind to make sure he behaved himself, and with the nurse trailing quickly after the escort he was soon left to his own devices. He knew he didn't have much time, as soon as one of the officers realised he had been left alone someone would come running back as fast as they could. Quickly he spat on his hand and rubbed the saliva all over his fingers. Then, raising himself off the bed onto his shoulders and ankles he gingerly pushed his hand into his backside. He winced as it went and very carefully, very slowly eased out a swollen condom. It had a knot in the end and in the wonderfully elastic red bag there was a not indecent amount of white powder, caked but still good. Just at that moment one of the officers came hurtling round the corner and Phil quickly shoved the chemicals under his pillow, pulling the covers up around him. The policeman stopped at the door, seeing through the glass that

Phil, to his eyes, hadn't moved. He put his hands on his knees in relief and tried to catch his breath, shaking his head at his own lack of fitness. Inside, Phil lay back and smiled.

The two guards waited outside the bathroom door. Phil was evacuating his bowels and Charlie had been allowed a wash bag from the hospital shop in order to clean himself up. The guards grumbled to each other about the situation, ignorant of the duplicitous nature of the two addicts tandem requests. Naivety was no excuse.

Inside the toilet, Phil and Charlie were enjoying the fruits of their wardens' stupidity.

"There you go buddy, enjoy!" Phil handed a rolled up piece of paper to his new friend and got out of the cubicle, sniffing and rubbing his nose as he did so. Charlie knelt down by the toilet and looked at the line of powder on the seat. He blinked and pushed the paper into his nose. Snorting harshly he felt the burn as the spice raced up into his sinuses, his eyes watered slightly at the sensation. It had been a while since he'd had anything this bad, it did the job though. He felt the familiar buzz as the drugs did their work, softening the world around him, and at the same time leaving everything as brilliantly sharp as he had ever seen. He felt good, the stimulant adding to the hubris of outsmarting his wards. He sat back on his heels and let his body steady itself.

"Shit stuff!" he said.

31

"Yeah, I know, but you get what you can and when you can right?" replied Phil.

"Yeah, yeah. No problem, no problem." Charlie paused and gave a sniff, rubbing his nostril with his fist and dropping the paper tube down the toilet. He flushed. "Thanks, I needed that, calm my nerves a little bit. We'd better not stay in here too long though, the pigs might start getting a bit sus'." He glanced at the door shiftily, as if by the very mention of it they would be caught out.

"What, them two?" replied Phil sceptically, "You're joking right. I mean, who the hell puts two of *us* in the same toilet together and doesn't go in with them." He looked over wryly, Charlie smirked quietly at the rebellion.

"Good point. Wankers!" they laughed together, tough circumstances and bad drugs mitigating circumstantial feelings of doubt in both parties.

"So what *do* they want you for then? You never said." Asked Charlie after a while.

"Oh, right yeah." Phil paused, things had been going so well. "I'm a witness... Protective custody, sort of... I dunno." He gave another short laugh, nervously this time. "I think they're trying to pin something on me."

"Pin what on you?" Asked Charlie.

"Nothing, it doesn't matter. Something I might well have done." Charlie leant back on his haunches, eying Phil with a strange laconic smile that Phil didn't find entirely comforting. But

32

even though it put all of his senses on alert there was still a depth to the others mans gaze that drew Phil towards it in a manner he had never before encountered. It was as if for the first time in his life he was feeling the love of another creature. And aside from that, in a part of Phil's mind that was still active he heard the silent commands to ignore it, to let it cloud the mind but not to enter the soul. He felt dislocated, as though only himself and the other existed in the whole world.

"How about you?" he asked eventually, "Why did you do it?"

"Do what?"

"So much in so little time... it's only going to hurt!" He chuckled slightly, lightening the conversation somewhat. Charlie turned and slumped against the wall.

"I knew it wasn't good," Phil glanced around the cubicle door, "But somewhere deep in my mind I though I might find a truth." Charlie sighed and shook his head, "It sounds stupid... I feel like something wants to open up in me, but I just can't quite get at it." Charlie stopped talking abruptly, embarrassed at his candour. Phil was staring at him thoughtfully. "Come on," he said, "I think I can hear those pigs banging on the door!"

That night Phil lay awake in bed. He was thinking about what Charlie had told him, thinking about some of the times before. But above all else he was thinking about that night in the house, when

33

the girl had died. Charlie had slipped into somewhere else, into the deep recesses of his mind. Only to the margins certainly, but he had seen the edges and it was enough to make Phil wonder. That the man still had a long way to travel was obvious, but that there was also a beginning in him. A distant potentiality that was trying with all of its might to burst through. Perhaps, thought Phil, redemption lay for himself within the hands of this gaunt stranger. That in saving him from certain sorrow he could somehow redeem what he had already done. That he would not kill again was certain, he would make sure of that, but who knew what evil he had already unwittingly released upon the world. As such he would put the one and the one together and make two. Charlie could minister to Goeth in his dotage, the sage who had directed Phil's dreams through the great Ether, the *Annwn*, and shown him the truth behind his eyes.

For some strange reason he felt an affinity with this Charlie, some kind of connection. Besides, the guy was nearly there anyway; one final push and he'd be out of the unknown. Then maybe, just maybe he would escape the oncoming darkness. If Phil could save one, give one a chance then maybe there would be a chance for others. But *that* meant that Charlie would have to *see*. Would have to *really* see, only then he could guide the rest. Who knew what would happen if he, Phil couldn't end his own life. If the fates intervened and prevented his very blood from flowing. Then would stand Goeth with Charlie at his side. All he needed was a healthy dose of Lycerin and a bit of direction and then he would realise, then he would know that it was best to run. As Goeth had said, don't get curious about what you see, because they really *are* after you.

Chapter Seven

They were coming more and more often now; he had to be so careful. They knew he was aware of them. They knew that they had to get rid of him. He should never have... But he hadn't been himself and that was an end to that. That the darkness in him had lifted was true, but it had left something cold in its place. A reality only truly understood with the door wide open. Goeth had given the key willingly, had welcomed what he had thought the end to his life's quest. But instead of the enlightenment he sought he had become a servant. Had set events in motion. The book should be destroyed, he knew that, but much as he'd tried it just wouldn't let him. His mind clouded like a fog. He was never meant for the red leather, it was always meant for another. He stroked the ginger tom that had sidled over for attention. It was *his* cat. Well, not really, but certainly it kept coming back. He would need protection, of what sort he had only a vague idea but...

But it wasn't right leaving him like that was it. He had seen the edges of things, but he hadn't seen it all yet, and that was the dangerous time. So he'd pointed him in the right direction. It was better than the alternative, to half know in the back of your mind what they wanted, what they were. That was the place where insanity hid. The full truth was better than a half-truth surely!

Goeth looked down at the cat he was holding and absentmindedly gave it another stroke. It was going to be hard doing this while he was away. But the alternative was inconceivable. The cold reality of sobriety. He could never handle that, he was just too scared.

Goeth looked the cat in the eye and sighed. He tickled it under the chin making it purr in the way that he had become so used to. Then, grasping the animal roughly around the shoulders and at the base of the skull he pulled sharply and gave a twist. There was a slight crack that made him wince and then he gently lay the limp body beside him. Eyes stared dully.

The world is an odd assortment of stuff. Energy zips around the place in various forms, and amongst the plethora of living creations there are a myriad myriad little bits of *stuff* that make us all up.

When the universe formed millions upon millions of years ago there was much less in it than there is today, much against popular belief. That the universe could occupy the same little bit of space all at once is ridiculous, the sheer size and weight alone... But I digress: There is a pop and the universe springs into being. At this moment there are no stars, there are no worlds, there is just the *whap* and *fizz* of stray atoms as they ping out into the newly fledged cosmos. Is it any wonder then that at some point, through divine providence or simply the nature of causality that some of these speed demons might find companions of other sorts. That atoms might form communities, and from that they may form molecules and so on until eventually you have suns and worlds and a myriad myriad life forms. And about all of this the energy of the universe zips and zings. If this is the case then we are both people and planet... and dog and cat and mouse. If this is the case then we are all made of the same: Stars. And if so then we are the potentiators to worlds.

He finished his tea, gulping down the last few mouthfuls in quick succession, and then turned his attention to the assortment of dried mushrooms on the opposite side of the now deceased cat. It was all very well listening to traditions and legends, but you had to know exactly what worked. There was so much corruption of the old tales that it was hard to tell sometimes. He selected three medium sized fungi. They were extremely long in the foot and had small delicate heads, creamy in colour, but heavily mottled with variations of deep blue. He had spent three days drying them and now he placed his chosen three into the mortar he held between his knees and began to grind them. They crumbled easily, their dry husks breaking under the pressure of the pestle. Goeth then picked up a small corked bottle, no longer than a thumb high. It was a decoction of ill ease and he was uncertain about using it. He had been given it many years ago and had doubts to its efficacy. A medium amount of this liquid was even so added to the powdered mushroom creating a bright electric blue paste.

He considered this for some time. It seemed good, much like he had been led to believe it would be. A little unsteadily because of the rough he'd smoked he leant forward towards the floor and picked up a small piece of charcoal. This too was added to the mix. As it was ground in, it darkened the blue to a deep navy.

Carefully, so as not to spill any, Goeth poured the liquid into one of the many empty food tins lying around the room. It had been thoroughly licked clean by the cat and shone brightly in the dim light. This was then carefully balanced on a haphazard, homemade tripod and placed over a candle so that it would thicken and congeal in the heat. After a moment he added the yellow-white fat of a rat killed earlier that day to the mix, not too much but enough to cover the top of the beaker and bubble gently as it floated there. Once it was at a consistency that suited him and he could no longer see any blobs, he wrapped his hand in the sleeve of his jumper and poured the mixture back into the pestle.

It had taken him a while to prepare for this ceremony. When he had first come across the practice he had been backpacking, many years ago this was, to the far north. He had just glimpsed briefly… but it hadn't stayed with him and he had struggled with what he had needed. The information and ingredients used were almost irrelevant, it was the sheer *belief* that cornered the practice and made it whole. He needed it to be a success. At least this way there would be a part of him they couldn't get. But Goeth doubted.

"Charlie! Hey idiot... wake up. Come on, be quiet." Phil hissed, his eyes bright in the semi-dark of the room.

"What? What do you want Phil, it's quarter past bloody three?" murmured Charlie groggily.

Phil looked at him annoyed, "You don't say! Come on, wake up. Those two bozo's have dropped off outside on the chairs."

"What is it? You've got some more snuff or somethin'?" Charlie was still half asleep, his eyes glued together with tiredness. He raised himself up onto his elbows all the same; "We'll have to be discreet about it if you have. I'll bet they won't be asleep for long, especially if that nurse goes past again. Here, do you reckon we could maybe nick something off of the drugs trolley?"

Phil thought briefly for a moment before he spoke, he seemed to be halfway through a thought process, "Although, I suppose... but not for a while anyway, and I've got some work for you to do before that."

"What are you talking about?" Charlie scratched his head with the palm of his hand, his hair made a rasping noise as it rubbed against itself in the dark, "I'm not doing anything, I'm in enough trouble as it is."

Goeth felt the familiar knot in his stomach and knew that the tea was starting to take effect. He relaxed and let the trip begin. Focus, that was the key, become a part of the ceremony, don't let yourself become interested in anything else. No matter what, he would know they were there now if they came for him.

Taking out a knife Goeth carefully began to skin the dead cat. He started at the base, near to the tail, and delicately worked his knife up the underside of the animal, careful to keep the blade no more than a few millimetres from the surface of the skin. If he pushed too deeply he might catch on something that he needed.

Cats often came to see him, the place was popular with mice and therefore held many a healthy snack for a lazy feline. Of course, the Inuit had used reindeer sinew, but he had found that it didn't actually matter, it was the ink that mattered, and the process of tattooing. The skin slid easily from the animal, it's subcutaneous fat acting as a lubricant and he gagged as he worked. After he'd completed that particular task he set about choosing a nicely elastic tendon, it would pass more easily through his flesh this way. A tight one would be knotty and would be painful. The dead animals' fur seemed to glow in the radiance of Goeth's hallucinations as he worked. Twitching and spreading like grass on a windy battlefield.

He couldn't recall now what the process was called, but he knew what the result would be. The ancient Inuit believed that the soul was located physically within the human body. They believed that there was not just a single, but an entire and separate soul for every joint and muscle and then if that part of the body was damaged the soul would escape. However there was a way to stop this happening, to keep the soul in its correct place no matter what

41

tried to take it. Whether it tried to escape of its own volition or whether the devils themselves tried to steal it, it would always remain where it belonged. The soul had to be *pinned* to the body by way of a certain form of tattooing and in certain positions over the body. This was done in a ceremony very similar to the one being carried out at that moment.

Goeth focused again, shaking his head to dislodge the images. He needed to visualise the rites, needed to know that what he was doing was exact and proper but he had to stay in the here and now as well. The adrenaline would help with that, and the pain. He knew it was going to hurt, but it would be worth it.

Taking the Achilles tendon of the cats right back leg, Goeth took his knife again and halved it lengthways. Then he did it again. This created a length of material approaching roughly the same width as a piece of darning thread, which he then squeezed as much of the blood from as he could. Technically this wasn't the way it should be done. It should be dried and beaten into strands, but there wasn't time for that now. The rest of the cat had been placed in a bag and set off to one side, there was no knowing what might be useful. It had also been weeks since he'd had fresh meat. After this he took out a large needle, probably originally used for sewing leather or similar and threaded it with the animal fibres, struggling a bit with the elasticity of his skein. This he then placed into the home made ink to soak for a while and lay back to concentrate on his trip.

Phil frowned towards Charlie, though surely this was what was meant for the man, what Phil saw to be the mans future in some respect. It was at the same time not something that seemed the natural course of things. Phil faltered for just a moment, his mind brought back to his previous few hours thoughtful sleeplessness. Finally he spoke the culmination of those thoughts. "I think... I think I want you to get out of here. And when you do I want you to do something for me, you understand that. There's an old man..." For a moment he paused, unsure of how to progress. "I've got a debt to repay, I left and now I can't go back. But you can go." Phil's face was bright in the darkness, there again was a glimpse of something within Charlie. That the edges had been revealed was sure. He was breathing heavily, the excitement of his salvation battering the sides of his brain, wanting to come out all in one go. He had to take it slowly though, he had to make Charlie *want* to get out. More importantly though he couldn't tell Charlie too much. The guy had caught a glimpse of things to come, but Phil could still scare him off. Once he met Goeth, then it would be okay. Goeth had this way of making you want to know more, even though everything inside you was screaming at you that he wasn't right in the head. That you should get out while you still could.

Chapter Eight

Goeth picked up the needle and looked at the flesh attached. It looked well soaked, almost black with the potion. Having never done the procedure before he honestly didn't know whether it was supposed to look like this or not. He sighed deeply and silently prayed to whoever might be listening that he was doing the right thing. For a moment he gazed at the wall opposite, and then without so much as looking he jabbed the needle sharply into his ankle.

His eyes grind against the intense sensation. His perception is already heightened and at this point the pain takes up his entire world. But this focus, this taughtness in the fabric of this man is even so not quite enough to stem the small, almost immaterial speck of doubt.

Hands shaking and blinking with the perspiration springing from his brow he took hold of a pair of pliers and, placing them on the protruding metal pulled the sinew through his body. The ordeal over Goeth relaxed and looked at the result of his work. Two small black dots were plainly visible at the entry and exit points, and just below the skin there was a pale line of dark blue where the ink had passed through his flesh. He wondered how well it would heal. Goeth shuddered, the adrenaline had taken the edge off of the tea and replaced it with an altogether different sensation. Sort of cold, but with the edges still blurred and the centre now as sharp as daylight. Just another twenty-six more dots to make, another thirteen nails for the soul and he was done.

"It's not just about you though you see..." Phil saw the look on Charlie's face.

"What makes you think I give a shit?" Charlie was in no way impressed by Phil's assumed authority. "What makes you think I won't just rip this old guy off and steal his crap? I'll tell you what... *nothing!* Don't pretend to know me!" Phil's face hardened, his knuckles clenched automatically and yet... there was a sense of distance in his mind. A woolly cloudiness mugging him inside and leaving him naked. It *felt* like love, of a sort, and yet it wasn't, it very much... wasn't. "He... he holds quite a lot." Charlie perked up.

"I could get a hit?"

"And more," Phil's eyes were glassy, still his own but... not quite. "If you would he would keep you I'm sure."

"That's what you want isn't it? Why, why do you want me and him together so badly?" Phil faltered at this, despite his dumbed state there was a limit to truth.

"Because... because you'll need each other." He paused and swallowed, *something* was willing him on, something dark. "I am the catalyst... Through me the demons will be brought back to the world. The darkness will out." In Charlie's mind the wolf paces on the shore, to and fro, to and fro. It bides, but it listens, it pushes the mind that holds it. Charlie speaks.

"What *on Earth* are you talking about? How the hell... you're mad mate!" And although the words communicate nothing, the sense of them communicates much to the mind listening. In the fug of pinkness Phil's centre perceives what is meant.

"The book is there. He has it. He showed it to me... The... the book is there." Tension leaves the air. Both parties seem as though they have come out of a trance.

After a moment Charlie turned to face the ceiling, he needed a hit badly, he could feel the cold sweats already. To be sure, he didn't quite understand what had just happened, or indeed remember much of the preceding minute and a half. And yet he was left with the overriding compulsion to acquiesce to Phil's wishes.

After what seemed like an age he spoke.

"Go on then." He said "How do I do it and where do I go?" Phil let out a huge breath and a grin split his face from ear to ear. His debt was settled, and the peculiar Charlie would soon be gone.

A conversation has taken place. Words have been passed from one to the other. That Phil considers himself both killer and coward remains unspoken of. That he cannot return because of his apparent fate is spoken fact yet hidden to consciousness. Darkness clouds all, and misinterpretation hangs on the edge of realisation and ignorance. The wolf gives a nudge, the task is done.

"Here, take my jeans. Maybe you can tuck the gown in or something and it won't look so different." Charlie looked at what he had just been handed. Oh well, never look a gift horse in the mouth.

"Cheers!" he said and pulled on the ruined material. They were stiff with dried sweat and mud but they were less suspicious than what he was wearing at the moment.

Cautiously he headed over to the door, slowly, bare footed, his feet making quiet slapping noises as they landed on the cold laminate. He could feel how they peeled away as he lifted each foot back up, the sweat on his soles sucking to the floor. Phil got up and moved over so that he was standing next to him, the springs of the bed making slight grinding noises as he stood.

"Don't worry buddy, I'll cover you." He gave a soft chuckle and patted Charlie on the back. Charlie glanced once more at the still sleeping forms on the chairs outside and reached for the door handle. Phil winced as the door swung open, biting his bottom lip. He hoped to hell it didn't make a noise. It didn't, and Charlie turned for the last time to his roommate. He nodded and gave a smile. Phil winked back and then nodded towards the open door.

"Go on then, bugger off!" he said.

Charlie slowly began padding up the corridor, his knees stiff with nervousness. He was only halfway up when one of the policemen started to stir. He froze instantly, unsure of what to do. The sudden

47

cessation of noise pulled the officer to full consciousness and Phil ducked quickly out of the doorway to stand square in the middle of the corridor. He gave the man a friendly pat on the cheek, his mind sharp with his joyful action.

"Come on then," he teased playfully, "you're it!" and caught the officer sharply in-between the legs with a clenched fist. Charlie made a dash for the fire exit as Phil scuffled behind him. Finally, as he padded out into the night he caught the sound of Phil's bare feet flapping off in the opposite direction and the errant fart of a raspberry. He smiled, and although his joy was pure and free there was also a seriousness inside of him. The wolf paces along the bank, back and forth, and on the opposite side sits a book, bound in red leather...

Chapter Nine

Stars spring into life. In galactic terms in the twinkling of an eye so to speak. And so we, humans as a species exist only for the merest fraction of the time allotted for life to take place in. In relative comparison. In this manner it could be considered that life is or can be recycled, born and reborn. Or inhabited. To inhabit another form, and from that have the potential to spawn truths and untruths. What then? The balance is shifted. But is this not the only way in which life can be used to its fullest potential. To monopolise on the life already present with the life that has ceased to or should cease to exist. To extend life, or to extend torment.

If we are all created from those same million myriad of zipping and zinging bits of stuff then this is surely the case is it not?

Cochrum pinched the bridge of his nose and tried not to look into the light. He'd had far too much whisky last night and was in no real state to be in work. Even so there was still necessity. Not regarding the case as such, although this was very much on his mind, but for a different reason. Certainly, there was a concerted effort being made on someones part to push him out. Insomnia aside he needed to *focus*.

The forensics lab swam into view, a blurred bright mess of light and white walls. There was always a distinct *smell* about places like this. In his years on the drug squad Cochrum had smelled this smell on so *many* occasions, there was no description for it. There was the usual crap lying around as well of course. Some things he recognised, some things he didn't. It didn't really matter anyway, it wasn't his job to know. There were people for that, and *they* gave you the answers. At least you hoped they did. The DI glanced down at the occupant of the table in front of him. He repressed the urge to gag.

"She's not been fed on then?"

"Just like the others." Replied Doctor Joseph Frankson. He was the police pathologist, and through necessity more than anything else Cochrum had found himself working with the man quite closely.

"Why do you suppose that is?"

"I don't know Richard," sighed the doctor, "And no matter what theories you have we've found no traces of a handler. There just isn't one." Cochrum looked down at the dead girl in front of him again. "Oh her, yes, well we did get something from her." Cochrum immediately perked up.

"What do you mean?"

"I think it's best that I show you. We've er... we've also managed to get some saliva from the wounds... it was a spot of luck really. I should have the results in a few days, I've sent it off to the university to get looked at."

"Right, good, well at least that's something to tell the press. What's this?" Cochrum gestured to the table next to which Frankson now stood.

"This is erm... this is a casting."

"Right, plaster cast, yes. You get it from the girl?"

"Yes, we were fortunate again in that respect. It's only the second time the body's been found intact enough for us to take a cast."

"So what's the news then?" Cochrum was beginning to get impatient. He needed something to work with and he needed it *now*.

"Look Rich, it's not as easy as that. I've never seen anything like this before." The doctor picked up the cast and began turning it over in his hands. "I mean look at it, it's just incredible. *Possibly* a canine of some variety but I've just never seen anything this *big* before."

"We knew it was big Joe, it had to be big." Cochrum sighed, "Okay, to go back to a previous theory. Could we be looking at some kind of *engineered* animal? You know..."

Frankson paused before giving his answer, it was important not to give too much, too much could spell disaster, but still he had to give enough for curiosity to take hold. "I think we'll know better when the DNA analysis comes back." He smiled warmly, "Those guys at the university are pretty smart sometimes."

As Cochrum left the room intent on seeing Phil, the youth from the cupboard Frankson paced back over to the girl. He took his glasses off and cleaned them fastidiously on the hem of his lab coat. He hoped he hadn't overdone it. But what better way to temp out a demon than by offering the companionship he desires most.

Beep.

... on the life already present with the life that has ceased to or should cease to exist. To extend life, or to extend torment.

If we are all created from those same million myriad of zipping and zinging bits of stuff then this is surely the case is it not? Or is it more the case that life can be accosted, adopted and deranged by those with the will to supplication? Maybe so. But that a life can be a restraint as well as a blessing cannot be ignored, should not. For it is central to the concept of freedom. Freedom of speech, freedom of thought, freedom of body. Wolves howl to the night, entombed in their mortal prisons, used and tormented by masters unknown in a world on the edge of knowing. Wolves howl to the night, their jaws slack and snarling. Not all are happy with this situation.

Chapter Ten

Marks is staring at the wall. There's nothing special about the wall as such, perhaps it's what he's thinking that we should involve ourselves with. He's usually a calm man, or at the very least he should be described as contained, for the time being. But the potential can definitely be heard all the same. Cogs whirring, making sense, counting. One, two, three.

The little evidence that can be relied upon that Marks has seen, makes no logical sense to him. But then there are a lot of things that make little logical sense. The trouble arises when Marks realises that he cannot break. But this is yet to be seen. For the time being there is a necessity for discussion, for elaboration, but the principal, the principality of this situation is elsewhere. Marks stands.

Beep.

Phil lay once again on his hospital bed. The chase had been rather exhilarating, but it did mean he was now definitely facing criminal charges. That was something he could've done without. But then it wasn't just him that was taking the rap. The two officers, on reporting what had transpired had both been suspended. This meant however that the next lot to come along weren't taking any chances. He was not only an accessory to escape and an irreplaceable witness, he was also a hardcore drug addict, this meant that he had not only been handcuffed to the bed, but also to both attending officers forming a neat chain through all three of them.

"Come on guys, I need a piss!" he hissed earnestly.

"Yeah, okay, I'll ask the nurse to bring a bottle next time she comes along!" sneered the guard on the left.

"What about civil rights and all that!" whined Phil.

"Not likely mate."

Damn it! Somewhere, deep in the recesses of his mind he knew why he'd done it, but it just wasn't surfacing. It was like it had been crammed down as far as it would go and it didn't want to come back up. He had just wanted to help the guy, either that or he just wanted him gone, he hadn't made his mind up yet. He felt connected, and that was the overriding sensation, not to mention his other little problem, and of course Goeth was a nice man. Even so, it kept going over and over in his head, it wasn't that he had particularly liked Charlie, just that somehow, he had felt that something linked them. There was a sharp rap at the door, Phil's train of though became completely derailed. Before the guards had time to un-cuff themselves from the over-subjugation of the drug addict Cochrum entered the room. He looked flustered, things weren't quite going in the directions that he had pre-supposed and this was causing an *issue*. A solution would be found and he was pretty certain that at least an element of it lay with Phil. For the first time he looked at the ridiculous situation in from of him. He sighed.

"Sod off you two, I need some time with the witness."
The two constables looked at each other warily. After a moment one of them spoke.

"Erm... Sorry sir, Detective Inspector Marks says you're not to see the witness sir. He says this is his interview."

Cochrum gave the man a blank look.

"I'm sure he didn't *quite* say that now did he."

"Erm... no, not quite sir no! But it was the same general idea."

"Yes, alright. Don't worry, this isn't a formal interview, I'll let Marks have that. I just want a chat with the bloke... To make sure he's okay." The Detective Inspector gave a brittle smile as the officer began to frame a complaint, he glanced up at the DI and silently thought better of it.

"You two can go and have a coffee break, I'm sure me and... Phil wasn't it." Phil nodded dumbly, "will be just fine. Won't we Phil!"

The two uniformed men reluctantly un-cuffed themselves and set off down the corridor towards the canteen. Cochrum turned to Phil and pulled up a chair. As he walked over he pulled at the knot of his tie to undo the button underneath.

"I hate these damn things." He said to himself quietly. He turned to Phil and looked at him stonily .

"Hello Phil," he said, "now... my name's Detective Inspector Cochrum. I expect you'll have heard from the media that I'm one of the officers dealing with this case." He didn't even feign a smile. Phil grunted in response. He disliked this man already, and not just because he was a copper. He gave off an arrogant smugness that made Phil want to jab a hot needle in his eye. Cochrum continued, the stolid gaze the kid was giving him was making him edgy.

"I need to know what you saw in that house." He said bluntly and leant back in his chair awaiting a reply. Phil looked up, eventually.

"You don't want to know." Not the response the policeman had been looking for.

"Look you little shit," the snap was audible, "Something messed up is going on in this city and you're the only goddamn lead I've got so start talking."

"Why would I talk anyway..." whispered Phil, "Word from the guards is you're off the case come Monday." Cochrum blinked. "Not that it'll matter very much."

"What... What the hell *do you mean by that?"* Cochrum was blazing now, Phil had scored a hit. He smiled and... and he felt, not for the first time the invasion of his mind. He struggled against it but... but this was different now. This was *Ap Nudd!* He felt the urge... he needed to... to speak. "The wolf is in the stories the stories of the dark the times of the oldest ones when the oldest

56

ones ruled the land when man met beast and beast bit hand you must to the oldest ones the tales of 'r *Mabinogion* you must go... *go!*"

Cochrum closed the door behind him as he left the room. He would talk to the doctor, he was the kind of man that knew about this kind of stuff.

Chapter Eleven

The man Goeth sat, ignoring the dull ache through his joints. His was a world to be pitied. He knew that they would come for him, knew that it would be soon. He sighed and put down his paper. The scrawls whirled on the page with a life of their own, as did Goeth's vision. Images passed in front of him, fizzing in the stillness. He'd seen them thousands of times before but they never became any less terrifying.

He had set things in motion, things that were not of his conscious decision, but things that he had done nevertheless. He wished he'd never come across the damn book in the first place. He had no idea where now, his thoughts were too addled, too clouded by darkness.

"My time draws, doesn't it friend?" He patted the book, red leather bound in front of him. His vision was flickering now, blending realities with a viscosity that was unnerving. He had accepted his coming death, and yet he hoped still in some respect that his vain attempt at remaining alive bore at least some manner of fruit. "Have they always been so hidden?" The book didn't reply. Goeth's voice was broken now, distant and at the same time frightened. "At some point... at some point... p...perception is refused, debunked... refused." He trailed off. "They don't stand a chance."

Things stand in the corners of Goeth's reason, taller than a house and as thin as bedposts. Their gaunt faces stare at their feet, as arms twice the length of their bodies' drag massive hands along the concrete. Grotesque parodies of the human form stare out through soulful eyes.

A bright chittering noise hits the wall in front of Goeth and suddenly he becomes aware of the space around him. It's too crowded, far too crowded. The creatures of his paranoia force themselves into every nook and cranny, claustrophobia pressing itself into every pore. He spins around frantically, unable to discern what's real and what's not, what was alive only in his minds eye. How could he tell what was after him, how could he know when all he could see around him were enemies. Something scuttled across the wall in front of him, naked except for the tight skin that wrapped around its skeletal body. Goeth backed away, turning towards the doorway, but that too was peopled with monsters. Thousands of tiny *nadredd, 'n anniben yn cyd-doddi* merging, crawling their way inside to form a solid squirming mass of tentacles.

*...Neidr 'n gycyllog chreadur...The air thickens...*He dashes back into the centre of the room, his heart racing with the narcotics inside him and the fear outside. Instantly as he turns he is forced to his knees by the most dreadful screech he has ever heard.

59

It pummels the very cells of his brain, gibbering into the centre of his fear itself and then expanding.

Darkness.

Goeth lay cowering on the floor, he didn't know what was real. Tears streamed down his cheeks and hysteria gripped his soul. His face contorted into a grimace of pain, it felt like his head was going to explode, the pressure was so immense. The capillaries in his eyes burst and blood gushed out alongside his tears, veins stood out on his neck and his face flushed with the blood of horror. His body tensed in one final effort to rid itself of these images, and a massive fatal haemorrhage in his brain stole his heartbeat, leaving him as a lifeless shadow on the floor.

Chapter Twelve

Charlie ran through the now night darkened streets, the elation of his escape streaming through his veins, energy beating itself into his animus.

It was as if sheer joy had taken him over. A release and... direction. Something inside of him was yearning to follow the direction that Phil had given. Find this... Goeth. But the man is unimportant, the man is superfluous, to the ignorance of Charlie. The wolf paces on the bank, the book opposite, the river between running dry. He can feel the tendrils of tender knowledge pouring over his skin. He snaps, there's something he has to do first. His palms are itching and his skin sweating, what to do what to do? Go back to the flat? Carry on to an unknown? *Shit!* The police would be waiting for him at home, but there was another option...

...Drug Maker make your... Drug Taker hide your...

Chochrum gave the double door in front of him a sharp shove, he was thinking hard and wasn't paying particular attention to...

"You're working late?" Frankson's face was weary.

"I'm not the only one."

"Yes well, I had to wait for the DNA analysis from the..."

61

"What are the results?" Cochrum almost took the doctors head off with the speed of his inquiry.

"You're keen. Well, okay then... I don't know." There was a pause, Frankson put his glasses down on the desk in front of him.

"What do you mean you don't know?" Cochrum's voice was quiet, confused. "Don't know what?"

"I mean I don't know what this is dammit Richard! The university doesn't know either. The DNA's unreadable, it's... it's *weird!*" Cochrum sighed and slumped into the chair next to the doctor.

"I went to see the boy today."

"The one from the house, how was it?" There was a pause before the policeman answered.

"It was... *weird...*" Both men looked each other in the eye. "And I bet that twat Marks has a go at me as well." He sighed and returned his gaze to the wall.

"What did the kid say?"

"Oh, nothing much at first. And then he couldn't tell me enough. Random crap mostly, didn't really understand it. But he did mention a wolf!"

The doctor was silent, things would continue along their path and the trap would be sprung. Although there were certain pieces as yet that he was still unsure of. There was an integrity to maintain and there was a distinct possibility it could have been

62

compromised. "Well that fits in with what we know so far." He replied.

"I did a bit more looking as well. I don't think the drugs have been good to him." Cochrum chuckled, "He thinks its some kind of Welsh hellhound!" The chuckle continued, Frankson didn't join in. "Its this book of Welsh stories, he said the name, can't remember it now, began with an 'M,' anyway, I looked it up..."

...face the world a day at a time, that and day will soon be mine...
...gwynebu 'r byd ddiwrnod am adeg , a ddiwrnod ewyllysia 'n ebrwydd bod chloddia...

The Moon is full. Cochrum's eyes blink open sharply. He's surrounded by trees, by bracken and bramble. He scrambles, tries to move forwards but as he should fly he finds that instead he's tied. That his movements are sluggish, steps staggering, exhausted, puggish and brittle, his breath wheezing and spittle on his lips. There has been a chase and at the end of it he stands. He falls into longish grass. The night air is cold but there is a harmonic that holds fear. Taps into the soul of those near. The howl goes up. There is a rifle in Cochrum's hands, he raises the sight to his eye, that he would shoot instead of die is imminent, eminent and obvious.

Grass rustles behind, he turns fires, there is a yelp and as the suns light reflects from the silver pitted face of Mani from Sol herself and together cast their selfish gaze upon the ground below Cochrum fights for his life. That his sin is in his strife, his selfish desire to supersede, to survive, he derides himself for this. His fist smashes the face of the wolf to the fore, it strikes down raking its claws across mans midriff. And as Moon looks on, man is set free from his physical restraint and sent hurtling back to the place of his origin. Wolves tear at flesh and gnaw at bone. A rifle lies, tossed aside, devoid of ammunition and cracked through inside. Mani looks on, the moon tied to the man, and the wolves bay in hunger.

Nothing moved in this place, the building was calm. To a certain extent of calm. There was life in the air, a pent up vigour that seemed to challenge anything and everything.

Goeth's body lay still in the darkness, the room brooding with the bruises of the recent conflict. After a while the crusts of ink around the still fresh tattoos began to flake off, and in the sudden, oppressive silence a faint sizzling could be heard as the revealed flesh began to bubble. The skin around the marks blistered and popped and red stains of swelling ran around each of his joints. A black ooze slowly crawled out of the wounds, piling up in small lumps of tar before finally the tattoos were completely gone. There was an abrupt tearing of the atmosphere, like something invisible trying to escape at great speed, a sudden halt and a brief struggle before the air finally fell still.

64

Honesty is removed from the situation, the interpreter lies...
Two paths will cross, one will crumble. The final path cannot be
broken now.

Chapter thirteen

Charlie scratched in the dirt frantically. His voice was a hiss but there was definite urgency there.

"Come on I need a hit. Come on... come on..."

His flat lay opposite, across a road, and whether or not it was under observation Charlie had decided that the park was his best option. His fingernail snagged on something in the dirt and it tore across the corner.

"Shit!" His eyes balled up, he felt like he wanted to cry. It *really* hurt. He nibbled the corner of nail, tidying the rough edge, wincing at the slight... there was nothing... there was no... Charlie began digging in the dirt, the stricken finger lost from his memory. Finally he scraped something that felt familiar. Or at least should have done. A movement from the block opposite, it's been unoccupied apart from Charlie for weeks. The wolf freezes, completely motionless.

"He's buggered off somewhere into town, see his mates that's what I reckon." The voices were just on the edge of hearing.

"What are we gonna tell the boss then?" The question was stark, "Oh sorry, he's pissed off somewhere else?"

Consciousness begins to filter back to the host, sight is slowly, ever so...

"He's just a junkie, he's only gonna kill himself somewhere else."

Car doors slam. There is the sound of an engine starting and the thick smell of fumes as it moves away. Gradually movement begins to return to Charlie's fingers, little by little. His eyes however remain fixed on the road. After a while he relaxes and resumes his search. It *must* be the wrong place... But where else could it be? He was in a bad state now, his face was pale and the sweat on his forehead was... he wretched. To the side luckily, but unfortunately the movement in the air pushed Charlie just slightly too far.

Only moments went by, but as Charlie came round there was a definite struggle behind his eyes. His tongue *clicked* involuntarily. After a while the tension subsided. *Shit, shit, shit he needed...* Quickly he got to his knees once more, there were more pressing matters that he needed to get to... he felt this, this urge, as though he were being beckoned in some respect. Which was utter nonsense *shit he needed a... Dammit!* His scrabbling fingers once more found what they should have done some possibly fifteen minutes ago. A heart flutters with adoration, love it could be said. Slowly his grimy fingers edge their way around the soft wooden box. The plastic bag is torn, he rips the rest off as he slowly eases his find to the surface. More moments pass. This time these ones are taken with puppy dog eyes. He feels the smooth sides. Not so smooth. Pitted and slightly rotted down one side. *Damn!* That must be all the rain at work.

Charlie quickly gave one last look about the place. He was pretty sure there hadn't been anybody about but... you had to know. You had to be... *shit he needed... sweet warmth* quickly he stood up shoving the box into the crook of his arm. He brushed himself down briskly and then headed off in the direction of inner sanctuary... safety... bliss...

Goeth's body lay in the gloom where it had fallen, the small piles of tar around him slowly solidifying into cairns around the mountain of his redundant form. The door that he had only recently tried to escape through swung open alarmingly. There was nothing behind it, and yet it had acted as though given intent by a cautious but determined hand. The door bounced back slightly as it rebounded off the opposite wall and finally came to a halt not so far from where it had begun. The bare wood, rotted by age and the damp that permeated the building creaked ominously as an invisible finger lightly tapped on it. The bearer was obviously intent on gaining a better view of what lay within but not confident enough to show themselves fully to the room yet.

A scuffle freezes on Goeth's desk, a rat, the movement of the door triggering its base reflex. Something squat runs from one side of the frame to the other, quickly making it's way to the better vantage point. Gingerly a face appears around the edge of the woodwork, making it's entrance at roughly two feet from the floor. At first only a flash is seen before it retreats, but little by little, ever so slowly a face appears around the doorframe. Fingers hold tight to the wood, a face nibbles a fingernail gingerly. She's only eight or nine surely, blonde hair and striking green eyes. A girl, small for the age on her face.

The rat begins to quiver, from nose to tail unable to take it's eyes from this fairly average child. *Tick... T..tick...* The head moves, odd, reflexive. She crouches as she walks, although perhaps *skitter* would be a better term. Perhaps she's playing a game? She giggles to herself at the sight of the recently defunct corpse and her light, bright eyes flick unnaturally towards the still quivering form on the desk. At once it's shaking stops and again it steadily begins to preen, taking especial care of its whiskers and ears. The child enters the room and moves to the rodent before gently picking it up. She stokes its soft fur absentmindedly for a second, enjoying the feeling on her fingers. Quick as a flash her countenance changes. She stares fiercely at the animal, lines of crimson arcing across her features, her eyes sinking evilly to a dull blood-ochre and her hair rising in a crest of sinuous scales around her ears and the top of her head. The rat squeals in sudden fear as her small milk teeth become the needle pointed tips whose venom would end its short life.

Almost immediately the creatures face regained it's calm exterior, and she threw the mutilated creature to the floor. *Krvoses.* She skipped happily over to Goeth's body and, just as any small child would tug at the arm of a parent she gradually pulled his remains out of the door and away.

The plunger sank, and finally Charlie felt the opiate cascade through his veins. His heart rate hammered and he felt a warm tingling spreading through his body. He lay back on the coldness of the grass and let the comforting uproar in his body overwhelm all his other functions. His hand slowly released the tourniquet and placed it back in the box by his feet, joining the needle that had already been re-sheathed. As his heart settled to a lull Charlie stared up into the magnificent branches of the oak tree he was under and let his mind unravel. *This* was what he had needed.

The box contained a number of other things as well as the ambrosia, and although paranoia could have been attributed to something else there was never any harm... a first aid box for the addict you could say. Ready money, a good stash of smoke, a few hits for the times on the run. Charlie's minds eye was alive, and yet there would soon be cessation. Oh, erm, and a chocolate bar... in the box.

After a while Charlie stood up, conscious of the fact that there were police not so far off and that he was still wearing laughably conspicuous clothing. A quick jaunt to the twenty-four hour supermarket was in order. Pulling himself up sharply into the branches of the tree Charlie stowed his box, fixing it securely into a hollow provided by the base of three high branches. This would

70

have to do for now, no-one would be looking too hard in a place like that at this time of night in any case.

Dropping to the ground he took stock of his situation. It wasn't bad considering. He had forty pounds in his wallet, leaving ten in the box and had also taken a small bag of smoke. After a brief scramble through the pockets of Phil's jeans he was also delighted to find the young man had been a smoker and promptly produced a small packet of skins and the remnants of an ancient and dilapidated bag of tobacco. He deftly rolled himself a stubby and set off towards the supermarket.

It was a fairly simple journey, half an hour through a reasonably neat residential district before reaching the main road. This could then be followed up in the semi-dark shadows provided by the orange streetlights until it met the turn off for the shops. And off Charlie went, puffing innocently away until he reached his destination.

He received a few odd looks from the late night staff as he stepped through the automatic doors, but Charlie was used to this, he generally got a few funny looks no matter where he went and he proceeded unperturbed. Rummaging leisurely through the racks the unkempt escapee eventually picked out a pair of loose fitting stone wash jeans and a rough flannel shirt, these coming to twenty-two of his forty pounds. He also chose a cheap pair of trainers, which brought the total to his limit. He thought, if briefly about the

71

morality of what he was about to do before setting off towards the changing rooms. After about ten or fifteen minutes he came out in the new clothes and shoes. If you looked closely you might just see the rough holes where the security tags were ripped off, but not without effort.

Charlie continued on to the counter and gave the checkout assistant a smile, humming lightly along to the slightly annoying music playing in the background. A morose re-recording of a '90's classic. He rocked back and forth on his heals as he tossed Phil's knackered old jeans onto the counter. The girl at the till looked at the jeans numbly, her shifty eyes flicking first over the security tag inexpertly attached and then straight to...

"Yeah, you're right," muttered Charlie, "I think I'll just leave it."

He thanked the girl and casually made his way out, nodding to the security guard as he did so and wishing him a good night.

Almost five hours after his escape, Charlie returned to his tree. The sky was beginning to brighten now, dawn was approaching. He plucked the plastic container from its waiting place and yawned. The edges of his vision were blurred with tiredness, the sleep deprivation increasing his inebriation. His mind began to people the waking light. Vague images of creatures slinking back to where they came from swarming through his mind, showing him the safety that light held. Shaking the images from is head Charlie made for the only shelter he knew at that moment.

Chapter Fourteen

Light filtered through the cloud and haze of the morning. Mist hung heavy in the air as though it knew its time was coming, the heat of the day would boil through it with no care or understanding of what its presence meant. And yet through it stalks a centrepiece, in one respect or another. His mind is busy, and yet exhaustion covers him like a blanket.

Charlie walked the slowly awakening streets, his mind mussily contemplating what would await him on his arrival. He had no idea of what this man was like, and therefore what kind of welcome he could anticipate. The matter stood that he felt compelled to go to a man that for some reason he knew…now. He just knew, although hours earlier he also knew that he hadn't… Inside Charlie the wolf lies, tense, it senses its time is coming. Direction is true, it no longer waits at the banks pacing, now it's carried. Now it knows. Charlie smiled, he didn't know why, he was tired, just tired, his mind was wandering. There was no sense to any of this, it felt like a dream, as though something were caring for him and cradling. Smothering, encroaching. He took a deep breath, it must be the ambrosia, just breathe, stand up straight. The feeling fades, slightly. Charlie continues to shamble along, the label on his new shirt itching furiously with starch. The mist that remains whips about him, it pulls him from behind, trailing like a cloak... more pushing than trailing. Encouraging him forwards. There is a sense of the fated in the air, and the question remains... if he is not, then where is the *First?*

A figure rounds the corner, it seems darker than it did half an hour ago, more hunched, tired. It seems as though although it's walking at the same time it's being pushed, pulled by what remnants there are in the orange-red sky. Light boils the vapour away as a sigh on leaves. Not that there are many of those around here. Leaves or trees. The walker continues, his mind fatigued but aware that he needs to reach his destination. The reason for his compulsion has long since left him, he no longer cares in all honesty, in his own mind he walks to walk, his destination is arbitrary, although the safety that presumably it will provide is a consistent if minor consideration.

A tree, long bereft of leaves stands at the side of a sharply pointed fence, obviously designed to keep out any would be trespassers when the building beyond it had still been in use. Past this, turn off left down between these two buildings and carry on down the street. The instructions shouldered their way to the forefront of Charlie's mind, shoving aside the intervening years of chemical abuse that had so rotted the majority of his memory.

There were times late at night, times when sleep had eluded him or withdrawal had taken hold when he could almost touch his dreams, touch his memories. Not all of these memories were his, not all of the dreams were his but they were his for that time. He had never understood, had always been lost in that drug-induced miasma and had never even considered... The wolf growls on the edge of perception, Charlie's mind drifts and returns to his route.

As he rounded another corner he came to a halt. The building was in a pretty bad state, there was no doubt about that. He could find nothing to suggest the once thriving religious community that had worshipped here. They had long ago moved their establishment to the centre of town, a centre that had at some time occupied *this* space instead of three or four miles further over, where it now lay.

The building was a shell. Rusted railings made their way around a small patch of littered earth, a few ragwort plants forcing their way to the surface through the aeons of crisp packets, coke cans and the varying detritus of drug related society. The walls were green with moss and lichen, the long blocked gutters overflowing onto the masonry. It had forced damp into the marrow of the building, giving the plants purchase on the once solid sandstone. It was astonishing to think that this was where someone actually lived. Charlie shrugged to himself and steeled his nerve. Carefully he traced his way around the building, eventually finding the entrance. It was locked. There hadn't really been any windows, none that Charlie could fit through in anycase, and there definitely weren't any other doors. Gently he rapped on the woodwork, half hoping that no-one would answer. After a while he knocked again, it looked as though no-one was in. Charlie tried to peer through the greying glass of a thin window, careful to avoid the needles and crushed beer cans that lay strewn about his feet. There was a room off to one side of the main hall, the door was ajar and the interior looked lived in.

There was hesitation in Charlie's mind, and although sobriety had come back to the man the wolf still willed him onwards, still persisted despite... but there was little weakness now in its being.

The morning was in his bones now and he could feel the dew condensing on his hair. Probably best to wait inside, a short nap and a mug of coffee couldn't do any harm to his powers of persuasion, and he was going to need them if he wanted to stay for any length of time. No matter what his hospital mate had... but he hadn't had he. And this bloke looked like he generally preferred his own company to judge by his accommodation and the glimpse caught through the windowpane.

Putting his shoulder to the dilapidated wood Charlie gave a sharp shove. The rotten material gave way more easily than he had expected and he crashed into the room taking the door with him, it's entire length ripped from the wall.

"Shit, not a good start." He muttered darkly as he propped the fast disintegrating wood back up against its frame. For a second Charlie paused, he took stock, took in his surroundings. He now occupied a bare hall, which had probably once contained a great manner of pews and rails, all the fixings that a church should have. It lay empty now, it's furniture had either been auctioned off or taken to the new site for reuse. Even the great organ had gone, leaving only an empty hole where it's brass pipes had lain. Through this he walked, carefully making his way over to the half-open door. Considering the state of the building he was astonished to find he didn't fall through the floor.

As Charlie approached he slowed, his heart was beating fast, and as he craned his neck to see around the door he tapped lightly to move it, just slightly. Not that he could ever have known, but there was a perverted similarity in his movements to a young girl that had entered the place not so very long ago. The room was a mess. It had obviously once served as a vestry area, but any sanctity that it had obtained during that time had patently vanished the moment the dead man had chosen it for his lodgings. There were papers scattered everywhere, Charlie reasoned that the majority had fallen from the immense desk that occupied a large section of the room. He picked one up and glanced at its water stained dialogue. Little was visible under the grime and blotching of the damp, but he could just about make out the etching of what appeared to be a snake, and it was,... He shuddered and dropped the page. There was little else in the room, that is to say that there was a huge amount but that the majority of it was covered with papers and mess. Despite this and after much rough tidying Charlie managed to find what at some point Goeth must have called a bed.

The wire and springs creaked as Charlie lay down, and as he closed his eyes for some reason he knew that this was the right place.

At exactly the same time, Richard Cochrum was brushing his teeth. Bags surrounded his eyes and his face was pale. Much to his mirth he greatly resembled the witness that he had so recently interviewed. He gazed at himself for a while grinning and injected his arm with imaginary diamorphine. He rolled his eyes to the backs of their sockets and made a face of mock euphoria. Chuckling to himself Cochrum began to shave.

"Not likely I don't think!" he said as the thin blade rasped across his cheek, He gave another chuckle and then a sharp intake of breath. Cochrum dabbed at the spot of blood by his chin with a finger, "That'll teach me, won't it." Tearing a piece of toilet paper from the roll he took a small patch from the corner and pressed it to the cut. That should do for now, he thought and fastidiously dropped the rest of the tissue into the bathroom bin. He finished shaving quickly, his jovial tone lost as the business of the day overtook his weary body. The disturbed sleep would make him highly irritable today, he could feel it already.

Chapter Fifteen

Heads were down as Cochrum entered the station offices. He'd done nothing wrong, and yet he kinda *had*. There was a protocol to follow, there was always a protocol, especially in an office as large as this. And especially considering what the kid had said. Off the case by Monday. Marks was junior only by his time in the force, they were both Detective Inspectors. It was complete chance that Cochrum had been serving longer but it *did* give him seniority. All the same...

"You're a shit Cochrum."

"Thanks Marks, nice to see you too. I heard you were a shit as well."

"Bastard!"

And that was all he got. *Something* was going on.

Marks was shaking with anger as he sat down. That shit, that sodding *shit*. Well at least he hadn't got anything either. He'd have had to go through hours of gloating, but there was none of that, so Cochrum got jack as well.

Of course if Marks had interviewed the kid first himself he might not have let on either, but Cochrum was nothing if not an open book. Marks had a feeling about him, it was hard to pin down, there was pressure going around *sure*, but this guy wasn't acting right. He was falling off, disappearing, he was going to have to be careful.

Marks leant back in his chair, lost in thought, slowly twirling a pen between his fingers. He fumbled and snapped out of it, dropping the pen. He worked better at night, but this was a difficult one, everybody had to work. Double shifts already, triple shifts soon he was sure, they just didn't have the manpower to search the city in the way they needed. But Cochrum had *something*, maybe not from the kid, but Marks just didn't trust him enough to think that he didn't. Neither did the Chief.

Dulled light shines in through a grimy window, slowly warming Charlie's brain. Recollection of the previous night creeps back to him as he cracks open his eyes. There's barely light in the room, but enough, it's as it was before. Nothing has changed. He pushes himself to his shoulders and looks up at the window. Standing on the camp bed he uses his cuff to smear some of the grime away. The sky looks blue outside, just about, but who knew what time it was. There was maybe a hint of orange creeping in at the edge... and he knew it couldn't be morning...

Looking round the room now it looked a lot bigger than it had when he'd first found it. It had been dark he guessed, and he'd been very tired. Amongst the scattered papers and rubbish he caught a glimpse of what he'd been looking for. Stashed in a corner, a little dirty but still... Charlie glugged and chomped down the baked beans, there were loads of them, and soup, mostly mushroom, which was disgusting but at least he didn't have to go hungry. After a little further exploration Charlie found a small bathroom through a tiny door off to one side. It was truly wretched, but he slurped from the tap thirstily. He felt like he hadn't had a drink in days. The cool water was beautiful on his tongue, and although he struggled to get it down his throat, bean sauce still clogging him he forced himself until he thought he'd split... There was something on the desk. Something... Charlie gazed at the massive wooden desk through the doorway. There was leather. Just a glimpse on the dark of the varnish, but it set his heart thumping.

The room had darkened to almost black by now and Charlie wondered how he could have seen anything in the murk. Scrabbling around in the drawers eventually he pulled out not just one, but three smutty white candles. One was snapped and rolled as it dangled in a lackadaisical slapdash. He lit it anyway, and the other two. They were quite large and cast some pretty good light as it turned out. Even so the shadows seemed to jitter uncomfortably. Charlie wasn't used to candle light, it seemed far too organic. But that didn't matter, he couldn't keep his gaze away from the book. He'd pulled it out from under all the papers now, resting it on the desk proper. He couldn't place it, but he knew that... what did he know? That he'd come into another mans home. Even if it was a shit-hole. And now this book, this...

Before he knows it Charlie is sat down. The wolf inside, unbeknownst to him is baying and scratching in eagerness. The frustration is testament to the lengths employed... Charlie feels warmth, feels a deep warmth come over him. He feels safe, feels like... like he's loved. He smiles. The room seems to be more orange than grey now, and his skin feels as though it's fizzing. He doesn't know why but he knows that he's got to open the book.

As he does the leather creaks with age, it seems to suck at Charlie's fingers, and as his eyes settle on the first page, as he sees the swirling mass of writhing text, the stories pinned to the parchment the wolf begins to learn. And as the wolf learns the man catches glimpse after glimpse, although he doesn't really understand. That his mind could never recall, or even *accept* the threat... The wolf smiles, unknown to Charlie so does he.

Chapter Sixteen

"What did you mean?" Cochrum pushed the door shut behind him, Phil was tucking into a huge plate of pie and chips. Hospital food was never as bad as people said. "Last time I was here... What *was* that?"

"What was *what* Detective Inspector?" Phil carried on eating, hardly seeming to notice his own voice.

"Sir, I've got to ask you to leave I'm afraid." One of the constables in the room plucked up some courage. Cochrum glanced over his shoulder.

"Don't be stupid, I've got work to do. Go get a coffee. What happened to you last time I was here Phil?"

"Sir, DI Marks has taken..."

"I said go and get a coffee." There was force behind Cochrum's voice, it was unquestionable. It was as undeniable as the tides, and yet it was a force that was past the understanding of simple coercion. Both officers left, puzzled faces and blank minds willing them to the door. Cochrum's mind returned, and as he tilted his head back towards the boy for some reason he understood that it was no longer Phil McCearney that he was speaking with. Not that his conscious brain would ever register this, *could* ever register this. But certainly there was *something* inside of him that

understood, that began to listen as the rest of his body slumped down into the fatigue of the moment.

"Temptation is in you soul," Gwynn Ap Nudd's voice is tainted with earth, *"You could not comprehend at this point, not without... cataclysm."* A grunt escapes Cochrum's throat, there's something in him that hears. *"You seek further guidance."* Another grunt, *"Then follow the wolf and lead the lone hunter."* This time Cochrum speaks, although his voice is a whisper.

"You seek Mani as bait." There is silence for a while before Ap Nudd replies.

"Yes."

Charlie rummaged around in the filth of the room. There was more than his addiction willing him on, and in some manner of speaking he knew, but even so his search was frenetic. The wolf inside was pacing on the bank once more, impatient. There was a distinct requirement for control, for biological interaction with the world. Trapped inside the wolf can do nothing. Can bend mind to its will but in itself has no more *actual* presence. But when Charlie... lets go.

Papers flew across the floor, scuffing and rucking, folding and tearing. *It was never this soon.* Surely the last hit should've kept him going longer, but he was sweating and shaking from head to toe. He blinked a salty drop from his eye. He felt burnt out, like his energy was being used for something else but he had no idea what. *Shit he needed a hit.* The wolf willed his consciousness out, expanded his process of thought. There was nothing in this room, *nothing.* Just the book, and as yet Charlie hadn't dared touch it since he woke up on top of it a short time ago. His head still burnt with images that he couldn't understand. An organic swirling mass of words. Finally Charlie stopped churning through the papers, he wasn't going to find anything in here. That left only one more place to check, although the prospect was slightly daunting, but there had to be something, *anything* that could help.

The hall of the church was derelict, almost and most certainly to a definite extent. But despite everything that was wrong with the room it had managed to stay the challenges of time in some respects. The roof was still on for a start, and the walls. So at least the floor wasn't *too* rotten. Not as rotten as Charlie had expected anyway. Even so he trod carefully, there were probably all kinds of pipes and stuff that he did *not* want to stick his foot through, if nothing else it would hurt like hell.

Suddenly Charlie's right foot jerks down. The phrase best laid plans of...

"Shit!" He draws his breath sharply as he pulls the splinter out. He didn't even know rotten wood *could* splinter. Luckily it didn't go too far but it's still managed to tear a small hole in Charlie's ankle. As he pulls his pain away from the wood he hears the dull clatter of rotten fragments slapping the ground. Be more careful is the thought that goes through his head. But unfortunately

Charlie at all times has failed to spot the crowbar marks on the planks, hasn't noticed the dulled pathway from the vestry where the varnish of the floor has been pushed back by years of treading the same path. He *has* just looked up and spotted the missing tiles. He's also just felt the drip land on his face, and as he licks the sweet water from his cheek he wonders how long this has been happening. In just a moment Charlie will have a much better idea... ah, there he goes.

Charlie crashed through the floor. There wasn't even a moment to balance himself. First he felt the wood shift, then he was through. He moved slightly, aware that he was at the bottom and yet still only waist deep to the floor and pulled the remains of a plank away from his thigh. It had been an odd action, stuttering, and he'd half sat as he went down meaning the wood behind him had broken as well. As he straightened himself he lifted his leg to rub the graze that had sprung up along his shin. Well there was solid wood in this place *somewhere* at least. Stepping back he angled himself to see underneath, flicking a spider from his shirt sleeve. There was definitely something solid under there, and after the breath and adrenaline of the floor he hoped...

Charlie was desperate for a hit when he finally managed to haul the box out of the hole. More than a few more planks of wood had been removed, not that this had caused much of an issue, and now sitting, panting, wiping the sweat from his mouth and forehead Charlie opens his find. The wolf inside is not disappointed.

Cochrum sat in his car outside the hospital. Eventually the two constable's had come back in, one of them, the one that had spoken had handed him a latte with a very confused expression on his face. Cochrum blinked and looked down at his hands. He was holding an empty cup, funny, he didn't remember... it didn't matter. There were more pressing things to attend to. If he had it right then very soon he was going to lose all control over this case, and although he didn't understand the reasons he still knew that he couldn't let this happen. It was... It just *was*. It was *his* and there was no way that he was going to lose control just because he was being reassigned. Whatever it was that he had found from Phil, and that area of his mind was as blank as his expression ten minutes previous, it had given him more than he could ever have anticipated. His mind no longer needed the logic that... all he knew was that he had to follow, and that in turn *everything would work out*. Although how he knew this and the processes in his mind that led to these conclusions will continue as a mystery.

What was the kids name, he couldn't remember? Charlie. There was already a team on that case, not his, he had no especial focus. Maybe he could get a case transfer? No, there wasn't time for that, not if he wanted to stay ahead of the game. How could he get the information he needed without... He'd just have to wing it.

Cochrum's eyes were unfocussed again. They kept swinging, unable for the constant to remain inside the physical realm. His mind was slipping, although to where as yet remains unsure. Ap Nudd has forced something. There is a greater edict within Cochrum than his own. He dials on his mobile.

"Oh, hello Christine. Richard Cochrum here," a tinny voice replies, he continues, "I was wondering if you could tell me where the kid that escaped from hospital lives?" He paused for a second while he listened, "No, I've not been put on the case, but I'll owe you a *huge* favour if you can get me that information."

The prospect of having one over on Cochrum won over Christine's shallow mark. "Right, okay... thank you very much Christine, you're a life saver. I'd be obliged if you didn't mention this to anyone for the moment please... yes, that's right. I don't want to... Yes... I think I might have had an idea about where he's gone... yes I'll tell the officers involved as soon as I know anything for sure."

He hung up, resting his hands on the steering wheel. After a moment he turned the key, the ignition flared and Richard Cochrum drove away.

Marks slammed his hand down on the desk in front of him. He was seething, and although struggling to hide it he refused to let his anger get the better of him. Besides, Christine already had tears in her eyes.

"I didn't think it would do any harm, I'm really sorry!"

"Look, that's okay," Marks voice was stern but gentle, "Requests through me in the future though, you know how tricky Cochrum can be."

Quietly Marks turned to look out of the window. The sun was bright at the moment, but there was a definite density to the air. Cochrum had found a link, that was obvious, something that Marks had been struggling with himself. He had strung all the cases together, he had to have, otherwise why would he be looking for...

Marks was due to take over the whole portfolio on Monday, and he'd bet anything on Cochrum having a lead.

Chapter Seventeen

This room is dark. Not necessarily through a lack of light but dark even so. Deep in this darkness, this comfort there is a book, tattered and dogeared, yellow paged with its own years. Even though sight can relay no other sense, all the same it looks as though it smells musty. Grime has become encrusted slightly at the top and tail of the spine, but even so for some inexplicable reason it seems lighter than the rest of the room. The rest of the room is in fact rather dark, as has been mentioned, but this doesn't seem to deter the eyes reading. No, not reading, the word doesn't encapsulate the sense coming from the eyes. Drinking, even soaking, drawing...

Cochrum drove in silence, allowing the rumble and white noise of the day to surround him. He'd driven down these streets countless times, they were almost comforting in their familiarity. It was as if...

Cochrum's eyes stare apparently at nothing. Nothing much in any case. Slowly, almost gently a misty sheen pulls across them, glazing, half-glazing. These streets *are* familiar, but now he drives down them with an unfamiliar confidence.

The place was a dump. Boarded up windows and graffiti decorating most of the buildings about. There was all the same, a modicum of tidiness about the place. There was life, just about, and such as it was it demanded the civil liberties that all peoples demand of their governments. An off-license and a skip hire company. Even so, the police often found it hard to find volunteers to patrol this area. You could say the dilapidated buildings and cheap rent attracted a particularly strong-willed character.

Cochrum pulled up to the curb. Behind him was the scrap of parkland that Charlie had so recently used as confidant to his addiction. The Detective Inspector cracked open his door and felt the cool afternoon air lace its way in. He inhaled and his eyes closed automatically. On the case until Monday. And more than that, as his forgotten instructions led him ultimately to what would be his submission.

Quietly Cochrum smiled to himself. Even as his subconscious pushed him forwards his *conscious* mind leapt with the familiar smell of smoked narcotics.

So if Charlie *had* been here, had supposedly seen the surveillance and decided upon another objective then where would he go?

Although no dog he, Cochrum had been a copper for a long time. Too long perhaps, but some things experience could tell. There's a click and a slight whir as the car door gently closes. He wants to question, wants to wonder at this obsession but something larger is willing him on now. *Something has breached the Otherworld.*

Ink stands out in bright green tracery on the page. For some reason this is familiar, this is comforting. There's nowhere else for the drawings to go, they feel safe in the minds eye, and it's safety that they long for right now. There are words as well of course, there have been words for as long as the reader has sat. He drinks in the pages as they drink back, mind in decisive coitus with what he sees. So much to learn, so much to... It pours into his head in torrents.

Charlie sat staring at the page. His back was hunched, elbows at angles, his feet were planted and his mind was racing. He felt a darkness pushing him on, but a warm darkness, there was no malice, at least not to him. He was tired, so tired, he felt as though he could almost slip away entirely, let this *comfort* take charge. It was the book, the more he read, absorbed, the easier it felt to take this back seat, to let the darkened warmth take charge. But not yet, Charlie eyed Goeth's box cautiously, on the bank the wolf began to dance.

The supermarket looms ahead of Richard Cochrum. It's all that the consumer industry needs at two in the morning, a big box full of late night munchies. Slowly he walks in through the automatic doors and makes his way over to the customer help-desk. It's blue.

"Excuse me sir, police," He flashed his badge as he addressed the gangly youth in front of him, "I was wondering if you could show me the security videos?"

The kid at the desk stared dumbly, unable to control his surprise, finally he stuttered to life. "I... I'll have to get the manager to come down." The young man smiled nervously and Cochrum nodded in acquiescence to the half-spoken request. The youth left hurriedly, not wanting to hang around and left the Detective Inspector to his own devices.

Shortly an almost equally young man, Cochrum guessed he was only in his mid-twenties, approached and introduced himself as the duty-manager. Cochrum almost raised an eyebrow but satisfied himself with a sigh as he was escorted to the security lounge.

"What exactly are you looking for Detective Inspector?" Asked the manager. Cochrum looked over his shoulder, already thumbing through the tapes. "Police business." The manager was curious but also a little scared, and as Cochrum's stare tightened it was enough to put paid to any complaints the manager may have had.

Three hours later Cochrum was drinking another cup of coffee. It was sheer chance that out of the corner of his eye he spotted the blurred shape of a strange individual. He downed the rest of the cup quickly, the hot liquid burning his throat and he wound the tape on a few minutes. After a seconds watching he wound it on another ten minutes and then stared as Charlie headed out of the middle door, turning right just before the scanning area of the camera ended. He rushed out of the room and hurried over to the youth on the help desk.

"Out of this store and then right." The words tumbled out, "What's the first place you're likely to get to?"

Chapter Eighteen

Charlie stared at nothing, his pupils fixed and dilated, gazing at things that should never exist. *Could* never exist in reality. He knew, or at least, he thought he knew. There had been no option, it had been as though a part of him... *Some* of the chemicals had been familiar at least. Nothing like this could be real, it worked against everything he had ever been taught. Don't be silly, there are no monsters under the bed!

Icicles slid through his brain, piercing his doubts. Pushing in, pushing deep, encircling the last vestiges that he had always considered to be the centre of his rationality. Every way of life society had taught him. Every law and rule, created for his safety. They were all destroyed, and in their place lay something similar, but not quite the same. Don't swim in the deep water, it's not safe, you'll get tired, you won't make it back to the bank. Don't swim in the deep water!

Then suddenly there he was, watching himself. He was young, so young. There were no bags under his eyes, his skin was smooth and fresh, devoid of the track marks and stains that his grown up habits had produced. But he *wasn't* young at the same time. He was older than comprehension. Older than any living thing. His age stretched back through the aeons to a time when fact had been so much simpler. When cages had been made not of iron and steel but in human form, not that Charlie would know this. The apparition growled slightly under its breath and grinned wolfishly.

Charlie's mind was dimmed, pushed by the age. His youth accepted this age and followed it, knowing no better, down, into the water at his feet. The best way to warm up was to get your head under the surface, that way you became accustomed to the cold quicker, and so he dove off the sharp shelving of the bank and plunged into the blackness beyond.

Down he swam, down, further and further, until he could almost touch the bottom. He was running short of air now though, he would have to return to the surface soon. But the primal part of him, the aged and guttural part, the part that had seen the world through different eyes kept him down. Panicking, he struggled, he couldn't breath, he needed to get to the surface, but it was stronger than he was. Charlie tried to fight, tried to gain control of his own muscles, but it was no use.

In the murk something moved. Slowly it was swimming towards him, it's claws outstretched in anticipation. Charlie tried again to move, but the primitive, older part of him kept him steadfast. The thing was on top of him now. He had seen it before, and he quailed internally from those razor sharp talons. Quickly a single one flicked towards him, jabbing forwards with astonishing speed, ramming its solid point deep into his sternum, splintering bone and severing flesh. The creature opened its mouth and let out a stream of bubbles, slowly dragging its finger through the front of

Charlie's tiny, childlike form, willing him to scream, to swim away. But he couldn't, and this time he was in the monsters own, wet world.

With a guttural crunch it threw open his rib cage, exposing his still beating heart and wrestling lungs to the water about him. Clouds of black blood serenely floated away into the dark water and the greying, shrivelling mass of his organs pulled in the current.

Once more the beast reached a long bony finger around his bronchial passages, hooking the slender tool easily around the back, and *pulled.*

Charlie felt a sudden rush, everything in his body convulsing at once. Every muscle and tendon screaming at him that this wasn't right, that their need for oxygen outweighed any other problem at present. That he was, in fact, dying. And in that moment, in the terrifying few seconds of dire need before he passed away, his subconscious broke through the final vestiges of his rational mind, the two things mingling into one solid coherent whole. The primitive man, the larger, stronger being that had known, had kept him safe, had padded on the bank waiting for its moment, waiting to be let in, fell into the scared, confused child that lay on the waters bed. And opened their eyes.

For the first time in his life Charlie saw everything. He saw that perhaps he *didn't* need his lungs, even though everything he had been taught had pressed him that without them he would die.

Logic, he found, wasn't the path to true enlightenment. How could you be enlightened if you didn't consider all of the options? How do you know you can't survive without lungs if you don't try!

He stood up from where he lay below the water, at once feeling primal and strong, and also young and naive. His older self telling him the stories, and his younger self accepting them now without question and learning. He grasped the two sides of his chest and pushed them together, feeling the bones cracking as the splinters resettled themselves. He felt the blood rush at once to fill the gap left by his lungs, the platelets forming scabs on the surface wound and coalescing into great lumps of muscle within him. The bones of his chest knitted, overlapping each other, he was all, he was everything, he knew all he needed to know and he was stronger than he had ever been.

Charlie glared at the creature in front of him and it cautiously withdrew its hand, the tip of one finger drooping with the fast disintegrating remains of his lungs. It flinched under his gaze but held its ground, not sure whether to flee or attack once more. Before it had time to decide Charlie reached out and grabbed it. It seemed so much smaller now, weaker than it had been. His grip tightened as he considered what to do next, his eyes dark in the recess of their sockets. Even as he stood his nails dug fans of blood into the now still water and as the creature struggled and twitched, a slow, toothy smile spread across Charlie's face. Darkness was in his mind now, his soul superseded by another and as he finally snapped the beasts neck the wolf knew that *this* time it would not be returning to the bank.

Charlie's eyes flickered, and in the dark of the vestry he sat up sharply, his mind still flashing around his skull. His brain focussed on the world around it and tried to recall where he was. In the church, he was in the church. Didn't he have somewhere to go? Did he still have something to prove? It was all slipping away so quickly, fading as fast as it had come. He needed something to focus on, something to centre the new memories quickly, otherwise they would leave him for good. Blinking he turned once more to the book, but there was something wrong. Somehow he knew that for now its job had been served, but that its teaching would be needed again to bring something greater, darker than his own altered person.

Phil sat on the sink in the hospital toilets, his guards waiting for him patiently outside. A swirl of thoughts were going around in his head, none of them particularly positive. He was thinking back to that night, the night they had found him cowering in the cupboard. He was scared, he couldn't really remember it. The bits that he could remember flooded through from shrouded areas of his mind, telling him what it had seen, but it all seemed so far off. He had been outside of his body, watching his body, then not watching it, then watching it again. Then he had been watching *it*. There was no other explanation, it was completely illogical and yet it still made perfect sense.

The human mind was remarkably adept at preserving itself. Phil brushed an errant tear from his face, *"Cŵn Annwyn"* he said, almost chuckling, his voice cracked as he spoke. His mind had been fizzing and he had known. He would bring the darkness, he had known. By his actions countless lives would be lost, and he knew now for sure how it would happen. Even now his mind was on overdrive, buzzing with what he had felt and seen. All that he knew was that he couldn't remember, that he had blacked out. All he recalled was waking up in the cupboard, and finding the place swarming with police and drenched in blood. And it all made sense to him. He had watched his own body, he had come through the front door, Launa had let him in, and then he had watched the creature, all hair and blood red teeth, both through the stop-start miasma of drug-induced hallucination. Like a very slow strobe light, sometimes showing images and sometimes in the deep darkness of unconsciousness. Why shouldn't they have been the same thing!

That's why he had set Cochrum on the trail. Indirectly, or so he reasoned, giving clues. Telling the Detective Inspector that he was from that other place, that darker place. He hadn't liked that other one, Marks, there'd been something odd about him, a quality that had given Phil goose bumps. Cochrum was a bastard but that's what he needed. Marks on the other hand made him feel naked, exposed, and that was not a safe position for Phil to consider himself in. There was something about Marks... but that was unimportant now. He had passed on just enough of what he knew.

Underneath it all however, there was more. That there had been additions communicated by another he was still oblivious, but that an obligation had been satisfied he could feel. He'd liked Charlie in an odd, entirely unnerving way, and it was a shame because no doubt he would be put away for a long time. But Goeth... he would be condemned unless he succeeded in turning the policeman. It was only now, since Phil had fully considered what he had started that he realised how slim the chances were, and that meant that for him, Launa would never find peace.

Tears stung his eyes and Phil looked down at what remained of the crap snuff he had shared with Charlie. He chopped it into lines quickly on the toilet seat, using the blade from a disposable razor and snorted them quietly. An instant head rush sang through his skull and he sniffed the remnants up through his nostrils, letting them trickle down his throat in little globules of mucus. Then, slumping against the toilet basin he took the blade once more, and barely pausing, pressed it hard into his neck. He breathed in shortly as the thin shiv broke the skin, and tears cascaded down his face as he continued to push. He bit his lower lip against the pain and bright blood stained his teeth as he crushed the skin. Finally Phil gave the small weapon a last abrupt shove into the side of his neck and felt the taught fibres of his carotid artery spring back with released tension. Masses of thick blood spurted from the wound, arcing to the ceiling and painting the walls of the cubicle. He wouldn't kill again, and with a lopsided grin of satisfaction on his face, Phil McCearney silently died.

Charlie walked through the night time air, still half dazed after his ordeal. Lines danced through his vision, bright and alive in that strange way the drawings from the book were. The dregs of the narcotics fizzed gently through his veins, peopling the night with the yellow haze of his minds eye. He could have died, through all of that he could have died. How stupid could he be? But there had been more to it than that, more to him. Just as now but at the time clearer, more in control by the riverside.

As it stood he was alive, although to what extent he wasn't entirely sure, but within him the vitality of knowledge burned. Not quite so brightly as before, but bright enough. He knew that next time it would be easier to find this place. His dreams had broken through, they had found a passage, from now on all it needed was a short sharp shove to send them on their way and all that ancestral memory would flood back into his head. Deep in Charlie's hindbrain the wolf lies, still in this acquiescence to its wishes.

Charlie rounded a corner and came to a stop. He was sure this was where... Somewhere, in the back of his head he knew that this was where they would be. It was perfect. Nobody came here, nobody had come here of their own volition in decades. It's occupants never invited guests. They chose instead to go out hunting and scavenging, leaving their stagnant abode with an essence that kept even the strongest willed away. And stagnant it was. It held the rank odour of rotting flesh. Weeks and months of decomposing meat, scavenged and stolen, rotting gently. The flies that swarmed over them made a buzz that was audible at least half a mile away for any that were willing to come this far. This is how the *Krvoses* chose to live, and in this way they could hold fort for weeks.

Charlie crouched by the doorway, the place was larger than he'd thought. Carefully and quietly he removed the fragment of bone stopping the door. He gave a push, just softly, and instantly swung himself back around to the side of the warehouse, out of sight from anything that might become curious. The buzzing of flies was almost deafening this close to the building, and with the door open the smell made him retch. Trying to breath through his mouth, and his heart beating hard in his chest, Charlie carefully peeped around the edge of the doorway. What greeted his eyes was a sight nothing could have prepared him for.

It was a feast, of sorts, although not the kind of feast one would usually associate with high living. Insects weren't the only things filling their bellies at this unholy banquet. Seven or eight small children lay at various intervals within the mass, stuffing fistful after fistful of putrefied flesh into their mauls. Small, innocent hands covered in the grime of blood and gore, sating the malign appetites of their owners.

Even though Charlie knew what they were, knew they were creatures of pure evil, each and every one of them, something about them made him want to shout out. It was only the wolf that held his tongue, all of his human nature called him to take the children away and cradle them in his arms. But silently Charlie watched, his mind holding his body in check as a small girl, loping on all fours gently approached another. It was almost endearing the way she moved, aping the innocence of a chimp in her strides. She looked at the lump of greying meat the other child held in his hand and reached out to take it from him, stroking the back of his head with her other hand, smoothing his hair as she did so.

As soon as her fingers touched the fare however, she screeched. It was a high inhuman voice that made Charlie's ears almost numb with pain. Her arms and face cracked and gullies of crimson sprang from beneath. Her teeth, once blunt and human became pointed barbs and three crests of tight, fine scales arched over her scalp, viciously tearing through her skin as they went. She slashed at the underling with ferocious claws, tearing through the layers of his cheek with ease. Her opponent hissed, a flash of razor teeth and the beginnings of those blood red channels. But he subsided, skittering to the opposite side of the warehouse to nurse his damaged flesh.

The female returned to her childlike cast once more, and happily began to chew on her newly acquired maggoty prize, tearing at it with her young, childlike milk teeth.

Charlie eased his way out of the door once again and pressed his back up against the brick behind him. He ran his hand over his head, tugging on his hair as he did and breathing heavily. He hawked and gagged at the night air, trying not to be sick. He couldn't focus, his mind seemed to be pulling him... but... pulling him...

The memories of a long past ancestor, imprinted on his own memory many millennia ago suffused Charlie's own thoughts. His mind clouded, and for a time at least felt love. His body convulsed involuntarily, *these would be a beginning.*

Chapter Nineteen

Cochrum stared at the papers in front of him. How the hell was he supposed to find anything in the industrial estate? If it wasn't that this had turned into far more than just another case Cochrum would have handed in the information he had and let the teams go in. But that couldn't happen, there was far too much at stake. What choice did he have. The evidence that he had was insane, and yet at the same time it all seemed to fit. Even this chase, this pursuit. It didn't *feel* like the wild goose chase he knew deep in his thoughts that it was. These facts aside however, Cochrum was no longer in control of his actions. He was now being driven by something much deeper, deeper even than his ambition. There were no half measures anymore, everything was an option as long as he got a result. He had to lead the wolf, himself as Mani mere bait at Ap Nudd's request.

He folded up the map in front of him and checked the list on his notepad. There were six buildings within the first three miles of the area that fitted the bill. Cochrum took it as fact that this Goeth was a 'long-termer', it seemed to fit the pattern. There was a place for drugs somewhere in amongst this mess of facts, it couldn't be just coincidence. The first victim, and the last two had all been either dealers or users, or both, but that was where the links seemed to end. They had searched for weeks, but they just couldn't connect them. Cochrum was sure there was something else, something missing, and he was damned if he wasn't going to find it. He was going to find out what was going on, even if it killed him he would find out.

He returned from his reverie to the task in hand. For starters he was sure he could rule out the larger warehouses and buildings. This man from what he had gleaned seemed to be a bit of a loner. The fact that he had chosen to live in the industrial estate told him that, so he wouldn't want to draw attention to himself. Small places it was then. Cochrum hoped that he had done his research well and that his short-list was looking along the right tracks. He needed this to be over soon, something was niggling, and it told him that for some reason there wasn't much time.

The drive out to the estate was unbearable. What would happen when he found the people he was looking for? Should he arrest them? Should he even tell them he was a police officer? He tried to think how they would react. Phil had never remarked on a dealer, but it seemed the logical association to the current situation. No matter what there was no chance that he would have an easy entrance. No doubt he would be treated with suspicion whatever circumstances arose. This didn't really open up many options for Cochrum. Perhaps he could take them by surprise, that might be the best option.

"Best park you well out of sight my darling!" He said, his beloved convertible humming benevolently. "Don't want anyone spotting you now do we."

He pulled up just out of sight of his first location and got out. It had been a good home in its day, mass produced for the miners and their families, and like so many of the time. It was thin, and the mortar had blackened with the smog of the ages, giving a particularly unpleasant air to it. It's roof had partially caved in, and from the gap protruded the canopy of an enterprising young sapling, its errant seed had probably blown in and been lodged in the dirt of the rafters. This small fact gave a jauntily appealing texture to the otherwise lifeless remains of a once practical and staunch building.

Cochrum cautiously made his way over to the door. His hand shaking visibly with nervousness, he gently grasped the door handle. It was cold to touch and the shock of this jolted Cochrums mind to another place. His eyes glazed, and for the first time he wished he had worn some kind of stab-vest or something. No time for that now though. He brought himself back into the present and immediately put his shoulder to the door. Noisily he burst into the front room of the house and took in what lay before him.

There was no ceiling for a start. The back door lay on the ground in the centre of the room and a draft softly blew through the gap that it had once occupied. All of the internal walls had fallen in and the rubble lay scattered around the single, enlarged

109

space that had been the result. In fact, the only thing that seemed to have remained intact was the wooden staircase leading up to a high backed sofa propped on it's side, on top of which the small sapling had enthusiastically taken root. A draft blew through the building and ruffled Cochrum' hair.

"Oh well, number two here we come." he sighed.

At the hospital, Detective Inspector Marks stared unmoving at the scene of Phil's departing, the smell of the drug addicts blood flaring in his nostrils. His anger had long boiled over and now he resided in the calm of abject fury. Stood next to him was the guard who had found the body. He was one of the two that had been left with the man after the dismissal of their earlier, neglectful colleagues, and he was quaking with fear for his job.

"And you say that Richard Cochrum was the last person to speak to him, yes?" said Marks with brittle brightness.

"Yes sir."

"And Cochrum hasn't been seen for how long now constable?"

"At least a day sir. He was supposed to be on duty but he never turned up." The young constable stumbled over his reply but Marks didn't seem to notice.   His thoughts were elsewhere. Eventually he spoke.

"I think we need to have a little chat with Detective Inspector Cochrum in that case." Marks voice was quiet, disturbing, "Go and see if he's at his house. If he is, tell him I want to talk to him. Enough is enough!"

"Yes sir, right away sir." The officer left, gratefully.

Damn Cochrum! Marks was positive now that he was mixed up in this somehow. The man seemed to be blocking him at every turn. It had started fine, a bit of professional rivalry. It was this case though, there was something deeper in it, for both himself and Cochrum. And it wasn't just them, it had gotten to everybody, everyone seemed to be grasping now, withholding from their colleagues. Marks didn't neglect to include himself in this summery of ethic. Ambition was a seductive force, but at least he, Marks, had always stayed on the right side of the law, it was beginning to feel now that Cochrum had strayed over the rails.

Now to look at the facts. Phil McCearney is found with victim number four, obviously a drug related meeting as far as Marks could see. Another man with a similar lifestyle is found in an unrelated incident but detained in the same room. This man, after some time escapes and Cochrum comes to interview McCearney without permission. At this point Cochrum starts to act strangely. Then he interviews McCearney again, disappears and McCearney kills himself.

The facts started to bunch together in Marks mind, creating a pathway that had been missing a link for some time now, but he still couldn't quite put his finger on the whole truth. Phil obviously had an involvement somewhere. Cochrum had visited him.

Cochrum was involved too. They had talked, about what Marks had no idea but it had ultimately led to Phil's death, of this he was sure. That meant foul play. Was Cochrum bent? Was he on the take? It might explain why the case had been at a standstill for so long. Marks superiors certainly thought that this was the case. Marks himself had hoped otherwise but alternate options were getting fewer. It definitely felt as if someone didn't want the killer found, and the animal was almost ethereal. He needed more time to think it through. He had to find Cochrum, that was obvious, that this wolf would doggedly track the lone hunter, these were the facts. Something *other* drew him closer to this case. Charlie was involved in some manner too, and this was definitely under consideration.

Marks mobile began to ring, the jaunty tone clashing unnervingly with the gore that surrounded him.

"What is it, have you found him?" As he listened he pinched the bridge of his nose, his voice lowered almost imperceptibly, "Right, well I'm going to get into that apartment some way or another, I want to know what our detective's been up to." He paused if briefly, "Phone ahead to the station will you and get them to get me a warrant ready." Marks hung up and put the phone back into his jacket pocket. He would get the bastard yet!

Charlie still walks, digesting his recent experience. Blackness whirls around him. It isn't blackness in the sense of darkness, it's something else and it's infuriating. It is nothing. Its an absence, an area of null, it isn't dark, light, its nothing and in that nothing something is burning, is itching and screaming and clawing, and all the time the darkness draws it in, pulls it back so that all Charlie feels is the gap. He still has the edges of something in his brain though, niggling away at him. The edges of horror that have seared in through his eyes. But now that his commonsensical psyche has reasserted itself he can no longer see the core that has only recently contained so much understanding for him. Whatever it has been its obviously just been the result of the cocktail of chemicals that Charlie has put through his body. And yet, he still retains that curiosity that has moved him to take it in the first place.

The confusion this all caused in his mind was more than Charlie could take at that moment. His come-down was more than obvious, the motivation even for movement leaving him to his own melancholy. But even so he knows he must return to the church.

Charlie set out through the deserted streets, his flannel shirt flapping freely in the breeze. He gazed at the dead husks of the buildings around him, wondering how it had come to pass that the area had become so unpopular. It had blatantly once been a thriving and lively district, plenty of businesses willing to set up storage or concern in the warehouses. But now they were all gone, and all that remained was the lifeless shells, left to rot, not even worth the cost of demolition. Left to demolish themselves, time and the elements causing them to slowly decay and fall into their

113

own bodies. He staggered almost drunkenly and vomited against a wall, for a second a hint of canine is definitely visible.

Cochrum had chosen to walk to his next destination. It was a good distance, but the morning was only just coming to a close and the day was still bright and full of life. There would be time to knock at least four of his options from the list, hopefully one of them would bear fruit and he could get to the bones of this investigation before the day was out.

The Detective Inspector rounded a corner between two buildings and checked his map.

"Shouldn't be too far now!" He gradually made his way down the road. This was another area that had been affected by the introduction of better, cheaper buildings.

"Ah, here we are." Huffed Cochrum, unfit despite himself, "You're a pretty little building aren't you!" The irony in his voice was obvious as he looked on the edifice that now stood before him. It was the same one that Charlie had exited only hours earlier, and was now painfully making his way back to.

Cochrum walked watchfully up to the rotten wooded door, fully aware of his exposure.

He pushed on the door lightly and it rocked under the pressure and for the first time noticed its state. He took in the rusted lock and hinges and made a conscientious note of the slightly skewed angle at which it was perched.

"Who needs a nice clean suit anyway!" He smiled to himself.

Crouching slightly so as to not unbalance on the lift he took hold of the grips available. The handle on the right hand side, and the left hand edge, where the adjusted door had not quite met with the wall on Charlie's last exit. He grunted as he lifted the weight, the wood sodden with damp and heavy. Particles of damp mulch squeezed between his fingers as he shifted the weight.

With the offending obstacle out of the way Cochrum called into the gloom, trying to sound as inoffensive as possible. It was vital, after all, to develop a good rapport with these people.

"Hello? Is anybody there?" Nobody answered. Cochrum persevered. "I was sent here by Phil. Phil McCearney? He said he knew you. He said you might be able to help me with a few... details." There was still no sound from the darkness. The detective strained to catch something. The breathing of someone trying to keep quiet, or possibly even the sound of someone legging it out of a back exit. But there was nothing, and he made his way cautiously inside the building.

The main hall looked to be deserted. A few rubbish bags and bits of waste lay scattered here and there where the occupants had left them, but that was it. Cochrum bent to examine some of the detritus. Mostly it was empty tins, licked clean by some rodent or other, but just off to one side he noticed the gleam of something still damp and fresh. On closer inspection it was an almost empty can of baked beans. He knelt beside it and sniffed cautiously, it was still reasonably fresh, that meant that someone had quite recently eaten in this place. Of course, the tenants might not be the same people that he was looking for, but he could soon find that out. The only other room that he could see was on the opposite side and slightly to the front of the main hall, perhaps a vestry or similar from when this had still been a living church. The floorboards in front of it were broken, but still bridged the hole that had contained Goeth's box. Charlie had been very careful in replacing them, it was quite easy to trip and break something with drugs in your system. Hesitantly Cochrum also bridged the gap.

Charlie quickly looked once again around the edge of the wall. The suit was still there, he seemed to be very interested in the building. Shit, Charlie remembered the box. He shook his head, no more time for mucking around.

The man had by now removed the door and had stepped through into the main hall of the church.

"That's ok," said Charlie, "just don't go into the vestry."
He followed the rusted railing around the edge of the building and once more stuck his head out, this time to glance around the doorframe. It was wet to his cheek and he could feel the rotten wood crumbling under the small pressure that he applied to it. Charlie watched as the figure looked around the room, he watched

as it tapped on the door to the vestry, the door easily swinging open at his touch, and watched as it stared at what lay before it.

Charlie stepped silently out into the doorway. He had to do something, he couldn't let that man, if it *was* a man, he couldn't let him go to the police. He couldn't let him leave the building. Inside Charlie's hindbrain the wolf begins to sniff the air, but even so fear will hold the young mans hand.

He looked around himself, there had to be something, anything would do. His eye caught sight of a half brick buried under a sleet of rubbish.

Cochrum loosened the tie around his neck and undid the button of his collar. What should he do now? Wait he supposed, that seemed like the only course of action really. He didn't even know if these were the right people. Even if they weren't, it might be worth having a small chat with them about the stash they'd developed. This was obviously a long-term project, too varied to be a stockpile for selling. The box and items strewn about the room seemed to be small quantities of a great many highly intoxifying chemicals. Cochrum turned his gaze to the floor.

"And what's all this?" he murmured to himself, crouching down to take a closer look. Suddenly he became aware of a presence behind him.

"None of your business mate." said Charlie and hit him hard on the top of the head with his half brick.

Cochrum went down straight away, the blow thudding into the crest of his skull with bone crushing power. Luckily for the policeman Charlie pulled the blow, despite the wolf the man was no murderer.

Cochrum rolled away, his head spinning with pain and blood cascading down his face from where the brick had taken the skin from his scalp. He tried desperately to focus on his assailant, but to open his eyes and look into the light was torture. Charlie was on him quickly, his thin arms desperate in their punches, willing him to hold onto his newly found freedom. Strike after strike rained down on the officer, relatively ineffectual compared to the initial blow. Even so, moments later Cochrum slipped into unconsciousness. The last thing he saw before he blacked out were the wild eyes of terror. Ah, he thought, I've come to the right place.

Chapter Twenty

Detective Inspector Marks stalked through the living room of Cochrum' home. It was very comfortable, but a bit too tasteful for his liking. A bit of clutter was only natural, it made a place feel lived in. Not that his *own* place felt lived in. He'd hardly been there in days, but *this* felt like a show room. He glanced down the corridor, taking in the now defunct entrance. He had allowed the use of a battering ram. Partly out of necessity and partly out of spite. He supposed that if he had waited then it was possible a locksmith could have been called, but that meant time, time that perhaps he didn't have. Who knew what Cochrums place was in all this, but he was going to find out. There was a decisiveness in him, there would not be another death. Besides, it had made him smile, seeing that pristine white door smashed to splinters. Even the nicest people can be vindictive *sometimes*.

They'd been looking around for little over an hour now. For what Marks wasn't sure, he'd know when they found it. So far however, they had found nothing. Not a jot. Cochrum had been very fastidious. Finances were sorted by file, they were currently being analysed back at the station. But aside from that Cochrum had obviously been getting increasingly paranoid. There were no note books so to speak of. In the case of the lists and maps of the industrial estate, they were now in the pocket of his jacket, not that Marks would know that.

"Tear this damn place apart." He yelled, unaware of the futility of the task. "I want every square centimetre searched, do you understand me. Then, when you've done that you can bloody well do it again! There's got to be something here, I can feel it!"

He was well aware of what the press were making of it all, he saw the newspapers every day. On the street, the bus, they all said the same thing. The public were getting scared. At every crime scene they had found little bits of evidence, all pointing in certain directions. They had given a fascinating overview but frustratingly none of the specifics that right now they desperately needed. The circumstances of the killings had collectively made it easy to build up a scenario, but physical evidence was either nonexistent or could lead them no-where. Facts were facts, and the facts were that until this situation with Cochrum there was nothing that could incriminate anyone. Footsteps petered out, and eye witnesses lost all ability to describe what they had seen. But now Marks was seeing patterns. Some had been evident from the start. The regularity of the slaughters, the brutality, the fact that all of the victims had been involved with illegality in some way. And now Cochrum was involved, and it just seemed to fit. Little things were coming together. The precision of the killings implicated that the victims were hand picked but for some reason he couldn't see Cochrum fitting into that role, it seemed far too dirty.

Marks continued with this strange amalgam of thoughts, and while he did he absentmindedly picked his way around the flat. It didn't matter that nothing seemed to quite make sense yet, the overall *feeling* made sense. The feeling in the back of his head, buried away deep in his subconscious that said in following Cochrum he was going to find something. A feeling of dread that he got when he thought about the man and the situation, dread at the neatness possessed of the whole thing.

"His car's not in the garage sir!"

"What?" Marks snapped out of his reverie, barking at the young officer that had just addressed him.

"His car sir," said the man, a little reproachfully, "I went and checked with the car park attendant. He said that Detective Inspector Cochrums car had been gone for some time now, but he couldn't quite recall the last time he had seen it. They have security videos though sir, so perhaps we could find out when he left."

"Right, good work constable. Get onto it right away. He's been gone for some time I'd say. This place has been empty for a few hours at least, and he's driving his car, which I believe is quite distinguishable?"

"Yes sir, lovely motor!" Marks rolled his eyes.

"Well piss off and find it then!"

The subordinate vanished quickly, taking another superfluous policeman with him. No one wanted to be doing nothing around Marks while he was in his current mood.

121

Cochrums head felt like it was packed full of angry bees. They buzzed furiously at him and seemed to chatter incessantly every time he tried to open his eyes. He had been knocked unconscious, he knew that much. And he was pretty positive that he had come to the right place. The connection he had felt to that man, staring into his skull through those bloodshot eyes had told him more than he could have gained from a question. This guy *knew* something, he was positive. But was it Charlie, or Goeth who had attacked him, this he couldn't guess.

A trickle of bloodied saliva dripped from his lips, his head bent forwards at an entirely uncomfortable angle. Damnation, he was thirsty. That was the shock no doubt. Right now his body was full of endorphins and adrenaline, his response to the injury, but damn it hurt. He guessed that the blow had not been meant to kill. It had dealt him a lot of damage, true, but after he had fallen he could have easily been beaten to death, which he hadn't. And that was promising. His brain had so far not given up the ghost, and he hoped that the chemicals pumping through his veins would sustain him long enough for his injuries to sufficiently correct themselves.

After what seemed like an age he managed to get a grip on his bearings and the policeman raised his head. The tendons in his spine pulled uncomfortably, taught and stretched by the way he had been positioned. He was sitting up, and it felt by the way his hands were bound and the uncomfortable thing his back was

122

resting on that he was being propped up by the folded frame of the camp bed he had seen. Squinting in the apparent brightness in the room Cochrum opened his eyes. A fuzzy figure, wavering as if held captive in a heat haze was sat somewhere in front of him. Gradually, as the man's eyes became more accustomed to the glare, and the pain began to fade a little, the blurred figure resolved itself steadily into the form that had put him out of action. It was staring intently at him and drinking a cup of something that steamed.

"Would you like a cigarette mister policeman?" it said and proffered a small white cylinder. "Oh yes, I took the liberty of checking in your wallet. I might as well find out who you are, eh?"

It took another sip of the steaming liquid. Funny, thought Cochrum, the way his eyes don't seem as focussed as they were. They kept flinching to the sides of the room and fading slightly, as if they weren't quite seeing what the rest of the world was. He nodded towards the cigarette being held out by the youth. He didn't normally smoke, but he needed this mans help, and this sign of geniality was promising.

Charlie walked over and gently placed the tab between Cochrums lips.

"Now, I'm going to untie one of your hands so you can smoke this. I'm trusting that you'll use it only to smoke. Your legs are goin' to stay tied mind, and I'm just over there," he said, pointing to the patch of floor he had only just vacated. "So there's going to be no legging it Richard, understand?"

Cochrum nodded, not yet up to making any noise. Charlie untied a single hand, as promised and brought out his cheap plastic lighter to spark up the cigarette. The detective coughed with the first drag, and through his choking spoke his first words since waking up.

"Charlie?" He winced, "I imagine you're Charlie."

"Wouldn't know about that." Replied Charlie cagily.

"I was sent here by Phil!" Continued Cochrum breathlessly. "I thought," but what had he thought, the question remained in Cochrums mind, "I thought I would learn what I needed to know... I'm not here to arrest you."

Charlie stared at the wall in front of him for a few moments. The tea was beginning to make things considerably clearer. Suddenly he snapped back to attention.

"You understand that I can't let you go. He would never let that happen." Charlie looked pained, if only for a moment. "I don't know why, he doesn't like...... Piece of horse shit!"

Once more Charlie stared into the middle distance, his breathing felt shallow to him but that didn't matter.

"I don't think... I can't *tell* you, you wouldn't understand." He took a deep breath, his fingers were cold but that was okay, "He doesn't want me to try, he says there's another purpose for you. That there's no point. What do you think Richard?"

"I won't come back, I promise." An edge of nervousness crept into the Policeman's voice. The wolf was sniffing the air, he

124

tasted his prey close but by the hand materia he was prevented. By Charlie he was... Something was wrong, Cochrum had seen first hand what drugs did and even so there was definitely something wrong.

"Won't come back..." Charlie echoed the Detective Inspector, "You've always enjoyed the night haven't you Richard? The stars, the darkness, the solitude. Charlie got up and walked to the other side of the room, Cochrums eyes following him. "He tells me that the darkness has always enjoyed you as well. He tells me that reflector of Sol, the moon, stops his approach." He paused, "Would you turn, Mani?" He paused again, smiling wolfishly, "Or shall I let the *Vargr* start the end?"

Marks ducked under the plastic blue and white police tape that surrounded the car. It was more than comfortable. A convertible, leather interior, mock chestnut finish on the dashboard, and all just as clean as the apartment.

The air was starting to tighten, he could feel the gathering humidity in his head, making him tense and edgy. He ran his hand quickly through his coarse, dark hair.

"Right, what have we got?" he said.

"Well, it's his car alright." replied a middle aged sergeant named Morris. "We got a positive identification through from the registration number. We did a bit of door knocking and one of his neighbours, a Mrs Jacks from the bottom floor flat said she'd seen him going off towards the industrial estate! I come down with a couple of the lads to have a nosey around and we find this parked up here. No sign of the Detective Inspector though I'm afraid sir. Not quite sure what he could be looking for 'round here, but if he's gone into the district then we're going to have one hell of a time finding him."

"Thank you sergeant." Replied Marks, his tone terse and restrained. "Do me a favour would you, I want this car off to forensics first thing tomorrow. I don't quite know what I expect to find but I'll bet you there's something. Damn it though, it's going to take all week to go over it properly. There's no time to be mucking around." Marks paused for a second before continuing. "Get a surveillance team onto his apartment will you, I want cameras installed, the works. If he comes back then I want to know. If he doesn't then we'll have to start searching in this lot, and I hope like hell we don't have to do that"

As he was leaving sergeant Morris turned around, he looked sheepish.

"The press are looking for a statement you know sir. They want to know where we're getting. Shall I tell the press office to prepare something or do you think we can hang on a bit longer?"

"Shit Morris, we've *got* to hang on longer. If Cochrum knows we're after him he'll go into hiding and we'll never get to the bottom of all this. Inform the press office that I'll deal with it. Tell them it's in my inbox!"

Morris knew what *that* meant. Oh well, he thought, not my problem.

Chapter Twenty-One

Charlie woke with a start.   His mind was confused, almost...
displaced. He ran his hands over his face, feeling the pocked skin
beneath his fingers. *This* was real, he was positive of that, but with
his nightmares still fresh in his mind the rest of the universe
seemed ever so slightly out of kilter.

"I'm losing my grip." he muttered, and picked up what he
had rolled previous to his slumber. Everything would seem a lot
clearer after this. He inhaled deeply, enjoying the harsh flavour
sinking through the rotted bronchia of his lungs. There was
something malign in the air, something greasy and thick but he just
couldn't focus on it. Focus. Focus was central, he couldn't lose
focus, there was too much danger for that. To hell and back, he
really needed a hit! And there was that policeman as well. Well, he
had to start somewhere, and it was the only way. To turn the
incarnate body of the moon itself: Mani.

He sat up and perched himself on the end of the desk. He'd
spent the night on it and he shivered with the cold ache that it had
pushed into his muscles. Cochrum remained where he had left him,
although he now lay supine with only his arms in the air, held aloft
by the rope tying them to the bed frame. It looked entirely
uncomfortable.

There is a deep, hot flare in front of the policeman. It's only small but in the glumness that surrounds him it's more than obvious. Lips inhale deeply, a noxious mixture that smells heavy and unfamiliar to the policeman. Hot. And then a cloud of dark umber-blue smoke tumbles off and around. This is not a drug that Cochrum has had contact with before, his curiosity sneaks around at the back of his attention. There are more important things.

"Bet you've got well bad pins an' needles don't you?" Charlie grinned.

Cochrum pulled himself upright,

"Is there anything to drink?" The question hung in the air for a moment before Charlie answered. His voice was soft but even so the answer was no less cryptic.

"Not for the moment," he said, "Although you may need to purge later!" He crouched down in front of the policeman, his eyes intent on something, but not anything that Cochrum could identify. Eventually he spoke. "What are you here for Richard?"

"What do you mean?" Cochrum's voice was confused.

"You know what I mean Richard," replied Charlie, "Why did you come here... Really?" Cochrum paused for a moment before answering.

"I came for the truth... I guess. I don't care anymore, just the truth!"

Charlie looked down at Cochrum, there was something in his eye. Again the focus was there, was back after a fashion, but there was something with it as well.

"What is it?" He said, nervous at once at Charlie's expression.

"Nothing," replied Charlie, he smiled, "Nothing."

As he turned away there was a twinge, only slight, but as his cheek twitched he knew that the wolf was unhappy. Even so, for the time at least he had the majority, Mani would have the chance.

Snap to a wasteland. It's fairly large in size, flat, grey. Except that it's not grey, it's lots of colours, but grey is all that can be seen. There should have been something else here, but it doesn't look like its ready yet. Maybe if we come back in a little while. Maybe we were meant to come earlier, that would make sense. There *was* something, and it went and soon it will be back again. Perhaps. It's an illogical problem since there have been no parameters defined. But even so there's a thickness to the air. Not toxic, not intoxicating but liquid, fluid, almost tactile. How it sustains itself is a mystery. Perhaps it doesn't. Sustain itself. But in not doing so it deprives itself of the vital energy that is obviously required. This makes no sense. This is another land, another world. The Otherworld.

Charlie put down the two needles he had filled, the fluid inside so enticing. He walked over to Cochrum and stood in front of him.

"I smelled burning?" said the policeman.

"Yes, you did." replied Charlie. "Now, I'm going to ask you one more time. Is it really the truth you're after? Is it for you, or is it for your career, 'cause if it's for your career then I don't think you're going to want me to do this."

"It's for me! Do what? What are you going to do?" Charlie took out a scabby looking scarf and wrapped it tightly around Cochrum' eyes, making sure that he couldn't see. Then he went and got the syringe containing the opiate. It would have to be intramuscular, there was no way this guy was going to hold still for an intravenous shot. The thigh was the deepest muscle wasn't it? It would have to be that one then, he didn't want to hurt him after all. To the side of his mind the wolf growled, but even though it had control now it was curious, and there would never be another time such as this. Not to mention, Mani, the moon could still be destroyed afterwards.

The force of the jab easily pushed through the cotton of Cochrum's suit, and even as he was yelping Charlie had pushed the plunger.

"What *was* that you bastard?" But Cochrum was already shaking, the chemicals in his body pulsating to the new beat.

"Fucking hell." He said, this time in a much smaller voice. But by now Charlie was no longer listening. Instead he had

131

tightened a tourniquet around his arm and was busily injecting himself with his own long awaited hit. Charlie lay back and soaked it all in. He felt the familiar sense of lead in his limbs as the euphoria overtook him. His mouth was dry and his skin was warm. On the inside his fur itched as the wolf muzzled his way forward.

Cochrum was going through similar sensations, all entirely unnerving to the Detective Inspector. He was pretty sure he knew what had been injected into him, and it scared him. But the sensations, the 'rush' was so intense... Cochrum succumbed to the drug, finally allowing his body to enjoy what he had no control over at all.

Time ticks on a pace... *tick!*

He finished the sentence he was writing and spared a glance over towards the redundant form of the detective. He was less accustomed to the substance than Charlie, and as a result had been slipping in and out of consciousness since the very beginning. It wouldn't take long to build him up though, Charlie didn't intend to take the long road, there just wasn't time.

For a moment Charlie stares at the wall... at the cracked and peeling plaster in front of him. It's beautiful... beautiful in that same way that spiders are. It has a grace to it that at any moment could potentially skitter forwards and strike. This is unusual in that to all effects and purposes it's only a wall. A wall that has admittedly seen better days but a wall all the same.

Charlie shudders with claustrophobia. It isn't the room that's small. On the contrary, it's quite spacious but the air is thick and dense. Like grease. Familiar. There are also misgivings about the policeman.

One considers that it may be easier to kill him, and a lot less trouble.

The other looks at the situation and sees the policeman's malleability. He is susceptible. A path is opening before him. He thinks he might take it. Charlie thinks he might take it too, although it's not his path. Not his policeman. Is it the right one?

A bead of sweat drips from Charlie's nose and hits the page in front of him. Diffuse lines swirl around the sudden sodden patch, writhing against the page like so many drawings from another place. Like the wall. Sucking in deeper. Like the waste-ground.

Could he slip out for a moment? Surely it would be okay for a while, and what would happen even if he did wake up. Charlie stood up and rubbed his eyes, he looked over to where Cochrum was slumped. Something had to be done. This man had to be broken. He puts down his pen and turns the page.

Beep.

Edward poked his head out from behind a wheel arch. He was lying at present full length on a low, wheeled metal trolley. The majority of his body was obscured by the back end of Cochrum's car, the wheel lay off to one side surrounded by a multitude of nuts and bolts.

"We've been looking for over two days already sir," he said, addressing Marks who was sitting on the edge of a table a few meters away. "The team's exhausted, I really don't see that more time would achieve anything."

He rolled himself out from under the car and stood up, wiping his greasy hands on a cloth. He was dressed in a light baby-blue overall, marking out his rank slightly against the main body of the forensics team.

"There's got to be *something!*" said Marks in tired exasperation. He pinched the bridge of his nose against his exhaustion. They were all feeling the same he knew, they were all irritable. The team had been working constantly since they found the car, every single scrap of rubbish being analysed and traced. Marks knew he was pushing them hard, but it was about time this farce of a case was closed. Anything Cochrum had done in that car, they'd been over it.

"Well, anyway," said Edward, "this is pretty much the last thing I think we're going to find." He held up a small polythene bag, it contained a tiny amount of sandy powder. "Before you say anything, its mud! I found it under the wheel arch just now. It'll have to go off for comparison, but I'd say off the record that it came from somewhere up the parklands district."

"Didn't the drug squad do a raid up there a couple of weeks ago?" asked Marks, all at once suspicious.

"Yes they did, but don't you be getting any far flung ideas. He's a copper remember."

"Maybe," persisted Marks. " but it wasn't his case. He would have needed permission to investigate someone else's crime scene. Mind you," he added darkly, "Cochrums never really been one for getting peoples permission."

Marks stopped speaking abruptly, his internal monologue too full of notions to express any of them and he sat there at the end of the desk thinking quietly to himself.

"This is circumstantial at best sir." Said Edward after a short while.

"What? Oh, yes." Replied Marks, jumping at the interruption. "It's only a matter of time though Ed. He's messed up somewhere along the line, we just have to find out where."

Marks voice was far away as he spoke, distant and strange, lost in his own mind. "It all works in my head you see," he continued, "He fits into all this. There's a space in the pattern and *he* fits."

Edward slowly began to edge away from his superior. The man looked odd, his eyes were glazed and there was a thin veneer of sweat across his forehead. It made him look animal, violent. It made him look hungry.

"I think we should stop searching the car now sir." Said Edward nervously.

"Yes," replied Marks, "I thought you'd say that."

Beep.

Marks sat in his office gnawing on a pencil. It was beginning to get dark outside, the creature always attacked in the dark, as far as they could tell in any case, and there had still been no sightings of Cochrum. Had he got it all wrong? Maybe his peer had been onto something. *He* could have ended up being the next victim and they just hadn't found his remains yet. No, he didn't fit the bill. The circumstances were wrong. Their killing machine was predictable in some ways at least.

But Marks still had this overwhelming feeling that Cochrum was deeper in than any of them should be. Things were starting to get very hot, and Marks wasn't sure how much more heat the police-force could take. There were demands being made of them for safety, for assurance. The chief was gnawing at the bit for forceful implementation of law. Things were starting to get very hot indeed.

The Detective Inspector stood up from his desk. There wasn't much more he could do today, and besides, the emotional and psychological energy that he was using had left him completely drained. The gathering cloud on the horizon added nothing good to his condition, a storm right now would make things even harder. How could he be expected to think straight when the world around him was doing its best to bend him out of shape. A good nights sleep would do him the power of good. He couldn't actually remember the last time he'd had an undisturbed night. It was the pressure, it had to be. He got headaches that just wouldn't go away, and just recently he'd been having the most awful nightmares. Unsurprising considering the state of the crime scenes he'd been dealing with. Tonight though he would check himself into a hotel, have an early night with a book and get his head straight.

Marks grumbled inwardly at the weather and stepped out into the cool evening breeze. His hair tickled his temples as he strolled out into the quickly darkening streets. He always let it flop naturally whichever way it pleased, its fluidity a stark juxtaposition to the ramrod efficiency with which he kept everything else about his person. He grinned, his mouth turning up at the corner and revealing just a hint of canine.

Why not walk to the hotel, he thought as he neared his car. It's a nice evening and the fresh air will be good for my constitution. Already he could feel his grasp on reality being strengthened. He imagined the corners of his mind filling out to the full-bodied grey matter it had resembled before all this trouble

137

began. And with it, although he had no way of knowing this, the impression that had been worming its way through alongside his stress was pushed back, joining everything else that he had rejected so long ago.

Chapter Twenty-Two

Time has passed. There is an ache as well as the familiar pinch as the needle breaks the skin. A bead of blood bigger than usual swirls to the surface. A vein has collapsed. Charlie pushes the plunger, sandy fluid flows into Cochrum. There are bruises and deep scores in his arm already. He barely even resists. He thinks he might want it but he's not quite sure yet. His mouth tastes of tin and he feels warm… comfortable.

…unreasonable. The moon bows in homage.

His wrists were raw with pulling and tugging at the ropes now, his eyes were dark and thick stubble covered his chin. He was barely recognisable as the man that had entered the building... whenever that had been. He had lost weight as well. The drugs had increased his metabolism to such an extent that the food he took in burned up almost instantly in an attempt to keep the flow of energy constant.

Cochrum could feel his body rotting around his brain. Could feel himself falling apart, but even so his mind seemed stronger, so much surer in itself than it had ever been before in his life. He felt warm and safe with the narcotics in his blood stream, and then when they had gone he felt lonely. He felt as though he had lost something that, although it was just out of reach his mind was nevertheless holding him secure. He knew himself so much better with the drugs inside him...

...while the devil walked beside him.

But still he hadn't found what he had come for. Sometimes he forgot his reasons, when the drugs completely took hold... *and in doing so the red and black the dark shaped harpy the fugitive of time would whine and chirp in quick succession and pull the tangled cobwebs. And as they sweep aside they say their sweet deride and chide and fashion all their passion they force aside their hate and pride and push within the wolfs own skin a truth so deep so long to keep. That Charlie slips inside the cracks in his own mind. Remains concealed, hidden and so strands of his soul recalled at bidding. That he might survive to feel pride. Pride of the self, pride of the soul, pride of his health as a moonlit mole burrows beneath Vargr's skin. Seeks to withhold and prevent further sin...* At the end though, he always returned to that place in his mind, the place that craved the truth. And he still hadn't seen it as far as he could see. He had endured this psychological torture, watched his body start the continuing journey to complete atrophy and had been given nothing of the truth for which he searched in return.

"When are you going to tell me?" he asked for the thousandth time. Charlie didn't even look up from his task.

140

"It's going to take a while. We'll get you there soon though!"

Charlie was disconcerted by his current feelings towards the police officer. Cochrum was obviously his senior by a few years and yet there was a sense of age in Charlie that he couldn't deny. In essence Charlie claimed fatherhood for want of better phraseology. He would stand *tad uwch*.

Sandy powder broke easily. Chopped and re-chopped, shuffled and lined. And then something else. A distillate, greenish brown in colour, unrefined and viscous, yet to be fortified but strong in itself nonetheless. Charlie poured a drop of surgical spirit onto this and then added the powder, he blew on it experimentally and the alcohol visibly evaporated in a brief waft. He smiled to himself quietly and re-hydrated the material for cooking. Cochrum was still looking at him. This was an experiment in more than just chemistry, it was an experiment in dependency. He turned slightly so that the policeman's view was a little more obscured.

"Is... is there enough for me as well?" stammered the Detective Inspector nervously. Charlie smiled to himself. He hid his delight by turning even further.

"I expect so my friend, I expect so." He said.

With this reassurance Cochrum settled back once more. It had been an uncomfortable day and he was stressed out. He was sure that Charlie was aware, Cochrum had seen him watching. Not in a malicious way but Charlie had a way of scratching the itch. He knew when it was time...*mewn anobaith amser yn gwybod.* Somewhere, in the back of his mind a little light flickered, but it was quickly hushed away by his now rusted endocrine system.

There is a hush in the air, a stillness at the moment although it's barely perceptible in the dim light. A shadow stands next to Cochrum, it is outlined in magnificent electric blue, threads pulling tight to the policeman's skin. A separation. There is separation in the air as well. A gap has opened. No, not a gap, more like a void, a vacuum, it begs to be filled. A malefactorious essence is distilling in front of him, it doesn't seem all that bad, it will fill the gap.

The key remains within the proprietorial, of conscious thought detain. Remain cogent all the while, ally yourself for gaining truth and guile within the pastures bold. But be told, the separation of serenity and self becomes the open man, and he will need something deep within that seeks to hold his hand.

Over the last several days Charlie had systematically stepped up Cochrums drug uptake. He had been assaulted on a near inquisitorial scale, succumbing without hope of protest. There was no opportunity, but like so many others before him he felt less and less inclined towards seeking opportunity out. He had surpassed all of Charlie's concerns. More and more Cochrum looked at the world through Moon eyes.

After what seemed like an age to the policeman, the young man finally walked over with a syringe held firmly in his mitt. Cochrum closed his eyes and relaxed, awaiting the now familiar jab that would see the end of the itch. He was endlessly surprised then to feel Charlie fumbling around beside him. It was only when his hands suddenly flopped onto his legs that Cochrum realised he had been untied! His arms had become so dead through being held up for so long that feeling in them had been seriously impaired, and as the blood gradually filtered back through the half collapsed capillaries an intense and painful feeling of pins and needles spread though his flesh. Cochrum looked up at Charlie who had stepped back and now crouched on the floor at his feet, still holding the delicious narcotic lollipop.

"I think maybe I can trust you now!"

Cochrum nodded, and with only the barest hesitation he held out his arm, palm upwards, slightly bent at the elbow. Charlie smiled.

"So eager to go to school aren't you!" he said. He took hold of the man's arm, squeezing tightly and massaging the area around the hinge until blue veins protruded, naked against the slow onslaught of the thin needle.

"I think we'll have you out and about sooner than I thought Richard."

Cochrum stared into Charlie's eyes as the plunger pushed the liquid into his circulatory system. Charlie watched as the mans own eyes went from dark brown, slipping up inside his head until only the whites were showing. He grinned.

Beep.

"Okay ladies and gentlemen." Marks announced over the hubbub, he'd been gearing up to this moment for over a month now. "If I could have a bit of quiet please we can go over what's expected of us all today and get this show on the road."

There was a large crowd gathered in the main office room of the police station. Marks had acquired and cajoled forces from all departments for this task. There was no way in hell he was going to be able to accomplish it without them. Of course there would be a huge amount of red tape to go through later. Why so many coppers had been drafted to this department, and why as a result most of the city's policing resources were being fed into a single operation. But the Detective Inspector was confidant that he could win round his superiors. After all, it wasn't just the lower ranks that this case had captured. If Marks could wrap this up quickly, he would be a hero, a celebrity. The endless press conferences that his commanding officers found themselves obliged to speak at were creating more than a nuisance, they were a battle in themselves. The sooner the press were sated with some kind of result the better, and the glory would answer everyone's questions.

"As you all know, this is quite a roughly assembled plan of action, so please bear with me. I believe that the man we seek, one Detective Inspector Cochrum, currently suspended due to his suspected involvement is in hiding somewhere within the industrial estates to the West, section fifteen. We've all worked hard to get this operation on its feet, lets not waste the opportunity. We've thrown all our balls in the air now, *this* is the one we need to catch. He's been off the radar for a while as we all know, paper trail for this one's been long-winded but we're there now. We don't know who else is involved so keep on your toes. Finally of course there's the..." he trailed off momentarily and looked to the floor, a number of other officers blanched slightly at the thought, "and we all know what that can do! Now Cochrum, he's our key and he's opened the door. He's given us our 'in' and I sure as hell don't intend to waste it. Ladies and gentlemen, lets close this case!" There was raucous applause from the gathered assembly, the hundred or more officers involved shaking the tables with stamping and clapping. This was inspirational. This was motivating.

"The buildings that we are going to be searching over the next few days are spread out quite thinly. We've got a wide radius to cover. You have all been given a number between one and four have you not?" There was a mass of mutterings to indicate that they had indeed all been given a number.

"Team leaders have been appointed. For your own safety, stay within your team and obey the commands given to you. If you locate anything suspicious, call in to base. I will be running the control station from the Eastern quarter. I expect reports from you all at least once every ten minutes. If you come across the creature, treat it with *extreme* caution. If each team leader will come to me at the end of this briefing, I'll hand out the maps. If required, there will be an armed response unit available as well as unit animal handlers. Are there any questions?"

For a while nobody speaks. There is a small amount of muttering and coughing but on the whole the room is quiet. Marks tidies his papers and prepares to return to the relative safety of his office. There is a hand in the air.

"Yes constable?" he says.

"That's sergeant sir!" he says.

"Sorry, please continue."

"Just a couple of the lads were wondering how Rich got all mixed up in this?"

Marks feels a compulsion. The question is answered awkwardly and to the satisfaction of no-one, but Marks knows that it's right. He has to find Cochrum, and it doesn't matter how many rules he breaks or lies he tells to get him there. Cochrum has had similar feelings recently. Well, at an earlier point in time. We may not be aware of how long. But for some acceptance doesn't come quite as easily. There is rebellion, a didactic paradigm, an oxymoronic juxtaposition of attitude. It could cause an issue were

146

it pressed. Lets hope it's not pressed. He is completely close-minded to everything apparently illogical and this is worrying.

After twenty minutes of watching the room outside milling around in collective confusion, the first of the team leaders entered his office. They weren't happy with his explanation, but they knew their superior and they knew it was all they were going to get. There were over forty buildings to search over the next sixteen hours. Each group would do a shift on and a shift off. After that there would be another forty, and another. There were endless buildings in section fifteen. No-one knew exactly how many, or if it came to that, how many it would be possible to search before Marks favour with the chief ran out. There was a book running, and the stakes were getting higher and higher.

The morphine still hadn't worn off, the taste of tin lingering slightly longer than he was used to in the policeman's mouth, but Charlie approached once more, a syringe brimming with liquid.

"No, no more!" Muttered Cochrum childishly, and waved the younger man to disappear.

"Don't you want the truth Richard." replied Charlie, so close that Cochrum could feel his breath caressing the skin of his cheek. He spoke softly, and gently ran his hand over the side of Cochrum' neck. The feeling was intense, all his senses heightened.

147

"I think its time Richard. I think you want this now!" he paused for a second.

There is a sense of time in all of us, the pull of the wind, the force of the ground. When all abounds this we may say, that to pay the feeling deep within, to still the mind but yet fit in we must accomplish first a binding thought. Once wrought it tides for happier times, times of quiet certitude that can't elude the hostile charms that seek to waylay.

But bypass this to double layers, when ancient sayers soothe to charm to mediocre lovers given each and every deafening heart. When central discourse widening tor they count to tethra when foot to floor they feel the tan of hides, that clash and meet toward the middle. To twiddle their thumbs and hide.

A synapse flares, the heartbeat skips and minds begin to blend and fray, but stay. There is no choice, the harshest mercy to persist that those who started must force issue and embellish the cruellest living tissue. That rots and boils in definite contempt, for company we must lament. But without such base a receptor guides to distant parts that lose the chase.

Cochrum was apostate. His current mental state was confused and sublime all at once. There was a tearing in what he felt, his own

148

person felt disconnected. He was completely at Charlie's mercy and this was both comforting and unsettling.

A hand brushes Cochrum cheek. There is a whisper in his ear, it sounds lyrical like so many angels talking in unison. But not angels. No, not angels but something else. There is a quiver in the voice, it is excited. More touching, more physical contact. Fear and paranoia are unusual but not unknown. There is a hint that some may be near.

In matter of fact the atmosphere is close, humid almost, palpable certainly. There is tension. This comes primarily from the distilled, the mind of matter. The apostate seeks enlightenment but the cost is becoming clear. Colour whirls and patterns form and unform, the unity of blackness becomes paramount but the apostate isn't sure he understands. The purpose is recognised that's definite but there may be an amount of trepidation that is curious to the outward observer.

There are fluctuations in what the observer may or may not see, an aphasia of subliminal language, a structured synonym for the features presented in front, to the fore. The rear contains, as has been alluded to a principality of darkness, no sorry, blackness. This is key. This is a key. No, not a key but something else entirely, the matter of fact existence of...

Headless down a darkened hall, trepidly they creep, their little hearts are pumping and their jaws around their feet. But guide me child of light, into the water go, and lift my feet up high, let me ride the flow.

Around the spires and glass peaks, across the darkened floor, move with swiftness, care not leisure for closed shall be the door. And through with ram or lockpick, but open it you should, and never be afraid of a scythe and a blackened hood.

Charlie abruptly ended his tirade, taking the policeman by surprise and quickly grabbed Cochrum around the chin. He pulled his head sharply to the side, and stabbed down with the needle, jabbing it straight into the carotid artery. The policeman screamed in shock and pain as the drug addict drove the shot home, and he tried ineffectually to pull his head away. The addicts' grip was like a vice however. With a well practised movement the needle was withdrawn and Charlie's hand moved quickly from Cochrum' chin to his neck, clamping itself around the point of injection, making it impossible for any blood to escape.

After a few minutes the man at Charlie's crouched feet lay still, all struggling forgotten, concentrating only on his breathing. He slowly withdrew his hand from the stout neck. The hole had closed through the shear pressure of his fingers, and already platelets had formed a weak scab.

Charlie walked back to the desk and sat down. It was going to be a long few hours, but this was a vigil that needed to be kept.

There was a storm building outside, the pressure in the air was gathering, slowly but surely beating down anything that stepped out into its midst. Humidity hung from the walls of the broken buildings all around the policemen. It made them sweat, and stink. The air so close that it couldn't evaporate. Massive black clouds had been moving in for some time, pulled from all around by the void created by the heat of summer. They swirled in a huge anticlockwise mess of global perspiration. But any breeze that might have pushed them there was far above the rooftops. Everything below the cloud line was stagnant, as if seated in a city sized pressure cooker. People sat in their houses or walked down the streets, just waiting for the storm to break, for sheer Pascalic pressure to be such that it crushed itself and rain came tumbling down in great sheets. But that wasn't to happen yet. Instead the sky crackled with stored energy, and bided its time.

The policemen were nervous. The atmosphere was too familiar, and it boded ills that none were too willing to find. Somehow, they all knew that one of them was going to die that day.

Beep.

Two and a half miles away, Marks sat in the surveillance van that had been parked not so far from where Cochrums once forlorn car

151

had. The Detective Inspector told himself it was the spot most central to the search area, but really it was to keep his loathing of the vehicles owner tight and focussed in the face of the task *he* had instigated!

A multi-band radio, receiver and transmitter, with links to all of the team leaders was currently occupying the space around Marks ears. The independent teams each had a separate bandwidth the Detective Inspector could key into with the merest flick of a switch, and the team leaders themselves could do the same from their handheld radios. It all worked perfectly, but all of the comms technology in the world couldn't control the results.

The tension in the truck was incredible, the technicians assisting knew the risks of the operation. It was a polygamous march through the police force, multi-departmental and that meant jurisdictional queries and hierarchical buffeting. Marks was the most on edge, he continually barked commands and requests down the mouthpiece of his headset. Redirecting teams and ordering the rapid search of whatever the next building was. So far they'd found nothing, and this was certainly taking its toll on those involved. Anxiety levels on the field were as high as in the van, and the interchanges between the various positions did nothing to alleviate the situation.

The radio rattled one more time, the sounds of a muffled, interference stained voice crackling through from group one. There was nothing to report. Marks slammed his fist down on the surface in front of him.

"Shit! That's nearly all of the short listed options. If we don't get a result soon there's going to be trouble."

Silently the technicians considered this. Yes, there was going to be trouble, but they all knew where the buck stopped, and it wasn't with them.

Chapter Twenty-Three

It is getting dark outside by the time Cochrums eyes finally open, a deep nectar of blue pervading the room from what grubby windows can be seen. Spasms still occasionally judder through his body, convulsing within his diaphragm, making him wretch out the last contents of his stomach. But the night doesn't enter into everything. Most things certainly there is an aspect to be considered, but on the whole it is not the intention that it is the centre of things. There are other things at the centre. Time has eroded, cracked, battled with the ancient signs that hold it in place. Writing on writing on writing in confused commiseration.

Past this there is something further to consider, that the metaphysical is not the only element that may be affected. There may also be a certain amount of physical de-representation, a submissive genome that is easily waylaid. That is fractured. This can account for a number of the events that have been perceived.

But in what context they make sense is something for the self, for the avatar.

Cochrum' lip curled at the side, it was cracked with vomit and mucus. Something was open, he could feel the draught. His lungs felt swollen, processed like tinned meat but there was air as well.

"Is the door open?" whispered the air. Charlie gently picked up his hand and cupped it in his own.

"I know," he said, and the confidence that he exuded made Cochrum smile. "Do you think you can stand up yet? Only, I think we ought to take a short stroll, there's something I want you to see."

Cochrum nodded, and unsteadily hoisted himself into a sitting position.

"Steady, steady, you alright, yeah?"

"Yes. Thank you!"

"Don't think about it." said Charlie urgently. "Don't push it away"

"But... I wanted to ask you something. I can't remember... There's..." Charlie listened as the man talked. It was hard not to condescend towards him, he was so childlike, still so unformed. Form could be added later of course. What he was saying now was interesting but bore little relevance to the task in hand. Charlie let it wash over him, through him, answering when he thought it possible. For the most part Cochrum had few questions, but the

154

necessity for speech after such an experience was overwhelming. Compartmentalisation was tantamount to understanding.

Cochrum kept muttering to himself as he walked across the hall, trying to remember something that was fading far too fast. Much as he tried though, he couldn't quite grasp it. He had this vague feeling that there would be another dead body in the morning, but he didn't know where, and he didn't know who.

A shadow passed in front of the window. Both men froze, concentrating on the movement. It was a group of people, about ten or so, walking along the path outside the church. The one at the back paused for a second in front of the window. Cochrum could feel his heart thumping, it seemed a long way away, but incredibly loud all the same. There was a crackling noise, as of someone talking into a radio, and then the figure moved on.

"What the hell are the police doing here Richard?" said Charlie, his voice urgent against the echoing walls of the hall.

"I don't know, I don't know." Placated Cochrum. "I don't know, I can't think straight."

"Shit! Alright, we're just going to have to..." A sharp flash of lightning lit up the room, blinding the two companions into silence, the storm broke. Thunder screamed from above, shattering everything that was able and beating paperwork across the floor. It cracked high above them, starting at a disconcerting baritone and breaking into an explosion of roaring air. Unseen in the murk of

155

the sky, sheets of rain swamped in on themselves, filling the void left by the earthed electricity. Cochrum had ducked when the sound came, it forced him brutally down onto his knees, and he covered his ears. The storm was directly overhead, its eye staring down onto the church with baleful malevolence.

Eventually the thunder crumbled to a halt, but in its wake an equally terrifying noise took over.

The team of policemen looked nervously at the sky, the clouds towering over them like gigantic airships straining against the potential pull of the wind. It was going to break at any moment. The streets were steadily being encased in muggy darkness, men were stumbling and swearing as they tripped over loose bricks and odd bits of rubbish. They were jittery, on edge.

"Right," said Morris, addressing his team, " I think its time we got some torches on lads." There were some murmurs of agreement from the dark behind him, and one by one nine thin beams of light shrouded the walls in shadow. Morris shuddered despite the humid heat and tugged at the throat of his Kevlar vest.

Morris turned and looked behind himself puzzled. He was sure he'd heard something. A fork of lightning crashed out of the sky, lighting the whole alleyway with glowing white after images and a mass of thunder pummelled the gravel.

"My head, my head, my fucking head!" screamed Charlie. He scrabbled at his hair, his face a mask of pain and panic. The storm had broken. The pressure that had been steadily building in the sky had cracked with the lightning, and with it, Charlie's mind had cracked too. The sudden difference seared through his skull, breaking the ties that held his reptilian mind from the rest of his body. It took over, instinct overriding every other command. But just before he lost complete control... *In darkness they're buried, in sickness you see but remember the time that you came home to me, you broke me and beat me and I sat through the worst. In defence of your soul the belt wasn't bad but I was lachrymose to say, and apart through the doors you tumbled away and left me your heart till the end of the day.*

Richard Cochrum stared in sickening terror at the juddering form in front of him. His friend, his adopted ally, the man who had shown him the light was what he had searched for all this time, what he had longed to discover, to destroy. But it was only now, when his mind was finally open to what his eyes were showing him that he could see the real truth. There was no killing this thing. Even through believing eyes it was an impossible monstrosity. But he had advantage in his awareness.

Skin swells in powerful lumps shoulders cracking, gristle breaks down with an audible popping, his animal being in a rage of agony, but through disharmony, through the armoury of bestiality

he arms. In instinct based charms.

The pops of veins and muscle fibres were frighteningly loud above the torrential rain. They ripped and tore, the body's mechanism for healing sealing them back together in larger, grotesque lumps of their previous selves. Testosterone arced its way from Charlie's pituitary gland, forcing aggression into his very bones. It made the hair on his body grow and stand out in places where there had been no hair before, forcing the need for self-preservation into even this smallest aspect of his being.

Fusing muscle, taking shape and pulling, downward in a tussle.

Laughing dogs so full of muscle prize the arch disciple of the

principal example that covered the once meagre frame, it became

solid and tough, the tension held within them, pulling him in,

making him rough.

Cochrum whimpered in fear, he could feel paranoia, feel it sear through his body, that shoddy laboratory for drugs that weakened him, that in speaking to him stood him firm so that he could not turn. He looks, he feels the burn.

Unable to move, to scramble or run, he watches as it screams in anguish. And amongst the omnivorous, the superfluous there come sharp serrated blades of fun. They dull the sides with blood, tearing through the flesh-like hood of gums and jaw, forming a maw. Calcareous yet cancerous, growing from comparative stumps, watch as the blood pumps from open mouths. There were shouts, it was primitive and bestial, based on instinct and survival. It *was* human though, but deeper, much deeper.

The animal stood up, still obviously in pain from the sudden change in atmosphere, scratching at its head and creating huge gouges that self sealed as they were made, the same hormones that broadened the muscles helping to heal. It fought to keep its balance for a moment, staggering under the forgotten weight that its new muscles had to bare. The density of its brain tissue, that had slowly forced itself together with the pressure of the storm, adapting and hardening, protecting itself and the genetic information in its cells that had been violently torn apart. The wolf defending itself and taking full control of Charlie's body.

In the state that Charlie now occupied, he could never have recognised that it might have been an invisible enemy tearing at his brain. All he saw was that there was only one other animal in the room, and it must be that which had caused him to hurt so much. Deep in his hindbrain the wolf directs, pushes with all its might. Now is the time for the Moon to cease.

Cochrum stared at the monster, cowering back as it approached. "I... I found it," he said. "You're what I was looking for all along! Charlie?"

Beep.

Marks sprinted down the street, following the noises that his brain still half refused to recognise. Something though, something inside him was telling him to keep going, to keep running. And so on he ran, the rain whipping at his face.

Lightning split the sky once more, and a great howl emanated from an ally to his left. Marks skidded on the waterlogged tarmac as he changed direction, no longer aware of who was with him and who wasn't. He just needed to *run*. Blood pounded through his skull, his body screaming at him with every tearing step, willing itself forward, pushing itself to the extreme.

He rounded the corner onto the street where the church lay. He was completely alone now, his fellow officers following in the armed response vehicle terrified of what they might find. Because of this, they would arrive at the building a good five minutes later. But Marks was driven. His suit sodden and his eyes stinging with the downpour that surrounded him, he crashed into the derelict, somehow knowing without doubt that this was the place where it would all end.

The sound of crunching gristle met his ears as the splintering of the doorway died away, and his eyes followed the sounds to the apparition crouched in the middle of the room. Its head snapped around with inhuman speed, and a final crack signalled the complete settling of Charlie's new form.

160

"Don't move!" Screamed Cochrum from his position on the floor. He had a gash in his side and through it his entrails hung, splattered across the floor beside him in a stream of gore, the morphine in him the only thing keeping him alive. Great claw marks were raked across his face, and his bottom lip was swollen, the blow splitting it completely along one side.

Memories rammed themselves against Marks rock hard rational conviction, and he stuttered to a halt. His face contorted, an agony of inner turmoil as the monstrosity of bestial power turned its attention again to Cochrum. Once again, it roared, harmonics of the possessed human mind breaking through alongside the animal scream of pain as streaks of blood streamed from its mutilated gums. All Charlie was now was wolf, all thoughts of turning the Moon gone, all thoughts of collaboration forgotten. What he'd intended to show that night was now left to the wind. Others that would gather to his hindbrains cause. Its nose also bled freely, the result of the trauma to its brain, and fast-healing scars criss-crossed its face where it had scratched itself. This was the beginning, this was how it had to be.

Marks cowered back, shielding himself automatically from the creatures raised claw. But it wasn't meant for him! Its arm arched through the air, its eyes full of wild intent, and smashed brutally into Cochrum head. Claws ripped through the man's cheek, severing tendons and shattering bones. His broken body swung around, and lay limp.

161

The werewolf gazed at the damage as the man choked on the blood welling up in the back of his throat. There is a tug of energy and the creature screams, tearing at its eyes, Cochrum's grip on life is fading, the Moon feels the pull of the earth, tugging, dragging.

Marks watches as the wolf leaps with apparent ease onto the tortured form. It rams its claws hard into the shattered temple, plunging the talon deep into Cochrum brain and finally, thankfully ending the man's life.

A few minutes have passed, no more, no less. And now the wolfman turns to give the *other* address. Fear grips Marks mind and freezes him tight, so much so that he can't take flight. Paralysis in ambition and phrases seep through, from repression of forethought that he knew couldn't be true. That had been hidden and pushed to the deepest depths, but still images seep through, clinging to gaps.

Through all of this mess of information, a single phrase pushed its way in.

"*Cwn Annwn!*" he whispered. Dogs of the otherworld.

Suddenly the beast staggers to the side, scratching ferociously at its head. It falls to the ground, all its co-ordination vanishing into nothing. It falls once more, this time landing heavily against the wall, twitching and wincing in its silent agony.

Marks is no longer watching however. His iron hard rationality has broken the mind it is supposed to protect. The barrier that, in these circumstances would yield to the subconscious onslaught is too well equipped for what passes in thought. Impasse. All he can do is stare.

Armed officers are running into the building now, taking up positions around the defunct form. Hands drag at the Detective Inspector roughly, pulling him to the safety that the walls provided, but to Marks, all of this remains unseen…

…to mortal eyes the Earths grip on its satellite wavers slightly. Not much, but enough. Fractionally the moon begins to decay, to succumb to our planets endless attraction.

In the corner Charlie convulsed, lying unrecognised deep in epileptic spasm, the synapses of his brain struggling to reconnect their torn tissues. The pain of the last few minutes steadily subsides and pours away into the unconscious night time of instinct. None can see him, between worlds he lies, and as the wolf dances it sniffs at the skies and he remains hidden.

PART II

Propensiate dolmanic structures. That rupture, and grow and glow in unborn shapes along that red-grained frame that shields the soul from eternity. A rock that in maternal bliss, though battered and striated, hated by its kind may find that deep and soulful entity not entirely of its faculty and actually quite grave.

But multiply propensity, a bacterionic focus of the elementary. That in greatness stood for centuries without a foot upon its head. But instead, instead a thousand stand beneath the ribcage on the ground. That settles where it fell. That without nook or shadowed knell will blast and blow around.

To mitigate an exponate of dust, to trust. Without concern we can see, we perceive, we discern what's red and yellow, brown. What drowns the soul in what perception breeds, and the seeds, the seeds stand so tall upon the shore as the Dolmans breed.

But that which we acquiesce toward must heed the warning. That red and yellow, brown will not be mourning.

Chapter One

There is green, it flows across, not stopping for a second. It's quite beautiful really, fluorescent tracery on an otherwise bland backdrop. Its no wonder that people come to watch, come to see. Not that they just come to see that, they come to do other things as well, but they always save at least a glance for the colour. There's something about it, something that makes it important, but for some its exact meaning is lost. There is a vague meaning, held within collective consciousness like so many things, but like so many more there are hidden meanings. The world is built on rules, or at least that's what we're led to believe. In truth it could be said that rules are imposed on the world, which in itself is timeless and doesn't really care. It's in this way that humanity both justifies and measures its existence. Amplitude, longitude, latitude, X, Y, Z, the axis of nations. But they all stop to stare at the green tracery, even if it's only for a second. Seconds count though, they multiply, they breed, they breed in such a way as to make bacteria jealous at their methods of propagation. There are many things a second can do that bacteria can't. For one, seconds have the potential to contain conscious thought, after a fashion.

Beep.

They are perfect in smallness, although they haven't always been. Without blemish. Almost undetectable, insignificant. Almost always all one colour. Red and yellow, brown. A collective of billions without differentiation. Soft, warm, comfortable. Never static, always moving. Almost as light as the air that pushes them along. Tiny. Miniscule. Reflectors of light. Snow without the cold wetness. A million shades of one colour. A dry sea. Sharp. Irritating. Blinding. Ever invasive.

There are two grains. They itch. Abrasions in miniature, but as yet, disembodied. There is a desert. Immense, and for the most part empty. A few thorny, low lying shrubs grow here and there. Their leaves are waxy, succulent, with an almost grey-blue-green flavour to their texture. On the horizon there are mountains. They look tiny against the sky, but jagged and sharp peaked all the same. Some of them have snow on the top, some are coated in deep green, but not the green of before. They seem terribly out of key with everything. The mountains surround everything, as if the desert is nothing more than a sandpit, penned in on all sides by watchful parents. At no point is there a break in the ring. There are no passes, no valleys or glacial gorges. There is a waterfall, it sparkles, but that makes no difference really.

Beep.

Marks has sand in his eye. His lips are chapped and his head aches from dehydration. He blinks, once, twice. Almost blinks, his eyes are screwed half shut by the bright sunlight. Never the less the two grains of sand work their way over to the corner of his eye, and eventually out onto the sweaty grime of his face.

Simon Marks sat up. Too fast as it turned out. His head swam, contriving to both buzz with irremembrance and ache with all too much clarity both at the same time. He leaned back slowly onto his elbow and pinched the bridge of his nose with his free hand. He personally wasn't yet ready to vocalise what he was feeling, but a groan escaped his lips all the same.

"Nnung!" he said. He winced at the dry pain in his throat. His jaw ached as well. He swallowed a glob of thick spittle and whetted his stinging lips with his swollen tongue.

"Wha' the…" he said, slurring slightly. He pulled a sharp face as he swallowed again and ran a sand covered hand through his thick hair. "Shit!" He felt the sudden graininess against his scalp and took stock of where he was. Sand. Shrubs. Mountains. Shrubs. Sand. Shrubs. Waterfall. Mountains. Shrubs. His eyes were having trouble focussing, something else out of the ordinary. His head was still mussed up as well. Waterfall. Water…fall. Water. Something to the side of his mind gave a nudge. Got to get to water. Desert, mountains. Desert, mountains. Water.

Beep.

He stares at a white wall. It used to be white, it's a sort of yellow cum cream now. The plaster's old, very old. It's riddled with damp, and periodically large chunks of it disintegrate to the extent where there is no hope that it will stay on the wall anymore. At the base of the wall there is a bank of yellow white dust, not quite swept up. The wall is therefore also a patchwork. Unfortunately the new plaster bonds quite badly to the old, damp plaster and has, on a number of occasions, had to be replaced itself. This in turn has led to a rather entertaining layering effect, occurring by default from various attempts at matching the old paintwork. New is applied as old begins to peel, thus cementing it quite effectively back in its place, until that is, the damp gets under that paint as well and begins making that peel as the latest batch of plaster crumbles. It's quite a complex system, and one that has been taking place for many years up to this point. The white wall has pox. It has the scars to prove it. In the top right hand corner a handful of mushrooms make a bid for freedom. Their stalks stick out at all angles, confused as to the way to grow by the obvious lack of windows. There is in fact a single window, but grime covers its glass so thickly that a mushroom could be excused for considering it a part of the wall. One mushroom even has the tenacity to grow upside down, although when one is sprouting sideways in the first place what is it that can effectively be considered upside down. In

168

any case, they are grey-brown, the colour that you'd expect mushrooms to be, and they ever so occasionally drip with the damp from the walls. Amongst the mushrooms there is a flourishing but small ecosystem of exoskeletal life. At least, this is what is assumed. Filament-like strands of gossamer span the fathomless lengths from mushroom cap to mushroom cap. Miniature Tarzan's must swing from them surely. Below, or to the side, mildewed meadows feed herds of grazers, while their warder's slumber beneath the fungal behemoths. It's a pleasant thought to associate with such an environment.

They make the air smell of damp as well, musty and entirely unpleasant. Quick, look, there goes another piece of plaster. That'll be the best part of a days work no doubt.

Beep.

"Well, what else was there to do?" Marks mumbled to himself as he trudged across the packed sand. It was warm under his feet, even through his shoes, although the main effect of this was to make his feet sweat profusely into his socks. This in turn made the sand already in his sock's seem even worse than it did on its own. It was a vicious and cruel trick.

Already he had begun on occasion to externalise his internal monologue. It seemed almost a waste not to. There was no-one else to hear, no-one to call him crazy, and it was worth it for the little comfort the sound gave. It was a break in the never ending rustle coming from his feet, the hiss that surrounded him and filled his ears. Did sand *never* stop moving? It set his teeth on edge. Got in between his teeth too.

"Shut the hell up!" he screamed, his whole body tense against the glare and the roar and the never ending sandpaper wind. Words felt familiar but unused in his mouth, like he would achieve the same effect by any guttural sound as by a word itself. It was a logical consideration, after all he knew exactly what he meant and what purpose could a word give to a world without people. "*Shut up!*" he screamed again, and ran as fast as he could, yelling into the wind, his arms flapping and body turning at an unassailable foe.

Finally Simon Marks collapses to the floor. He curls up tightly into a ball and tries obsessively to catch the tiny tears flowing in rivulets from his eyes. Eventually he falls asleep.

Chapter Two

Beep.

The day is still young, but already Simon's footsteps stretch far off into the distance. He woke again with the same headachy nausea, but this is something that's being dealt with.

"Not as windy as yesterday." He remarks idly to himself as he walks, but even so he has fashioned a serviceable headdress, scarf and mask from the silk lining of his suit jacket. He sings songs to himself while conducting the flies with a stick he has found. It's about two feet long. He doesn't look behind himself anymore, not like in the beginning. Not that he's travelled for that much time in an actual sense of the word, but experience breeds creation, imagination, and why therefore should Marks not have been the breadth of some epic in his minds eye. The mind has no reference point. Experience breeds creation... fast... doesn't look behind himself anymore, not like in the beginning. The beginning. Is there time here? Everything just stays the same. It doesn't matter when he sleeps or when he wakes, doesn't matter how long he's been walking for. If nothing changes then how can there still be time? This is why he doesn't look back, there's no point, it doesn't matter how far he's walked if it takes him no time to walk it, and although this perplexes him, how can he be perplexed with no time in which for it to take place? Perplexion that is.

171

There's a lot of room for thoughts like these in Simon Marks head. There's nothing to look at after all except his goal, and that's still too far away for it to be lost effectively in perspective. For now at least.

At least. At least. At least the translation remains without compunction, that the central aspect with much emphasis placed upon it, may lead to the recognition of an ulterior, a synthesis. And through mitosis or meiosis, the choice is unimportant may place the thought directly at the forefront of the mind, the centre of his kind. And with pressure coming from the rear, from behind we feel direction.

His head is dizzy. Sometimes he would like affirmation. In his actions at least. He has to sit down more often now, sometimes he falls down and wakes up later on. Presumably later on. He reasons that he must need the sleep.

"Not hungry though." Mutters Marks out loud, voicing the end-most thought of his daydream. It was true as well, he felt this unquenchable burning thirst, this ache for moisture almost playing out of the very dryness in the air, but no hunger whatsoever. Marks trips on a rock and falls hard onto his hands and knee's. He forces out an expletive, it's crude but he feels that it's something the situation requires. "Shit!" he examines a graze on his hand before continuing... walking here, I'm actually still lying on the... "...

floor somewhere over there." He finishes and walks backwards, shielding his eyes with his hand to see where he's come from.

"No time." Mutters Marks, "No time like the present." He laughs breathlessly to himself and pauses for a moment, hands on his hips, to catch his breath. As he stands, something on the ground catches his eye. He stares for a moment, transfixed. So rarely does something come along to break the monotony, a shrub or low lying tree can cause a stir in him for an hour or so as it becomes visible on the horizon. Everything is the same, there is no change. I'm significant here, but only because I break the landscape. I'm insignificant because there's not more of me.

Simon Marks bends down to the shiny piece of metal. Who knows what it used to be, or how it got there. It's equal however in importance to Marks, it breaks the landscape.

A figure bends down on the horizon. He's a long way away. Not as far as he thinks though. The sun is behind him, the sun is always behind him, burning umber, forcing the landscape into a beautiful sepia.

The figure has picked up something now. It must be hot from the sun, he's dropped it and is making an awful fuss, holding his hand and shouting at the sky. He's finished dancing around now though. Now he's wrapped his hand in the cuff of his shirt and has picked it up again. It shines bright.

It's copper, and only discernible from the landscape by its size and shape. No small grain this, a long oval about three inches in all and worn beautifully smooth by the ever-moving sand. It had been half buried, but not anymore. It's rising now, high into the sky, higher still. And then quickly down again. Now it lies on the surface, fragments of burnt skin curling on its small face. It's about half a centimetre thick and has been eroded to a sharp edge around its entire circumference.

It's rising again now, except that this time…

Marks holds the metal up to his eye. It's plain, but beautifully so. He can see every molecule of it sparkling in the ever-present light. It's gold to him. So smooth, so smooth that all he wants to do is stroke it against his cheek, feel the softness as it strokes his skin. Too hot though, he looks painfully at the raw tips of his fingers. At least there's no chance of infection, the heat will have cauterised the flesh on contact. Silly mistake really, but pain clarifies the mind so wonderfully.

Marks runs the sand blown artefact edgeways over the back of his hand, just lightly. It cuts deep but not a drop of blood is spilled. Marks mind fills with the blue sparks of electricity. His heart thumps momentarily loud in his chest and his eyes fill with energy. He carefully slips the blade into the pocket of his trousers, and urges his legs once again into effort.

He travels faster than before, placing his steps rather than letting them just swing. This hasn't affected his frivolity however, and only a hundred meters or so along the way he begins to hum a jaunty little song he remembers from his childhood. He has a small smile on his face.

He wakes with a start, didn't realise he'd even fallen down this time, let alone gone to sleep. He never feels tired, he just falls.

His hands are covered with scars now. A criss-crossing of noughts. Sometimes he needs to be reminded that he's alive, it's hard to tell, sometimes. The pads of his hands are calloused with the constant sand abrasion, and the skin of his face has become hollow and weathered. His scarf is more securely fastened as well, but no less makeshift than before.

The mountains are big now, the waterfall is big too with regards to his perspective, but still a lot smaller than he expected. Truth be told, it's probably no more than two or three feet wide. He can see now too that at its base, where he expected a pool, the water shallowly circles a large boulder, behind which however who knows.

Marks turns over onto his back and sits up. The mountains in the distance on the far side are tiny now, minuscule as the copper, but not as small as the sand. Large as the sand. Or rather a smallness that covers everything, all that the eye can see.

175

He holds his thumb up to the horizon, directly in line with the row of mountains and closing his right eye, switches his thumb backwards and forwards. Now you see it, now you don't. Now you see it, now you don't.

He moves himself around again, this time onto his side, and looks hard at the waterfall. He doesn't think about time at all now, can't fathom how close or far he must be. He tries the trick with the thumb, but all he can fit behind it is the boulder. It's confusing, he doesn't understand.

Beep.

There's a man on the horizon. Is it a man? Yes, it's a man on the horizon. No, not on the horizon, by the big boulder. It's a man, but by the big boulder. Is it a man though? Yes, chapped lips, drenched in sweat, skin sunburned, hair a mess, hair full of sand, eyes full of sand, socks and shoes full of sand. Eyes staring at the water. There's a man by the big boulder staring at the water. Looking at his reflection? No, looking at me. I'm looking at my reflection in the water. I'm looking at my reflection in the water around the big boulder.

It was damnably odd, thought Marks as he looked at his never quite right reflection. It felt like he'd been there all the time. Didn't feel like he'd ever moved. Time. Time was different here. Everything was different here. But that water looked so refreshing, more refreshing than he ever could have imagined. He had hoped, did hope, will hope, had hoped that there would perhaps be, or is, a small pool behind the boulder that he could bathe in. Unfortunately he had, or has had no such luck.

As Marks skirts the edge of the rock, even before taking a drink, there is something wrong, malformed in the landscape. No, not quite malformed but something is calling in his mind, noticing some terrible distortion. There is something horrific in his eye that for some reason he can't pin down. There is no space for a pool. Perhaps this might not be an especially noticeable aspect when compared to the other intrigueties that the panorama has to offer, but the mind only has the capacity apparently, to digest certain quantities of information at any one time. This seems to be a reasonable place to start.

Life blood wash through sinewed crevice, blinding light of living tasked to those not so forgiving as they should. But not like those who wear the hood, the black and dark with blade and trail, that opposed to the snail will race and cut the flow. But if we sow, and pile rock high, we must surely understand, we must know the condensate of height will mitigate the plight and bring the freshest flowing river, that sets heart and mind a quiver for within the blessed darkened shaft, with water pounding fore and aft comes hope. Along with those who dote.

Marks sat on a small rock off to one side and closed his eyes. He could feel the fine spray bouncing from the boulder, whose side was green with algae and gently moistening his chapped lips and cheeks. He took his black leather shoes off, emptying them of the sand as he did so, and put them on the floor with his socks. It was much cooler here than anywhere else, so there was no chance of the sand burning his unprotected feet. They were covered in calluses and blisters in any case. Next he undid his slowly dampening shirt, and painfully bent his elbows to take it off properly. His joints were tight with dehydration, but all the same he got down in this half-naked state on his hands and knees and slurped freezing water from the base of the waterfall. His hair was plastered to his forehead, frigid water coursing down his sweat stained and sand covered back. He shivered and gasped a moment, winded by the cold, and an instant pounding headache drilled into his head from above. No sooner had he drunk his fill however, than Marks was sat, still with his trousers on, laughing like an imbecile and crying like a fool, fully submerged in the tiny torrent of water. It stung and burned where the heat had made his skin peel, but it was wonderful, it was perfect. A perfect ice-cold shower in this indescribable place.

"How the hell did you happen?" called Marks, raising his arms, palms upwards against the pressure of the water. Great big blots of water spattered the sand from his arms. "Where do you go?" he said, his voice tinged with that silence usually reserved for holy places and libraries, but even so not yet fully realising the profundity of what he had said. His words echoed up the cliff face, and the water froze his mind into stillness.

Beep.

Eyes, all around eyes. Looking and watching, never quite sure what's going to happen, but when it does they'll have seen it. They've seen it before, sometimes. But sometimes they haven't. They giggle in the silence at the others ineptitude, snickering at a half and half mess. But that's not always the case. Fear is relative, *a* relative, a relative to passion, and these things with their pale faces and scraping hands have so much passion. You can see it when they smile, when they grin. Their thin lips pulling back and showing the blackening and cracked stubs that used to be teeth. Excited and rich, pulling and jostling each other as all they could dream comes alive in their eyes. But only in the quiet of the world because in the noise of society they can't be seen, and that makes them sad. Ever so sad. And when they get sad the passion fades and they try, oh how they try to recapture it. Crying and shivering, mewing at each other as they paw at humanity with the fingertips. Infecting where they touch and blackening the skin, spreading a pestilence so vile that the body rots at the very place it was touched. And even this isn't enough because in the morning the light heals, which isn't right at all. But half and half and half and

179

half and half. And which way to swing is the question on their lips as they giggle into the wind. Blowing and pulling fetid air past them, taking their scent with it and passing it through the noses of all close by. They turn and walk the other way. Forgotten something, must turn the light off, where did I put the…

…and it amounts to nothing. It cancels itself out, which is the right thing to do at the end of things.

Beep.

Simon Marks lay, drying in the sun. His clothes were on the outward side of the big boulder, having been pressure washed, like himself, by the waterfall. They now dried in the desert heat. He didn't feel self-conscious being naked, who was there to see after all. It was immensely liberating, in a very actual way. This was an act that he would never consider proper in the usual course of things, in fact his modesty was such that he had found communal locker or changing rooms a problem on more than a few occasions. Gently he thumbed the small piece of copper that he had found in the desert. Just something he had needed at the time, to remind himself why he was still walking. Marks looked at the oval in his palm, and closing his fist tightly around it, he stood up and threw it as hard as he could out into the desert. He would never deny someone else the chance that he had been given, even if that chance bore the mark of darker things. After all, the first thing he had seen within it was the warmth of the sun, and wasn't that the importance of the moment.

Beep.

He was asleep. As soon as his eyes had closed he had been asleep. And now it was dark. When he woke up it would be light. As soon as he woke up. When he blinked it was dark, when he didn't it was light, it was that simple, there was no more to it. The land was naive supposedly. It didn't understand that light and dark happened whether your eyes were open or closed. At least, these were the principals that it understood, and in its very essence it was logic twisted and turned to its utmost. It made sense all the same. It was dark when you slept, so therefore, when you slept it was dark. And what was a blink besides a very brief sleep. The land was a child, no more, no less.

For now though, it was dark. No moon, no stars, because when you sleep you can't see them anyway. They don't exist. There was no wind either, no hiss of moving sand. No point if it couldn't be heard. But even in the stillness of Marks sleep, there was always something that kept moving, kept pouring through the sealed up recesses of his brain. True, there was something blocking its progress, but some was still seeping through. Water's insidious like that.

At the very edges, nearest to the boulder, the moat of water microscopically dipped down. Fluid dynamics dictated that this couldn't be, not unless something was sucking it down. There was *space,* and that was where the water wanted to be. Slowly. Grain of sand by grain of sand. Water can move anything if given enough time. Water in a crack can turn into a glacier. Just give it enough time. And lower the temperature slightly.

Marks watched the moat of water around the big rock. There was much that was odd about this place, as has been noted, but he could never when he thought about it remember why it all seemed so strange. Much as he concentrated, there was never anything from which he could form a comparison, no point of reference that he could dredge up. Instead he got frustration and whatever was, apparently was, there was no reason, no right or wrong that he could fathom.

Despite this however, there was something more about the water, something clarified, not vague like everything else. Even in his head things felt different nearer to the water. Not just cooler although that was an added blessing, but more solid. He felt more solid in himself, which to be honest he hadn't since he had first woke up, whenever that had been. These tricks with time were really starting to mess him up as well, not that he hadn't been messed up in one sense or another since he'd started walking. It was called desert madness, or desert fever, or blindness or something. The mind played tricks, blurred the edges of things. You saw every detail of every speck, every tiny speck, and it annoyed the hell out of you, burned the deserts never ending openness onto your eyeballs in brain-searing detail. So much detail that, at the end of things clarification in any sense became almost impossible.

Eventually he'd stopped seeing anything at all. Probably in part due to dehydration, sight was the first thing to go after all, but it hadn't been the blackness he'd expected. It had been like seeing nothing but somehow being able to see everything all the same. Then he'd found the metal, and the pain had solidified things. It'd helped him grow new eyes, and a path had been spread before him, no longer just the miles and miles of wasted land it had been. Options had been taken away, and suddenly things had seemed so much clearer. Clear like the water.

"But where does it go?" Marks murmured to himself again. This time however the words didn't just slip away from him like before. This time he stood up urgently and peered intently at the point where the water met the rock. The dip was far too minute for his eyes to detect, but all the same, there was something, an urge that compelled him.

Beep.

Water falls, wet and deep, or so we are lead to believe, but when shallow instead there is much to be read into where why and how it leaves.

So to think of it thus, that beneath the loose crust is a panacea of dispersal preparate, and if we negate the duplicitous state then in practical knowledge we propagate.

Digging deep and digging down, looking for the rocks own crown. And when none abounds the deeper we go so the seeds of hope begin to flourish and grow.

The question to ask is where does it go? If around the base there's space to flow but dry sand sits and quips and jipes and shovelled handfuls are thrown with spite but deeper still the life blood goes.

The freezing water and the scorching wind were new. Well, new in the sense that they stirred things in Marks. Where before they had burned and refreshed in their own independent manner they were now both refreshing, to a certain degree at any rate. Not that this wasn't infuriating, to enjoy something that you've so recently loathed. There had to be a better way of emptying the basin though. Shifting these tiny particles wasn't going to get him anywhere very fast. But were they tiny, really? They hadn't seemed so small to him out in the desert, they had been the world for him, had taken up the universe. He hadn't been able to see anything else, just the sand. Each grain had seemed colossal back then.

Simon Marks grinned wolfishly. It was really that simple wasn't it. Although simple and easy were two entirely separate things. Painfully he looked back out into the desert, and started to walk. Sometimes you just needed a new perspective, and he reasoned for the first time how young the land really was.

Beep.

Driving rain. Beautiful swollen splashes pummelling the ground, collecting and then dispersing as the affected area grows and grows. Grey tarmac hissing away the heat from the day, bathing in the great wash from the sky as glorious droplets of heaven massage away chewing gum and sweet wrappers. It scours chalk from the pavement and dirt and grime from the walls. No-one comes out in the rain if they can help it, but they stay snug and warm behind double glazing, triple glazing, their centrally heated paradise, watching the world drown outside.

A street light flickers. The stiff, sharp grass at its base sucks in the water like so much mana, pulling in the golden, glowing, softening liquid. Life begins to return to shrivelled roots. In a few days there may even be new shoots here, bright and green, pushing up through the broken glass. There might not of course. The scratching twigs down there might well be too far gone. If this is the case then so be it, there are certain things that are out of the hands of mortal men.

Beep.

Marks looked back at where he had come from. He had the advantage of experience now, having walked this route once before, even if it was in the opposite direction. Not that direction meant that much out here either. He had also started with a clear head, alongside the more practical knowledge, as clear as it could be in anycase. Of course, none of this made the journey any less arduous, but that couldn't be helped, it was a means to an end.

The wind had calmed to a standstill as Marks had set out. It was ominous, although that word is grossly overrated, but in this case it fits. Everything was still, and for possibly the first time Marks became aware of how accustomed he had become to the constant noise. The drone had stopped, and although this meant no flying sand, it also meant that there was no relief from the burning sun. He was already drenched in sweat, and felt the beginnings of disorientation from the dehydration this caused. His mouth had long since dried out, and as relief from this Marks now constantly sucked on a small pebble.

Footprints slurred their way back across the sand, stodgily smudging down dunes and around rocks. There was obvious method to them however. Occasionally they would track back on themselves if the going got too tough, but they would always return to their original direction eventually.

A man holds out his thumb in the direction he has come from and closes his right eye. He moves his thumb to the left a few inches, and then carefully twitches it back.

"About right I think." He mutters cryptically to himself.

For a moment Marks concentrated, focussing his mind but at the same time blurring his vision. Everything fused. The yellow of the sand. The silver grey of the shrubs, the orange of the mountains. All were nothing and everything. Then suddenly sharpness, and in that split-second in-between when nothing was quite sure whether it was the same or different Simon Marks made a snatch for the boulder.

Distance meant nothing here, time meant nothing, perspective meant nothing. Marks arms, his hands, for a fraction of a second were both many miles long, and only as long as they had always been. The boulder was immensely heavy, and so light as to be negligible.

A torrent of water poured down into the chasm. It was dark, and sloped downwards through and under the cliffs at roughly a forty-five degree angle. Convenient.

Marks stood on the edge, watching in fascination as the rock peeled back on itself, revealing more and more of the rusty brown emptiness. The rock didn't so much dissolve or crumble, more it compressed in on itself, shifting and tightening for an increasing distance from the edge. The sound was much like bone breaking. There was no rubble, no wastage, and at the end the hole stood neatly three to four meters wide, as if it had always been there. The water flowed nicely down it in a shallow but gushing stream. Marks carefully stepped forward, and down into the dark.

Chapter Three

There's a bed. It's a very complicated bed in fact, not in the way that it's function is in any way difficult to grasp, but complicated still in relation to other beds. Perhaps it's complicated in a moral sense as well, although that's really more for the individual to decide. All honesty be told though, it doesn't look like a very comfortable bed. Mostly in any case. The mattress looks plush in relation to the rest of the establishment, quite deep and with an attitude that suggests semi-comfortable springiness, but there's no pillow. Instead there's a thick brown leather strap at about forehead height. It looks worn, but incredibly strong all the same. At one corner it has been stained a deeper shade of brown by something, no attempt has been made to remove the stain. At intervals in the mattress there are holes where chains lead down to the bed frame. There are two for the forehead, the left of which has two links joined with a padlock so that it can be taken off if it needs to be. There are also holes for the neck, wrists and ankles, effectively spread eagling anybody that deserves strapping down. Beneath the frame there is a complex network of chains and pulleys. It is by way of these and the series of stop-cocks on the side of the bed that the straps can be individually loosened and tightened. The bed frame itself is cast-iron and extremely heavy, there are dents and cracks in the tiled flooring where the feet of the frame have crashed down during procedure. The patients tend to move around a lot on *this* bed. The inside of the frame is an insulating box of wood, the outside is polished to a healthy, clinical gleam. There is a voltmeter and cables on the wall, it is switched off. Paddles and a head-vice are alongside extra straps, ready for the next procedure. A wooden spoon-shaped object is also there, to stop the tongue being swallowed. This procedure is still quite experimental.

He hears the bed frame rattling later on in the evening. The lights outside the room went down the minute it started, one of the bulbs blew this time. No point requesting another room, likelihood was he wouldn't get it. Wouldn't remember to ask next time he was awake. Brain flickered, time to go. Silently he thanked God that the lights didn't blow on his account.

It was humid in the tunnel, incredibly so. In fact Marks had taken his shirt off against the heat, despite continually scratching his back on the cave roof. At least there was plenty of water, he thought bitterly. In matter of fact, he was up past the knees in the bitingly cold stream.

As he had moved deeper into the tunnel system he had found the passages getting narrower and narrower, meaning that now he was constantly bent double. Also, due to the restricted space for the water to flow through, the once shallow stream had gotten deeper and deeper. On top of this, the roof of the system was so hot that bizarrely, above the freezing lower half of the tunnel the top half was boiling, was humid heat, wrapping Simon Marks in a hot, choking mist. This also meant that he couldn't see the roof of the tunnel and therefore couldn't see when a nasty outcrop would gouge even more skin from his raw head and back. He banged his head again hard.

"Shit!" he swore venomously, "Shit, shit, shit. Would you look at that." Marks looked at his fingers, they had blood on them. His hand had automatically flown to his forehead at the bump, now he touched the stinging lump more carefully, wincing all the while. Carefully he sat back in the freezing water and lifted up a cooling handful of the liquid to bathe the wound.

The one consolation of the strange circumstances in the tunnel was an ever lightly blowing convection current. This mild, warm breeze now blew over his face, bringing a waft of fresh air with it. Marks had noticed a while ago that at intervals of roughly fifty meters a wide shaft shot up through the rock of the tunnel roof. He had no idea how they'd been made, or even how many he'd passed now, but they let in light and blessed air, and that was all he wanted to know.

It was a presumption of Marks, through educated extrapolation that this was some sort of magma-tube cum mine shaft. The main tunnel was smooth to the touch at the sides, and the glittering crystal formations that reflected the light so prettily were obviously volcanic in origin. At points this main tunnel would break open into a crossroads, where a much more roughly hewn tunnel would intersect. These, he suspected, were man made, and much younger. By looking closely at the corners of these crossroads Marks could see how the metamorphic rock, rock changed by the heat and pressure of the magma, slowly gave way to a much softer sedimentary rock. It must have taken a lot of effort to break through into the tunnel he travelled.

With this in mind, he *guessed* that the vertical shafts were there to encourage the convection that was bliss to him, but that was just a guess. It looked very much as if the old had almost been taken over by the new. Almost, but not quite, the stream now once again gave the old a pre-eminence that the new didn't.

"It's got to go somewhere." Said Marks to the misty half-light. "It wouldn't flow otherwise."

Carefully he got back up, his trousers sodden, but not caring he began once more to follow the flow of the water down the tunnel, his forehead still bleeding from the bump. The blood diffused magnificently in the remains of the water on his face, and in the dim light from the vertical bore shafts it looked just like some old tribal war mask, dripping easily from his chin.

No-one notices them. Who would, when living takes up so much time as it is. They creep around, scratching and scrabbling in the darkness. Because darkness is good, no-one notices in the darkness. There are feuds and battles that can go on for years between them. Them. In their own little world, so separate from the one that everyone else is so occupied with. People don't see them, people can walk right by them and completely disregard anything that might take place, even if it means they have to sidestep in order to do it. The capacity of humanity for complete and utter ignorance is incredible.

There is shame in their lives now. They shelter in the light that our society casts because any light of their own has been taken from them. Anger, humiliation, these are just two of the things that haunt them in their waking hours. The things that haunt them in their sleeping hours are much worse. Things that eat away at the soul and make it harder and harder to go back to anything that could once have been called security. What is security now? Now that they are part of another world, have been pushed into this world by collective consciousness. Collective ignorance. Conscious societal ignorance. They are part of a world that no-one sees because there is something about it that is so terrible that to know of it would drive them insane with fear, with the knowledge that is kept locked up for their very safety. And that's why they sidestep.

But that's also why they huddle together at night. In two's or three's. Because there's something about numbers. In numbers there's less chance that it'll be you, more chance that it'll be someone else, and in this world, slightly to the side of everything else, sometimes that slight opportunity for life can mean the difference between survival and feeling your blood drained from

193

your veins. But still your body remains to face the torment because this is only what you would like to happen, and this will never happen, because the warmth of your life is succour to them, and that's what they feed on. Life. Not your death. Not quickly anyway. Never quickly.

And the worst part is that whilst this is happening you're aware. Not like the rest of the population, those who live in blissful ignorance of the disgusting mess that surrounds them. It was by their choice that you became a part of this torturous world and by their choice that your awareness gradually grew. You knew less of the world you were once a part of, the suits and ties and coffee at that little place down the street. It became less important to you and something else took over. Something almost but not quite still you. Something base and primal, something bestial that was willing you to survive in this unfamiliar place that was filled with familiar things. Something old living in something new. And because of that you became different. No longer the person you were but not quite someone different. Just someone who could survive, and no-one could ever take that from you because if they did then you would surely die, and nothing in the world could stop that.

Sometimes the fear takes you. When you're alone in an alleyway, even if there's nothing around. And you know when there's something around. But there's a need to be close to something. There's a need to collect together and peel away the pain of life in the Otherworld. Peel away the pain. Numb it through alcohol and drugs. Take away the harshness by blurring the boundaries. Let the real world come in, come into the world that now consumes you every day, a world so full of violence. But through the drugs, and through the alcohol you can let in just enough, just enough to take the edge off of things. And just enough to push back the fear, because if they can't see it then neither can you, and that makes all the difference.

Charlie turned over in his sleep, his face twitching against some inner instinct. His clothes were soaked with foul smelling sweat. It smelt ill, the smell of illness exuded. It was one of the factors you had to deal with when you went through cold-turkey.

In the darkness his leg twitched, in his mind something entirely other was occurring. Wind blew through the darkened street, ruffling his hair seductively. For a moment it lifted the thin blanket that covered him and tickled his lower back. Charlie gritted his teeth, although his eyes were tightly closed, there was something alive in there, in the back of his thoughts, drawing his blood, leeching and growing, although Charlie himself had no idea. An empty can rattled across the paving, skittering away into the murk. The wolf lifted its newborn head and sniffed to the wind.

Peel back the real world for a second, let the darkness come back to you…for a second. Take your mind off things for a second. Feel the scars scabbing over in your mind, feel the pressure of living two existences disappear. But if you do this then there are other things as well. Things that you don't necessarily want. Things that crawl in the dark recesses of your mind before they skitter out of the shadows right in front of you, and that's not really what you want. That's not the way life should work out. They come, bit by bit, chittering through the night. Not all at once, but they're everywhere and that's the worst of it. They don't hide, not as such, they've got too used to not being there. But they are there, always, in the side of every brain on the planet. They stop in the dead of night, breathing heavily with the strain of the chase as toughened skin drips with sweat that stinks and for some unknown reason the figure at the other end of the road ducks their head down and keeps running, running, running. And then stops as their feet are taken from under them. A street light blinks out just in time, and the blood is washed away by the morning dew. Innocent only in that there is no intention behind its actions.

Knuckles drag on the floor in the minds eye, and fetid skin drips with black congealing blood as a blanket is pulled firmly across a shoulder. There are noises in the night. None of them are pleasant. There are noises in the mind, they are even less so. It might be said, and possibly is said, that the mind can provide so much more fear than the brain can compensate for. Pull down these barriers and imagine for a second what an instant of that could mean. Euphoria perhaps? Euphoria as claws tear into skin, pulling and ripping, and claws scrape across bone, feeding the body as the warmth of a soul feeds the darkness behind the eyes. And great joy fills the shrivelled hearts, barely functional, only to the point of necessity. Fear can be a great motivator.

The darkness only lasts for a while though, and instincts die hard even for the gross, mutilated wonders of nature. Because nature is what they are. But the light hurts. So long in the darkness, so long that the light burns, and with the light salvation as they take to the shadows.

Marks could stand fully upright in this part of the tunnel, which was a relief because he didn't think his thighs could have taken much more crouching. His back and neck certainly couldn't take any more knocks. All over he felt like he'd been used as a drum, beaten black, blue and finally red by the same inane and non-sequential beat.

Off to the right he spied a largish outcrop of rock and waded stiffly over to it. He knew from experience now not to sit down for too long, it made getting up afterwards far too hard. He left his feet deep in the icy water as well, they had gone through the painful state of cold that they had been in, now they were just numb, and probably blistered and bleeding as well.

The knots in Marks' back cracked painfully as he sat down, and he felt the tendons in his knees creak and stretch as they bent. The mist and wind were as unbearable as the sand had been now.

They chafed at his already raw skin. At first it had seemed that only the old tunnel held this disguised curse, but as time had passed and the water had gotten steadily deeper, Marks had come to realise that the stream was beginning to break up. It now split down into some of the lower lying tunnels, and because of this the convection winds were attacking him from more and more places. Not only that, but they were stronger too, and they brazed his skin most uncomfortably. Hate was welling up inside him. He found that slowly these modern intrusions were becoming more and more abhorrent to him. They disgusted him like a cheap whore, smiling sweetly even though he knew what they were. They broke the weirdly beautiful smoothness that otherwise surrounded him, and mocked it by their similarity.

Marks stood up and began to walk again. The bore shafts were becoming much less common now in the larva tube, only seeming to present themselves when it was intersected by another pathway. As such, the reflective crystals that had guided his path now only very weakly shone with the diffused light.

Carefully he moved forward in the near complete darkness, trailing his hand along the smooth wall behind him. It was a great comfort to his uncertainty, but all the same his body was tense, for a trip, a low rock, a drop. He shuffled forward slowly. It helped to keep his eyes closed he found. The body was so much more accustomed to moving when it deprived itself of light rather than when it thought there should be light and there wasn't any. There was a reverence to this place, although disfigured. He didn't speak now, it felt wrong, like running in a hospital. Whatever it was, it just didn't feel right to speak, even to himself. Despite the urge for silence however, the splashing and flowing of the water around his legs rang out clearly in his eardrums, and unconsciously he found himself making a low hum in the back of his throat and in his chest that was a perfect counterpoint to the sound. It was the sound made under the sea by a rip-tide, or even the dull *glumph-glumph* of a heart beat, the stream flowing as it did through atria of cavernous arteries. Occasionally Marks would notice and stop himself, but for the most part it would manifest in a vibration deep in his stomach, it felt natural and right, it fitted with the fizz and splutter of the water.

Which was now flowing much, much slower. Apart from at those rare junctions that it rushed to fill the lower lying tunnels. But before those, and past them as well, the under-tug at Marks feet was hardly there at all now. The flow was stopping, pooling, not that he would notice in his bedraggled state. What he did notice though, was when the rock began to change.

Shiny, smooth. Black. No, brown-black, black in places, brown in others, sometimes light, sometimes dark. All disgusting. Makes a bitter crunching in the minds ear. Rounded though, gracefully so, perfectly so. Plated, intersecting perfectly, flexibly. Squirm. No, not quite, but close. Scuttle. Skitter. Skitter on needle sharp little

199

legs, tap, tap, tapping almost silently on the cold, bed-time tiles. Tiles almost everywhere. Not on the damp walls though. Plaster has been noted. Skitter up the wall, sit on the roof, watch the world, the bulb, the electric light. *Flick*. It's on, skitter away.

It has been raining, the door has swollen with moisture. As it is forced open it crashes against the opposite wall and a lump of sodden yellow-green plaster slops onto the floor. The words, "Crap Mike, it's worser than we thought!" are said. Rivulets stream down the walls to the floor, taking any loose detritus with it. As the door opens the water pooling shallowly at that end of the room flows out into the corridor. There are *splish-splash* noises like footsteps through a puddle, and then hands are lifting. Strong hands, but they still struggle with a dead-weight.

Rain lashes the window from outside and seeps in surreptitiously through the gap under the wooden lintel. The glass is reinforced with a thin metal mesh. It is fogged, but still lets in light. The wire mesh means that it can be smashed and still stay together. There's no point anyway, there are strong bars set into the concrete on the inside, as much for the protection of the inmate as for that of the people outside. Society fears difference.

A voice says, "Screw that Mike, I'm not touching the light switch again with all that water about."

After a while a thick rubber glove is brought, it is usually used for surgery, and the light switch is finally thrown. There is a loud bang as the bulb blows, heated mutters and then the door slams. Before silence there is the sound of a trolley being wheeled away.

The cockroach sits again in the damp darkness on the roof. Its two antennae quiver, and it hisses softly into the gloom. Men will come in the morning, but for now, paradise is its reward.

Chapter Four

Finger tips on rough stone, hewn and seen to spew from tragic natural movement, not necessarily indiscrete, and certainly not to be seen. Deep grooves long and sharp as though implemental or implement made don't fade as he travels deeper, finger tips his only real keeper. Eyesight dim and sounds unformed he pushes through beneath the ground the layers upon layers of time immemorial that quiz his mind. And although he thinks that he might just find some meaning in this steaming and watery abyss, this kiss of natures bountiful lips, he knows that while a feeling inside him may well grow he may not fully understand when sometimes he sees polish and sometimes he sees sand.

It was man-made certainly, and it had bled out from its centre deep into the surrounding tunnels. It wasn't massive, but it was still inspirationally big in comparison to the tunnels. For the majority the cavern was obviously hewn by hand. The walls were regular and the dimensions careful. Deep score marks criss-crossed all over creating a quite intricate pattern, and the parts of the floor not banked in rubble were deep under water to a depth that almost didn't matter. Or at least so it seemed, but lost in his focus forever he gleaned perhaps the tiniest insight. Light fizzed in from nowhere, so dim compared to the desert, but bright as day in the gloom. Marks walked to the edge of the pool. The mist no longer clung tightly to the waters surface, instead it floated about as clouds at the very top of the roof some fifteen or twenty meters above. That wasn't the only thing that seemed peculiar in this place, and Marks had long since become accustomed to peculiarity. The water had an odd texture to it, a glossy sheen around the inlet that was almost unplaceable. He reached down curiously to touch it, and it sucked at his fingers desirously. No normal pool of water this, but a thick viscous liquid that seemed to be feeding from the water. As he watched Marks could see at the far corner as a heap of unrecognisable iron-oxide, probably the mysterious tunnel builders long disused tools, were swallowed by a slowly climbing thick film of the liquid. As it climbed higher Marks could see through the semi-transparent covering as the rust was carefully eaten away and dispersed. Much the same thing was happening to the rock face. However, instead of complete dissolution, the dissolved particles began to reform into the smooth, languid surface of the earlier tunnels. The tunnel was reforming itself, trying to heal, and Marks couldn't shake off the notion that it wouldn't have happened had he not let the water through. The liquid was crawling over the ceiling now, but it was struggling, it could only get to a certain point before gravity dragged it back down in great stringy gloops to glop back heavily into the pool below.

"Bloody hell!" said Marks quietly, the first words he had spoken for many hours. He rubbed some of the gel slowly between

203

his fingers to feel its texture. It tingled, but wasn't entirely unpleasant in sensation.

After a while he wiped his hand on his trousers, disillusioned with the obstacle in front of him. The thick black cloth steamed at the liquids touch, a deep purple cloud that fell to dust on the ground at his feet, and where the liquid had touched a loose mass of wispy white puffs now protruded.

"Cotton." Said Marks, "My trousers are cotton. And that's the dye." He indicated the floor in astonishment. "But it doesn't affect me it seems." He paused, "Damn being naked, I'm getting out of here." And he dove deeply into the strange pool.

When he surfaced again some five meters out his eyes were raw and bloodshot, tears of watered down blood stinging his cheeks from burst capillaries.

"Damn my *sodding* contact lenses!" he yelled to the sky, but even as he swam he felt his body being purified. City air hacked out of his mouth in gross green-yellow mucus, and his vision sharpened to how he remembered seeing the world as a child. Covered in the gel his hair was washed clean of scent and shampoo chemicals, the blood on his back and head congealed and was replaced by fresh skin. Scars faded and calluses softened.

By the time he had reached the spot where the rusted tools had been his body was flexible and lithe. His muscles felt rested and strong and the toxins ejected from his body had given him a healthy glow. He stood tall in his nakedness and tried to think what to do next.

Beep.

Dirty murmurs down a dingy corridor. The lighting is there, just about. Flickering neon fluorescent tubing bolted to the ceiling, greasy brown joints, decaying yellow-white plastic, just like the plaster on the walls. Hard to imagine that this can pass for clinical. The murmurs are less murmurs now but more like mutters. A bit closer, not hurried or secret but matter of fact and obviously moving steadily nearer.

"It's an interesting case." One said.
One said, "Really, how do you make that out then, one could say that all of the cases in here are interesting. To a certain extent of the word that is."

"Serotonin elevation hyperactivity syndrome. Here look at this." Replied one. A faint rustle of papers. Not even mutters now but conversation, a bit echoing, but still there, and footsteps too. Not hurried, even now.

"This is quite unprecedented to my knowledge." Said one, a small amount of surprise entering his voice.

"I quite agree." Said one. The footsteps stop outside a door in the sodden plaster. Eyes peer through a viewing slit.

"And there's no response to outside stimulus whatsoever?" Asks one.

One replies, "None at all, he just lies there. If it wasn't for that one fact then I would say that the patient is suffering from some sort of psychosis. Perhaps a dissociative disease of the brain. That might go some way to explaining the extremity of his condition. I'm afraid the catharsis of his catatonia makes it quite a mystery at present. I thought perhaps exposure to external chemicals?"

"What's this?" asks one.

One replies, "Another mystery. Yesterday tests showed a huge jump in serotonin, similar to that produced by a hypothalamic-pituitary reaction, but you can guess as well as me what the stimulus might have been. Since then the patient has been naturally producing a base rate of serotonin far in excess of the norm."

"How delightful." Said one, " A fascinating case indeed. Do keep me informed won't you."

There are dead flies and dust settled on top of the tube light. The plaster above is brown but in a far better state than the plaster elsewhere in the corridor. The heat from the light dries the damp up. The footsteps move away, the sound feels dense in the darkness, it is one of the few things to listen to. The others you don't really want to hear.

The ground was hard where Marks was, but he didn't really mind that much. Despite the relief of his physical fatigue by the pool, he

206

needed time to rest his mind. An opportunity to just switch off, just for a while. Who knew how long he had actually been moving for, time didn't make sense, didn't matter here. Perspective was an illusion. He had seen more in this interval of existence than he could have possibly hoped to in any other arena. It was a lot to absorb.

Again he ran his fingers over his knee, tracing the line of a deep scar he'd had since his mid-teens. He knew it was there, could still feel it at his minds fingertips. The swell, the coarse, tight skin, the small indentation to the left top edge. Right now though it wasn't there, right now he had been born again in the image of his minds eye, in the way he had always imagined himself, had always wanted to be, could have been. Not out of vanity, he made sure to remind himself of that. It was not vanity, just the way he looked at himself. The blemishes, the scars, they were all still there, but for the first time his view was not affected, not imposed, and for the first time his view was perfect and impaired by nothing.

The lake had by now enveloped almost every surface of the cave, climbing on all sides of Simon Marks. It crawled over outcrops, moving over hand-shattered rock. When it was there it undulated with energy, and when it was gone it left a healthy sheen of amalgamated rock. And then, at the very summit of the cave, at the very apex, gravity dragged it back down again and again. Time after time Marks watched as liquid dissolved rock and gravity pulled it down to be swallowed whole in a great splash of viscosity. But only at the apex. And, as Marks watched, he could see that in dragging the dissolved rock down only at that point a great ring of emptiness was being created where rock was not reforming into that smooth surface. Shiny rock was continuously reborn on the outside, the ever-increasing trough lengthening each time as the liquid failed to quite reach the rough rock centre. And as the dissolved rock fell, Marks saw rising like a stalagmite, a great ring heading up slowly to touch its rough rock stalactite.

In a daze Marks watched, transfixed, unable to remove his gaze. He was hypnotised by it and it called to him. It was strong, so strong, it called out to him and pleaded in an unknowable way. Quick as he could he swam out to the rising plinth and lay gasping with relief upon its surface. He felt weight spattering down on him and mesmerically raised himself up. Ever so slowly, bit by bit his whole body was covered in layer upon layer of rock, crystallising on his imperfections. It solidified with glacial speed, and then continued climbing and climbing until the whole massive structure was up to waist and then head height. Higher and higher it built, while the indentation grew deeper and longer, an ever increasing central spire pointing down at its core. A key that fitted directly into the cerebellum of Marks brain.

He stood frozen, directly at its centre, surrounded by tonnes and tonnes of everything that could possibly exist, and even then, even frozen for a billion years in rock he still felt the moment when the never ending lock and key met, and that was when he thought he had it all worked out.

Diary of Doctor Joseph Frankson

December 30th

Showed Doctor Beaumont patient 726. He was very interested, as I suspected he would be and has asked to be kept informed on the matter. Was hoping for a tad more insight. Will continue with the suppressants and Monoamine oxidase inhibitors (The age of science is truly upon us now). I am sure these will lower the serotonin levels, at least to some degree, although at present they appear to be doing more bad than good.

Note to self: I must surely be an acceptable candidate with this case study. To be published, immortality, but I must remember a pre-requisite of immortality is always success, and in honesty, should be in no way removed from such.

The number on the door is seven-two-six. It has been painted over a number of times, you can tell. Lumps stick out where emulsion has semi-hardened, semi-dripped. The texture is smooth and soft to the touch, almost silky really. But that's the only nice thing about the door to be honest. It's grey-green, a slight difference in shade from the walls, and it's covered in heavy rivets around a thin viewing slit. There are heavy hinges and a heavy lock. It doesn't look very worn, which is quite odd when you think about it.

Beyond the door there is a figure on a bed. The bed is an old cast-iron one, like a lot of things in this place, old with the new, an obtuse mixture of the modern and the age old. Mostly this pulls against the grain, it's not meant to be. Two things that for many reasons perfectly logically should never meet. But here they do. There's not much more to be said for it really. This place is a different place, things can get confused. If you think too hard. The mattress is also old, and thin. Thankfully there is no evidence of leather straps.

It's late at night, most of the hospital staff are celebrating the New Year, each in their own individual ways. Beside the bed there is quite a large amount of empty floor space, it is concrete, cold and hard.

His eyes stared blankly. They didn't exactly see, but then again, conjecture in the hospital said that they didn't exactly not-see either. Despite the fact that they were glazed, they were at this point in time apparently very much focussed on a small patch of concrete to the left of the bed, about three feet away. His breathing was steady, it always was, but despite the darkness and lateness of the hour there was something not usual. At quarter to twelve the turnkey glanced through the viewing slit. All was normal. He continued. At eleven fifty-seven, or not long after, the figure on the bed blinked, took a massive inward breath, and screamed.

Cracks hairlined along the concrete. It pushed, upwards, by millimetres, but it was enough. Tonnes of pressure compacted onto the underside of a few feet square of concrete merely a foot and a half thick. The cracks grew, seemingly from nothing. They were, and all at the same time were not, there. They undulated, forcing up a little further and then crashing magnificently back down in a fantastic wheeze of frustration. Finally the crust rose up a full foot, and as it smashed back to its base the sides crumbled and it disappeared deep into the hollow below. Arms, caked in dust and mud, torn from fingertip to elbow, but still strong hauled Marks body, spread-eagled and tired onto the refreshing reality of the frigid concrete. He lay there for a moment, breathing heavily, hugging himself to the floor, soaking in its hardness, its grainy greyness. After some time he pushed himself unsteadily to his feet. There was a bed in front of him, iron frame, thin mattress, it had someone on it. Someone gaunt and grey like the floor. Someone hollow eyed and bloodshot staring, someone hungry and thirsty, breathing steadily but deeply, on their back but looking right at him, eyes glazed over. Marks blinked, and took a massive inward breath.

Soon he wasn't the only one screaming, although his was the most distressing. Soon the turnkey came running, his nerves shot. Soon more people came running, in party frocks and suits. Soon he was on the *other* bed, strapped down but still struggling. Soon the diazepam was injected, soon it took effect, soon he began to fall into unconsciousness, even though the screaming carried on in his head.

Chapter Five

The cobbled streets here are strange, they're unruly and mismatched, bumps stick up like the straining browned tops of freshly baked bread. Made in the traditional manner of course. But amongst them there is a strange conglomeration of flagstones and the unmistakeable black of tarmac around a drainage cover. Drains, that's something new as well. Not the old cast-iron brittle ones, but different somehow. There's a lot that's different in this city, but even that is something that's becoming commonplace, if such a state can be considered to be so. The past years have seen many changes, the old traditional methods not so much thrown out but twisted and reformed into something that almost but not quite negates the previous. Something that would be quite disturbing one would think, but there are few people in this here and this now, wherever that might be. At least, there are generally few people, occasionally there are a lot of people, but on the whole it all depends on what is expected and where it is expected from.

Pull downwards towards the cobbles again, ignore the steaming, smoking metropolis. This is a place on the very edge of things, on the very cusp of science and industry, straining to move forward but aching to move back. That's something that doesn't agree with everyone as could be guessed by the intelligent thinker. There are of course pardons to the rule.

A cigarette hits the ground. No brand name, white butt, gold ring where the tobacco begins. A few sparks scatter onto the amalgamated paving before a well polished shoe, with spats, crushes it into the stone. There is a sense of hustle and bustle in this place but unusually there are very few people around. All the same the figure on the cobbles is jovial and apparently looking forward to something. It is spitting gently but the atmosphere is quite light all the same, not cold but not warm, and oddly enough not humid either, but its already been noted that this place is an unusual place in general.

The figure takes out a cigarette case and pulls out another of the unremarkable white tubes. The filter is cork, light and fluffy, solid between the lips. He places it to his mouth and lights it with a match. The case vanishes into a fold of clothing, although there might just be a glimpse of lettering engraved on the outside before it disappears. It might have been Dr. J.F. although in all fairness this could purely be conjecture, and even in some circles be perceived as slander, should such a thing exist in this place. In any case, he is standing in front of what used to be a very grand building, a beautiful building in fact. It's old, made of sandstone and as such it's quite worn by time, wind, pollution. Parts of it are covered in wire mesh, supposedly to stop chunks falling off in bad weather, for the public's safety of course. If there was a public. It's been unused for years, a decade or more it's safe to say. At one time it's obvious that a great deal of time, money and love went into this place, the old masonry showing through the cack of ages the work and care that went into its creation. Huge pillars line the entranceway, two on either side in the Roman style and above that can just be made out some lettering, smoothed by the passing of time. It's hard to read and sits on a panel to the front of the great entrance. The first letter unfortunately is almost illegible, but what remains of it looks like a reverse letter 'C,' the outside edge of which has been sanded down to a smooth slant. The rest of the letters read 'PERA HOUSE.' At the top of the stairs where the entrance lies there is a bank of dry leaves, but the door is open and for some reason seems inviting.

Doctor Joseph Frankson approached the door, his faded suit looking suave against the pained exterior of the building. There was a gentle pinstripe down the trouser and jacket that hinted at the 1930's, although it's a mystery how that fits in with everything else. The wind blew a slight gust and the dry leaves scattered in a tiny whirlwind in front of him, the odd drop of water whetting his lips from the clouds above or catching in his hair. He smiled to someone next to him. Who wasn't there. It wasn't strange to him, as far as he was concerned this was how things were done and had been done for as long as he could remember, for as far back in his addled and hodge-potch mind as he could go. It was customary, was it not, once the workday had come to a close and on certain special occasions to celebrate with friends. This was what he was doing.

The friend apparently made a joke. He laughed. "That's not usually how *I* do it!" he quipped. This went down well. Frankson held out his arm and puffed out his chest before stepping proprietarily through the great doors of the Opera House. He was apparently stepping out with a young lady, although, who could tell.

Mayhem overwhelms the senses. The walls are covered with incredible gilt, sparkling and glowing on art-deco moulding as chandeliers twinkle with hundreds of candles. Amongst this there are ushers in tail coats and bow ties ushering people through immense rosewood doors, selling programmes and taking pennies on the sly in return for a 'spare' ticket they may have laid their hands on. There are people everywhere, resplendent in the best clothes they could find, have made, steal. This is the social occasion of the year and nobody would be seen without the very best.

There is a man, he is wearing a slightly faded suit but all the same is smoking his unlabelled cigarette in a very genteel manner. On his arm there is a young girl. Not young, but younger. They're laughing together and joking. He leads her away and over to a spread. The table is magnificent with caviar and quails eggs, sugared rose-petals and any amount of conglomerated food stuffs possible. It's very unusual even for an event such as this. A champagne glass tinkles off to one side and the noise seems to intensify if that's at all possible. There are so many people in this place. Beautiful, beautiful people. They're everywhere, like stars in the night in their shiny dresses and twinkling cuff-links, diamond earrings and polished shoes. Frankson turns…

…to whisper something in his lovers ear. He hands her a glass. It's empty. The foyer is empty. The glass shatters on the floor, splinters of thin crystal skipping lightly away to the corners of the room. It's dark in here, hardly any light coming in through the boarded up windows. The door slams repeatedly, the wind's picking up outside, you can hear it just about in the silence, sighing through broken panes and chimney stacks.

"What a wonderful party, isn't it darling?" said Frankson, "I'm so glad we came here instead of staying at the hospital for New Year." He paused, as if listening to a reply. "Yes, I'm sure. I can't wait for it to start, it'll be superb, I've heard fantastic things…" The chain smoking continued, as it had done for the best part of the night. Not to say that this was necessarily the reason, but there was a part of Doctor Joseph Frankson that was unsure. Not just unsure in fact, but very unsure as to what was going on. He knew that he was on a wonderful night out with the lady of his dreams, at the opera on New Years eve. He was eating caviar and drinking and being merry, but all the same there was a part of his brain deep, deep down inside that was screaming out to him that something wasn't right, wasn't going to be right, hadn't been right at all in a very long time. Time, time was important in this place, as it is in all places, except that especially in this place it was important, because it wasn't. It should have been though, and that was the important part. Frankson's brain was torn, had been torn and would remain torn.

He stepped up to the great staircase that lead to the circle…

…no cheap tickets he, only the best. But not for his own sake of course, although he would enjoy it. It was admittedly out of his budget, but there were certain things that had to be done right and he was aware somewhere deep in his jaded romantic repertoire that this was one of them. He took a seat next to his sweetheart…

…the rest were empty. They had always been empty. Time aside they had always been empty. There was no-one to people them, but at the same time there were hundreds, just not here, not now, over there and then. The same but different. Somehow. Everything was somehow, no reason, no solid shape to this place. The building was hungry in this place, at this time. Doctor Frankson smiled and joked to his side, his arm draped gently over the chair next to him. There was love in his eyes. A very confused love, but love nevertheless. It was almost as if he wasn't sure why he was in love other than because of some pre-ordained decision, made for him well before he even began to exist. But the building was hungry.

The wind began to pick up outside, as rain hammered the solid lead roof. No-one could hear it, if they were there or not, the roof was far too thick. But soon the wind was pulling at Frankson's clothing, ruffling his hair, and still he laughed and joked.

The seats pulled down, wood and metal screaming and cracking into none existence. Folding and crushing. The stage buckled, electrical cables mixed with solid stainless steel supports tore from hollows and ripped from brackets as even the concrete foundations of the building began to rent and buckle. It was as if the building was afraid to live, afraid of the life inside and the storm outside. Lightning crackled in the deadened sky, flashing from cloud to cloud, and there was a memory standing there in the chaos. Even so, it made no sense, nothing made sense, a common occurrence in this distorted place. It was a memory of pain, of blood and gore, but mostly pain, and tearing flesh, teeth splitting and gums bleeding, and of fear and defence, but mostly of pain, so much pain. Through all of this the building continued to crumble whilst Frankson sat in the slowly disintegrating past glory, still smiling as memories that weren't his flooded through his mind, walls splintering masonry and brick, sandstone grinding on sandstone, heedless to the obvious pain of a noise just beyond hearing. Lightning crashed to the ground at the base of the pillars, burning flags shot past melted tarmacadam as a hole was smashed into the ground. The air plinked and pinged as the stone cooled, and after images blurred through the vision of the people who didn't pass by. The wind howled around the building, but just a few meters out was deadly calm. Rain was tearing down, smashing in great sheets on the sides of the building as great cracks ran down its length. Slabs of masonry crashed to the ground, crushing the paving and road all around as floods of water cascaded down the steps from inside the Opera House itself. The leads on the roof dripped not only with the water, but with the sludge of ages, the soil and detritus that had amalgamated through years and years of negligence. Through great rents in the lead it ran, thudding down all around Frankson, and he sat as the House enveloped him, the bones of his legs slowly snapping and breaking, blood seeping from lacerations as fragments of bone were forced through the muscle and skin. And all the while he smiled and sat, his arm draped around the beautiful girl to his side as the New Year passed by in memorable style.

Pull back, pull far back from all of this chaos and look at what has become of this place. The soot and smog of ages choking through the bright gleam of modernity and the naïve semblance that was once the paradise of the hunter-gatherer. What has this place become. No, perhaps that's not the right question. What is this place becoming? The battleground is set, but what the pieces are and what they represent is another matter entirely. Through this place of confused glory the ghosts of whatever scream and curdle their way towards each other, pulsing and spluttering through the noxious gasses that seem to strangle this city of all natural life. What remains? Too many questions. But what? *This* question remains hanging in the air, refusing to pick a side, refusing to drop its knee and submit to the glorified ramblings of something that might as well not and never have existed for the good it has done this earth, this city, this *place*.

Shrill tones come crying from the space left by the Opera House. High and desperate, in need of attention, but at the heart of it there is something else, something that the soul won't approach, can't approach. Much as might be attempted there is some barrier, some deep seated and steadfast fear that bears little resemblance to the skills of todays instinct. An instinct that doesn't simply stop, but point blank refuses to approach. There are terrible things skulking in those voices, high and wheedling things, things that should never be let out. Joseph Frankson knows this, he knows these voices, he knows them very well indeed. He should do anyway, he hears them day in day out. The voices, piercing the ears of madmen, pushing through into whichever mind might take the brunt of their collective desperation next. *Hear me!*

In the gloom, the man in the faded dinner jacket flinches. It's the first time he has done so all night, even as the bones of his legs were broken. Blood seeps from the mangled stumps now, thick and black, at the end of its attempt for freedom. To where who can tell, but freedom it is, of a sort. The skin is pale on the

221

man, but still kindly after a fashion, older than it was a few hours ago, more drawn. He looks around himself at the mess of masonry and wood.

"Where did I put my cigarette case?" His voice is faint from lack of blood, and his hand drags painfully across a fallen beam towards the inside pocket of his jacket. He glances down, the pinstripe is unusually bright right now. Red. He smiles to himself as he lights up. "Not much more to be done really."

Chapter Six

There are madmen in the madhouse. This is what society will always assume when it comes to defining a place such as this. To society its definition is its name, therefore: Madhouse. There's not much more to it than that really. But what is a house if not a home, of some sort at least. Not necessarily a nice home or one that a person would enjoy being in, but if you set aside society's notion that a home must be a comfortable place, that home is where the heart is, then a home can be just about anywhere. A home is a place in which something resides, a house is a place where something is kept. A home can be kept within a house, at least this is something that can be safely assumed. These points aside for a second, the question arises, what, besides madmen who are as society states by their name, the definition of their type: men who are mad, who are kept in a home for madness. More to the point, what by society's definition is mad, because those that are mad definitely have a different view of it, this is guaranteed.

Pan down into the sewers. The muck and filth of generations and generations of society's finest, lowest and most average citizens. Not much to differentiate them down here. From what floats by it's quite obvious, one thing looks pretty much exactly the same as another. So what defines mad? It's certainly not the diet because that would be evident at this level of existence that's for sure.

You can tell a lot about people when you go down to the lowest possible level of their lives. When you push through all the bravado and front, and get right down to the nitty-gritty. There's a lot that can be discovered. One thing is for sure, and that's that not all people exist on the same wavelength. This is to coin a popular phrase, but this aside, all life is built ever so slightly differently, if not then Darwin would have had a terrible time proving his theory. Chemicals rush through veins populated by reactionary lymph cells, enzymes are triggered and send messages through synapses, tiny bolts of lightning leaping from junction to junction, and in no two creatures will the same pathway ever be taken. On that basis life evolves, and on that basis life stays alive. People see things differently. So how does society define mad? A misfire of glorious electricity, pulsing through orange-red clouds on a purple-blue backdrop. Perhaps not. But fear is always a primary, and what can't be seen by the general population cannot be considered frightening when alls said and done. Not that there is a very consistent population in this here and now, but that's another story. Madness is relative.

Shadows skulk along the inside edge of the sewer wall. They're not new, they've been there for as long as the house. What's new is the light, because without light they're just shapeless, non-entities. With light there is suddenly a whole new dimension, a whole new perception, and perhaps it is perception that has brought the light. There's no other explanation. All the same the shadows skulk. They gather in groups around the filth of society and feed from the residual warmth, pulling in whatever they can glean and learning to be human in the worst of ways. How can you learn to be human when the thing you learn from has had all the human machinations stripped away from it, laid bare before you. That's not humanity, that's something else. What is left when you pull away all the taboo's, the do's and don'ts. Don't go near to the waters edge. But you go and then suddenly it has you by the throat and it's pulling at your lungs. They float away almost serenely and suddenly being alone is one of the most frightening things, because its one thing to learn how not to breathe, but its another to do it alone. And still the putrid yellow skin and the mud encrusted claws drag across your body, defiling it. Don't go near the waters edge. Madness is to live on the waters edge, skipping stones into the beautiful calm. Madness is the ripples on the water as the boatmen twitch along, almost but not quite in time with each other. Madness is the sun baking your back as you sit and just watch, minnows popping up and catching tiny flies from the waters surface. Madness is the beauty before the storm. Madness is living through the storm. Madness is wanting. Madness is living. Madness is life.

Tall trees surround Saint Austin's, it's what would be expected in this time and in this place. At least for now anyway. No, perhaps not just trees, perhaps a wood. If this was just trees then what would you call something smaller, but that's beside the point. There is a high wall and then thick, dense woodland, right up against the other side. It would be quite picturesque were it not for the screams of the insane coming from the madhouse, its like listening to singing, although not the kind that most people like to listen to.

The woodland is thick, and apart from a long driveway passing through the gates of the wall and out to the other side there are few if any pathways. There are plenty of nettles though. Nettles and brambles. It's a pretty standard woodland, lots of green and brown, what you'd expect really. It's been untouched for quite some time one would assume, the thickness of the thickets and the height of the nettles can occasionally in some patches reach completely unprecedented levels.

But there are men in the woodland now from the town. They're moving very quietly.

"Do you have the stick?" says one. The man in front of him stops dead in his tracks and straightens slightly from the position he's been walking in.

"I've already answered that question three times tonight Jack, if you ask me again your gonna get a thicker ear than that brain in your head, do you hear me?"

"Right, right, you've got the stick, I know you've got the stick, I've already asked haven't I?"

"Yes Jack you have," replies the man in front, his voice is older than the second, fatherly in fact. He's carrying a walking stick, although the handle has some strange notches and the shaft doesn't have the look of anything that was built to support weight. All the same, as he's an older man he must need the stick for walking. "Now Jack, it's getting to about that time so soon we'd better find a place to grub down in, otherwise they'll come out and be gone before we've even noticed them."

"Yes Dad," which explained the tone of voice at least, "Dad?"

"*Yes* Jack, what is it now?" Jack flinched back slightly, he was obviously starting to get on his fathers nerves a little.

"I'm just a bit nervous that's all, we're really close to the house Dad and I can hear 'em screaming and carrying on. I don't like it much that's all."

"Okay son," said the fatherly tone, "you'll be fine alongside me don't you worry. Besides, the turnkeys in that place are some of the most scrupulous people I've ever met. Don't think we're going to have a problem with the loonies if you ask me."
During the conversation the two men had begun once more to move forward. They were relatively close to the hospital wall at this point, the lights from the windows just visible in the half dark reflecting across the open grass and gardens. Of course they

couldn't really see any of this, and in all honesty there wasn't even a need for them to duck down, the wall being much higher than their heads. The most either man could see was a faint glow overhead that gently illuminated the tops of the trees.

There was a quiet moment between father and son, just a glimpse into the lives that hid behind business. There needed to be food on the table tonight, hot food, not oats this time, oats and milk could only sustain a life for so long.

"Dad," the silence deepened slightly for no apparent reason. The sound sucked in any other noise in the woodland, "Dad, this is okay isn't it?"

"Yes son, for now its okay. Tomorrow though it won't be so remember what I said. Soon as we have what we need we leave, we don't come back unless we have to, that's how idiots get caught. That's how idiots get hanged." A shiver tingled its way down Jacks back at the mention of hanging. He'd seen a poacher hanged only last month, but needs were plenty in this place, and those willing to provide for them were fewer and fewer. The only way an honest man could get by at the moment was by breaking the law and there was just something fundamentally wrong with that as far as Jack was concerned. Still, he would never have allowed his father to come out here on his own. There were rules when it came to family and one of them was that you never let them go *poaching* on their *own!* Stupid man. Jack derided his Dad silently in his head for the ninth time that night since they had left

228

the house. But still the fact remained, if not poaching then what else, and as his Dad had said, who else was going to eat them, because he doubted very much that the madmen were allowed rabbit.

After a short time wandering through the wood the two men turned away from the wall and a few meters into a thicket they stopped. Jacks Dad lay a blanket on the ground and hunkered down, Jack did the same, their faces almost completely obscured by the brambles and miscellaneous ferns that surrounded them. It was a cold night, both men had wrapped up warmly but there was frost in the air and their breath crystallised as soon as it left their mouths. A hip flask was passed silently between them, an expense but then the whole trip was a risk in its own right. Meat was so expensive at the moment, and no-one was willing to sell it even if they had it. The land was in a depression, deep and severe, and the government either had no idea about it or no idea what to do about it.

Jack motioned silently to his Dad, it was going to be a long, cold wait in the dark, but they had chosen a good night, there was a full bright moon and a cloudless sky, and in being near to the house wall they had assumed the trees would be thinner and let more of the light through. They had been wrong on this one score, but they would make the most of it, they couldn't afford not to. The older man passed the stick up to his son and attempted to massage some warmth back into his fingers, even with the dark sky he could tell that they were grey and he hoped fervently that they wouldn't cause him too much pain when the blood came back. Jack saw what his father was doing and immediately set to preparing the stick. If opportunity came along it might well be the last they had the whole night and it would be awful to have missed it. Unscrewing the bottom of the stick he took the end and opened up two tiny secret compartments. One contained a single lead ball that he slid down the shaft of the stick, letting it roll down the hollow middle until he felt it plink to a stop near the handle. The other contained a single small pouch of powder. It smelled of sulphur and cordite. Setting this to one side Jack set about the handle of the stick, lifting up three separate small panels, each covered in wood but metal on the inside just like the rest of the stick, one on the top to which he fitted a tiny flint taken from his top pocket, two to the bottom, all three clicking into place with quiet and well oiled exactness. His Dad had definitely been right about this at least, the stick was still in top notch order despite not having been used for at least forty years. He felt springs tighten as he clicked the final panel into place, a small one, no more than an inch long and sitting just behind a larger one around twice its length. These two together constituted the trigger and guard, much like any other rifle but on a more delicate level. Jack poured the powder into the top opening of the stick, just under the flint and got himself into a comfortable position to wait for a target. He reminded himself how sensitive the trigger was and smiled at the power he held in his hands. His father looked at him awkwardly, a mixture of pride at his son and shame at what he had brought down upon them.

Minutes passed, and then hours. Jack was beginning to wonder if the spot that his father had picked hadn't been the best site after all. And then there it was, just on the edge of his vision, movement. Quickly he aimed, and touched the trigger. Flame erupted from his hands. From the stick, but also from his hands, and from his fathers hands, and more, it covered them, covered their blanket, the flask, the stick. Jack watched as the stick began to creak and rust, as the blanket began to dry out, the oil on the leather fading to nothing and the leather itself becoming brittle. He looked at his hands, bright and young, and wrinkled and old, the skin becoming transparent and veined with age. He fell to his knees and looked into his fathers eyes.

"It's okay Jack, it wasn't your fault." There was a strain in the old mans eyes, both old men's eyes. "Good shot."

Time, like any other kind of energy can't just be made or disappear, it has to come from somewhere and go somewhere. The from somewhere is the important part. Time must be taken from another source in order for it to exist in another way. The new replaces the old. But not quite. The old becomes the new, in a manner of speaking. Time is absorbed and replaced where it is needed, where it is wanted. In this case searing light flashes through the woodland, burning and rumbling across the earth, churning up plants and animals alike. The catalyst fired and the fire continued, eating, feeding, changing the landscape. Trees were pulled down like great concrete behemoths readied for demolition, and just as soon as they had been they were eaten up by the earth in a stop-motion show of natures glory, death at the end of all things. Mulching down and composting. And from this compost came new life, a myriad of larvae and young shoots, heading out into the world or heading skywards to be the first to see daylight. But the daylight didn't come, the only light in fact was the light from the madhouse, the dim glow that barely illuminated the leaves at the tops of the trees. New growth sprouted, but for want of food, for want of photsynthesisable nourishment it became gnarled and underdeveloped. Instead evolution began to take hold and instead of chlorophyll capturing the glorious rays of light from the sky and turning it into beauty, the soil itself was drained of blood. Nitrogen flooded from the ground to whatever remained of this small stretch of the woodland, and slowly all of the outlying life began to die. Time was different in this place because of what had happened. Time has to come from somewhere, but what happens when it has nowhere to go. When it is trapped in whatever torturous universe holds it. Time fights back, it tries to move forward although all the willpower in the world may be needing it to stay back, and for what purpose. For understanding, for escape, for the blissful existence that lies terrified within the mind of everything, as everything tries its hardest to forget what can't possibly exist.

Chapter Seven

Diary of Doctor Joseph Frankson
  January 5ᵗʰ

I must confess that on this day, and in this New Year I've woken to something most spectacular within myself. For the first time in what must be countless weeks, months, years, who knows how long, I am excited at what may be held for what I acknowledge as my calling.

Things have most definitely become more interesting within the past few days. Since the waking (most spectacularly) of Patient 726 on a very memorable New Years eve (one that none of us shall forget for a long time to come) Doctor Beaumont has become my close ally and it is my opinion that he will soon ask to be appointed directly to my department. Naturally he would have his choice of case files, but to have such an eminent man request this would be a great honour indeed, and no doubt but it will aid my vain eagerness for fame (if not fortune, for a Hippocratic life is never well paid).

Patient 726 refers to himself as one Simon Marks, a name that he was not, most positively, admitted under. More than this even, he insists that he is a member of the constabulary, a high ranking one at that and seems in some trepidation towards his surroundings. These delusions are most interesting, and one wonders what occurred in the patient's head whist in his catatonia. It may suit to see how far this hubris shall go, although of course a cure for his poison would naturally be foremost in any doctors' mind.

Marks looked around at his new cell. There wasn't much else he could call it really, it was dark and dank, water dripped down the walls and on the inside of the small window there were heavy-set bars, firmly rammed into the stonework. No chance of escape that way, he thought. But escape to where in any case? What would come next, that was the question. The time in the desert, in the tunnel was already starting to slip away from him, but even so he knew that this wasn't right, wasn't the reality in which he was meant to exist. Despite this however, he could feel memories, not his but not someone else's, invading his head, taking his identity and moulding it into something else, just as his reality had been moulded into this one. He could feel in the back of his mind that he'd had a revelation, could feel in his thoughts that he was different, that somehow it fitted for him to be here, but for the most part he couldn't place why.

Bolts slammed back on the other side of the door, and Marks strained to lift his strapped head as a large key turned in the heavy lock. A man walked in, very properly dressed, but there was something quietly preposterous about the style. His eyes twinkled in the half-light and for the first time in years Marks felt pure hatred take him over and fill him up.

The doctor took a step back as the supposed policeman writhed against his restraints, he foamed at the mouth, and a very demon came alive in his eye.

Diary of Doctor Joseph Frankson

January 7th

A curious encounter, and an even curiouser conclusion from Doctor Beaumont today. Patient 726 seems indeed to be almost a celebrity now within the hospital. His delusions have reached a point now at which his psyche becomes transfigured at times (unpredictable I might add) into the very beast of the thing that possesses him. Doctor Beaumont informs me that the condition is known commonly as Lycanthropia. Not in fact, as myth would have us believe, the actual rendering physically from human to animal, but in actuality this is merely a psychological rendering of the same, and thus treatable.

The patients previous unconscious awareness remains a mystery, not uncommon in cases of catatonia. Similarly, the nature of the dissociation that I have long suspected has caused within this example a confusion of reality. In distancing himself from the problem of his psychosis another has occurred, and in deference his mind has created an acceptable alternative hypothesis. Not only this, but the aforementioned has completely broken down its previous. It will be a task to undo this damage and not destroy what also lies beneath. Should that still remain!

The increased serotonin levels are also very vexing to me, there being no continued outward agitation to explain it. This in turn suggests that perhaps there is an internal agitation, although what this might be eludes even my experience. The brain is a fragile thing in these beings, that I own, I know better than my family. To push too hard could be disastrous, and yet this is what my training compels of me. Reality in some cases it seems must be forced upon us.

In his moments of lucidity, however brief they may be now, 726 remains muchly confused as to his context, historical, cultural and actual.

Hospital business continues as usual. Patient 29 passed of a stroke earlier today, the result of an e.c.t. procedure, this is regrettable and also admittedly a setback for my plans, however not unforeseen and therefore acceptable within the limitations of the procedure.

Nonetheless I must file a report.

Diary of Doctor Joseph Frankson
  January 15th

A brief note, for I fear hospital business must surely call me away soon. There is both good and bad in everything it seems, for I can find no heart in these words.

Patient 726 is now completely enveloped in his Lycanthropia, no evidence (at least spoken) remains of his former 'world.' Whether this is a blessing in that we have purged him and he is along recovery's way, or that it hides from us in even deeper levels of madness I cannot tell.

Cerebellum electrolysis continues, as prescribed by Doctor Beaumont, however, I am dubious as to its positive effects. The more sessions the patient is exposed to, the more his madness seems to take over. More and more Doctor Beaumont is becoming a figure of anger to Simon. There is in anycase a definite antagonism towards him by the other and this is worrying. Although Beaumont may be unconcerned it does belie a direct antithesis to my own personal recommendations for patient treatment. But to return to the point...

... It seems that rather than burning the madness out, we are destroying the central human controlling the beast, the very thing that I have feared from the beginning. If this continues the only course of action will be lobotomy, a most undesirable cure.

Diary of Doctor Joseph Frankson

January 16ᵗʰ

Marks lay on the bed, finally still, but watching the doctor intently. There were red raw marks where the straps were cutting into his skin.

One said, "How do you feel... Simon?"

"Like my brain has an itch and my insides are covered in hair." One replied.

The doctor made a note of this in his little book.

One said, "Are you going to fry me again?"

"Fry?" one replied, " Ah, the electrolysis. No, I persuaded Doctor Beaumont that it was unnecessary today."

"Doctor Beaumont." One repeated thoughtfully. There was a pause, then one said, "Where does the itch come from... Simon?"

"Deep inside," one replied, "where I've never looked, couldn't see before."

The doctor made another note of this in his little book.

"What do you think the cure to your problem is Simon?" asked one.

"Cure?" one replied, *"I'm not mad you bastard."*

239

Marks threw himself hard against the side of the bed, anger giving him impressive strength, greater than he could have ever imagined he possessed. Doctor Frankson stood up quickly as the bed unbalanced and came crashing down on its side. He stood there watching as Marks struggled against his restraints, teeth gnashing and spittle flying from his mouth.

Beep.

There are worse things than homelessness, although for most this is something that is yet to be proven. Even so, some would argue that restraints are more frightening than rain. Rain, rain when it creeps inside your shoes, into your socks. It sits, lives, festers. This wasn't what you wanted, a thick jacket, soaked to the bone, and people just keep on coming until you *bite*.

And then a hostel, and then they see you, and then prison... prison, rehab, hostel... climb into bed with the government, become a bourgeois parasite of the nation and live from the side of things, never really tasting ever again. Institutional. But never what you wanted, so far flung from the freedom of the wind that steals your blanket. The one that you took to survive the ever-changing weather as the bailiffs take away your television, sofa, wife, dog.

Charlie mooched slowly down the corridor to the canteen. He'd just come from a 'group therapy session.' Not his cup of tea really, but then you had to stick with the program and that was what was on offer. He much preferred the individual counselling sessions to the groups they were expected to attend, he had been a loner for far too long now, opening up in front of a group of strangers made him feel vulnerable, exposed. It laid him bare to their open sockets and pulled expressions. Who needed scorn when there was so much self-effacing shame in the room. It felt damaging to be a part of. And there was something else as well, something that they all knew but no-one would say. It was disgusting and it had made the hairs on Charlie's hands toughen with any thought that he spared for it. There was fear in that room, real fear.

He'd sat in the corner in the end. Stopped trying to *connect* and *feel*. He'd slowly blended away, peeling back into the tasteful pastel wallpaper, becoming the calming pattern of mottled cream and blue. It was how he liked it.

On the plus side however, the nightmares were getting less vivid, especially since they had starting cutting the methadone down. That was the main thing to be said after all, the program was working, for *him* at least.

Charlie stopped and looked at the food on display in front of him. Oh well, he'd eaten much worse in the not so recent past. The TV in the corner had the news on, Charlie barely spared it a glance. Something about tides on the equator. As he picked up a tray a memory flashed quickly in and out of his head, he flinched at the sight, but that was all, for now.

241

Diary of Doctor Joseph Frankson

January 20th

Well, thankfully my request to the Central Medical Association has been accepted. After a tumultuous few days I am happy to write that Doctor Beaumont no longer has any authority within Saint Austin's. I am sure patient 726 will be grateful on some level. I am personally secure in my belief that this is the correct course of action.

Mr Beaumont will still, naturally, maintain a presence in the hospital until such a time as a new placement can be found for him, but I think it best that he be kept away from Simon. The patient seems to have developed a strong and devious hatred for the doctor, whereas I appear to be more a focus of trust. I think it best for now that I refrain from mentioning my part in the patient's previous treatment.

Apart from this, things appear to be continuing much as usual. Patient 129   (self-admitted) seems to be responding to his treatment, that being the same electrolysis as 726.

His affliction is a muchly different psychological disease to Mr Marks Lycanthropy. Of course there are still the legal ramifications to deal with, but I am a healer after all, not a lawyer. One must approach only those tasks in the world to which one is suited.

Despite this good news, the case of 726's, 'Simons,'
drastically prolonged serotonin hyperactivity disorder plagues
somewhat on my mind. I have found through my experience, that
instances of this unusual defect subside within less than a week. It
is no wonder therefore that Simon has enveloped himself in his
Lycanthropic persona after over two months of the affliction.

Beep.

He gritted his teeth through anger and doubt. Thinking straight was
hard, all he could feel was the painful fury, itching at the back of
his head, bypassing his conscious thoughts. His bestial mind had
taken over, had hot-wired the modernity of his usual, conscious
synaptic routes. All he felt was pain, pain at the world, deleting
what had always been such a strong sense of self. No, not deleting,
pushing it, thrusting it to one side. In some way he had allowed his
primal, animal mind to take control, and in some way he had to
force a compromise.

For days neurotransmitters had been corrupting his vision,
burning through his head in ways that pulsed painfully through his
glassy eyes. Beetles crawled over his skin, biting, chewing,
stabbing. He felt every tiny leg scratching into him, saw them burst
into flame in his minds eye when the electricity took him, felt them
take control when the diazepam felled him. He saw the walls

dripping with honeydew, and in running to sate his thirst felt his face torn from the bone, leaving him gasping, blood dripping.

Through this however his mind worked, his *real* mind, lost to the side of his brain, recognising things, taking note. And through the decay and fear it hinted steadily that there was something not right. That what he saw through his bloodshot eyes was a nightmare, but not entirely untrue. His rationality told him to compromise. Find what was real in his mind, find what was real and solid, and hold it there.

Past all of this lay Beaumont, a figure on the sidelines now, feeding the beetles, laughing and turning them to fire.

Chapter Eight

Diary of Doctor Joseph Frankson

February 1ˢᵗ

A great many things have happened of late, not all with entirely desirable effects. However, these things will happen nevertheless.

Following my letter RE: Beaumont to the CMA it seems he has followed up with his own, no doubt in spite! It seems that against my complaint of him he had an audit instigated against my person that for the past few weeks has quite brought the hospital to a standstill. A madhouse we may be, but our intent is still to cure, and I was quite taken away from all but my most menial of duties. And for the sake of paperwork!

I was not best pleased, and I found it necessary due to the extreme nature of the disruption to put my usual rounds on hold for the duration. Because of this my monitoring of certain personal projects has suffered somewhat. I have to admit to recommencing my duties with a certain amount of trepidation at what I will find. The turnkeys have kept me informed to a certain extent, but in truth their observations, although done in honesty, are those of a layman's. I have had them keep an especially close eye on patient 726, with rather extortionate monetary recompense I must say. From their descriptions he seems even more bestial than before,

245

and despite the unreliability of my sources I have found myself beginning to doubt my decision to cease the electrolysis. I have to remind myself however that these are the descriptions of the uneducated and I am sure once I have had time to assess Simon from a more educated point of view and over an appropriate period of time that I will see much improvement in his general psychological health.

I find myself over time becoming more and more affected by this man. There is an understanding in the corner of his eye that I can reach no more than it seems he can, and yet he has in his lucid moments maintained a self-belief that surpasses not only that of the average lunatic, but also that of most sane men. In a most disconcerting manner it gives one a sense of strength in his purpose, whatever that may be. In many ways patient 726 represents the perfect specimen. In him there is potential for greatness in some manner. It is my duty as a healer, a man of learning and of medicine to aid in the realisation of this to its full potential, whatever the outcome.

Brown. Red-brown at any rate. Dirty red-brown, almost to the point of crumbling. Flaking in fact. There is water also, it seeps in all around, forming rivulets down the crags and crevices of the red-brown. Close-to it's quite magnificent, you could almost say perfect were it not for the chaos of pot-holes and razor-sharp edges. And yet the corrosion seems targeted. An interesting conundrum, whether apparently random erosion can seem purposeful, but that's where its perfection lies, way back when the metal was first cast into bars. Small indentations that seemed so inconsequential, flecks and impurities creating minuscule sink-holes for innocent droplets of water, cute in their smallness.

However, the innocent are more often the most easily exploited, and those inconsistencies are now major gaps in the integrity of the whole. Specifically in two very important areas. In this way develops a new conundrum, a question of integrity greater than on the scale of this one relatively small item.

Beep.

It opened its eyes. Light hurt, although in its side-brain it knew that it was dim. Growled, slightly, words obscured though, a chatter in the head.

One said, "I'm sorry Simon, I'm afraid I didn't quite catch that?"

Acknowledged, but it still doesn't understand. Frustration, but for some reason there were things stopping it from moving. Frustration again.

One said, "I'm afraid it was deemed necessary for you to be restrained again Simon. Mr Agbert said he wouldn't like me to be in the room with you alone otherwise. He does molly-coddle us all. Do you remember Mr Agbert, the gaoler, he brings your food. I see that you've not eaten today." One kicked a food tray with its foot, "This is apparently the third day in a row."

It was confused, the noise was low and vaguely comforting.

Doctor Frankson missed the slight flicker of recognition in Marks eye, he left the room and made a note in his little book to very politely request Doctor Beaumont's assistance in a forthcoming lobotomy.

Beep.

Marks lay on the bed. Lay strapped to the bed. There were a number of things not right, a number of things going on that most definitely shouldn't, but Marks brain was so divided that no proper semblance of his consciousness could discern what. Despite this however, there were also a number of things that no amount of shouting had been able to drown out, his throat was now bloodied and raw from the attempt. There was hunger, a great hunger, a need for something, but no amount of eating could sate it. Eating, yes, he'd stopped that hadn't he. Food was bland, grey, there was no appeal to it, it felt bitter and dry in his mouth, he craved delicacy, the deliciousness of something that he couldn't put his finger on. Surpassing everything however Marks felt a desperate need to escape, at least until the moment when he had found what he needed to scratch the itch on his brain.

The itch, that was the other thing, the itch. Incessant, all consuming, infuriating, he had tried everything, that's why they had strapped him, not that he was conscious of that fact, not that the matter of restraints made any difference to his internal processes whatsoever.

There were footsteps down the corridor, they echoed slowly around the high ceilings of Saint Austin's. Two sets of footsteps, no, three, certainly no more than three. Marks brought his mind, such as it was, to bear. A need to escape, to escape, a need to escape, scratch the itch, find something to scratch the itch, escape and find something to scratch the itch.

"It should be a fairly simple procedure today gentlemen." Said Doctor Beaumont in a business-like manner. "Doctor Frankson, I believe you are familiar. Perhaps for Doctor Simpson's sake you could describe it's main features."

"Certainly Doctor Beaumont." Replied Frankson, gritting his teeth. Despite himself, he continued, "A Translobal Leucotomy, or Lobotomy. In completion we look to the insertion of two instruments in between the frontal lobes and the thalamus, effectively separating them. The easiest way to obtain that result is to insert each instrument just under the eyelid, next to the tear-duct. The trick is not to sever the optic-nerve, very difficult I think you'd agree Doctor Beaumont." He continued before Beaumont could pick up on this jibe, the number of failed surgeries had gone up dramatically since Beaumont had entered the hospital. "Essentially, we are severing the patients ability to emote, to give concern. It is a revolution to the psychiatric medical profession. Is that not right Doctor Beaumont?"

There was a long pause that hung heavy in the air before Beaumont could muster an answer. "Quite... quite right Doctor Frankson, quite right." He gathered himself quickly, "you have done well sir, this procedure is still not widely heard of."

"Well," replied Frankson simply, "this hospital aspires to be at the very forefront of medical technology."

Beaumont halted a few feet from the surgery door. There was another long pause. "Quite." He said at last, although this time his words were pointed and considered.

There was commotion within the surgery, a great crash and the scream of an orderly.

Run, thought Marks, run, escape this place. He hurtled out of the side door, leaving behind him the mangled body of the dying orderly, crushed beneath the great iron bed that Marks had so recently been restrained to.

It opened its eyes, grunt, something familiar in the air, makes its passions rage. Escape, return later. Marks charged, all fours pounding the floor. He smashed through the door to the corridor, splintering the frame violently and charging past the three doctors on the other side.

Doctor Beaumont was the first to collect himself. "After him." He screamed, and at once a number of orderlies came around the corner. Doctor Frankson stared as burley men ran to capture a person whom he had come to appreciate, whom he had charged to lobotomy.

Five hours later the search was still continuing, it seemed that patient 726 had somehow worked his way into the vast labyrinth of Saint Austin's Psychiatric Hospital.

In the semi-darkness it stood on its hind-feet, steadying itself on the wall, its nails had dug great grooves out of the sodden plaster. Now it stood, almost motionless, staring at the patch of failing sunlight past the corroded ironwork.

Carefully he put first one and then the other hand on a bar and yanked at it painfully. It shuddered at the treatment and shifted slightly at the top. Three more good yanks saw it crashing from the masonry, splinters of rusted iron zinging into the shadows. It pushed at the thick glass beyond and felt the wooden frame give slightly under the pressure. There were voices outside the door, muttering. Marks shoved hard against the glass, and as the woodwork splintered it rammed itself at the gap in the bars. The rusted iron scraped into its skin. Finally, just as the door burst open the corroded metal gave way and Marks tore away into the fast dissolving haze of dusk.

Beep.

Dogs barked in the darkness. To the right, now to the left as well, closing in. It roared into the shadows, dark and primal, tapping straight into the spine of anyone listening, any animal hunting. The barking stopped immediately, there was panting in the gloom, each and every beast still and aware. Marks burst into energy, throwing himself at the stone wall surrounding the hospital proper. Stillness greeted his frantic effort, and slowly the dogs padded away into the night.

Chapter Nine

Diary of Doctor Joseph Frankson
February 7th

After the startling departure of patient 726 all hell has broken loose at the hospital. The police have interviewed me personally several times, and I presume the rest of the staff similarly. Naturally I shall have to resign my position after such an incident. Doctor Beaumont I understand shall be taking charge of the hospital, and shall be utilising my office main.

Unfortunately the police dogs, our main method as I understand it for tracking the fugitive, are proving uncooperative and on the whole reacting in a completely uncharacteristic manner. So far our only clue is the damaged masonry to the west wall, where it is thought he scrambled over into Portland wood. If this is the case then it could very well be quite some time before we can track him down.

This being the obvious case to all, it has been decided that I should remain sanctioned here at the hospital for the foreseeable future. As a familiar figure it is thought that I may embody something of an enticement for him. In this way it is hoped that Simon may yet return, with my own person as a point of contact.

Beep.

Diary of Doctor Isaiah Beaumont
    February 7ᵗʰ

An interesting course of events these last few days. Unfortunately I am not as assiduous in my diary writing as I should be. It does help to keep one's thoughts in order, and serve as a reminder when necessary, but otherwise and on the whole it seems a tiresome duty.

*   Frankson seems to have taken his depositioning with good grace, and I have to admit that I shall enjoy sorting out his mess in this rather grand set of apartments. One can easily see how poor Joseph saw himself so far above his station with these facilities made so readily available to him. It now comes down to me, however, to restore equilibrium to the minds of the beasts interred. They must be shown that their indiscretions will not be tolerated by society. I shall soon instigate their new routine, once the orderlies have mastered the appropriate methods. If they did not learn under the reinforcement of Mr Frankson then they shall have it beaten from them like the distorted wrecks of humanity that they are. It is safe to assume that even though they cannot be cured, they can at least be trained.*

Chapter Ten

Eyes fluttering, body tensed. *Flick.* Body tense. *Flick.* Stomach convulsing. *Flick.* Sweat. *Flick.* Ferocious. *Flick.* Eyes flutter. *Flick.* dreams. *Flick.* Rage. *Flick.* Pain. *Flick.* Betrayal. *Flick.* Protection.

Charlie's hand shot out suddenly, catching the nurse's wrist as she tried desperately to insert an intravenous drip. His eyes crawled their way open, and his nails dug in as the nurse's skin began to break.

"Get him off of me." She yelled, pulling away. "When did we take away the methadone Harry?" she asked, addressing the charge doctor as she struggled with the unconscious man's grip. Charlie was still tightly grasping her by the arm, staring intently, although vacant of actual consciousness. Instead, symptoms of rejection had slowly over the course of his treatment been kick-starting a reaction in his hindbrain. Over months now the wolf had waited, biding its time. Mani was no longer an issue, but it had met Amaguq and now its moment was here, *now* it had its chance.

"Harry," continued the nurse, "Harry, he's hurting me." Blood was dripping around Charlie's fingers now, and a red foamy film covered his teeth as they began to slowly pop and crack under the pressure of his body's own resources. Blood trickled down his chin, and the whites of his eyes now showed brightly. He removed his hand quickly from the nurse's wrist and clamped his maul around the deep wound, tearing viciously at the flesh as if the blood would complete him. Men came hurtling through the door, pinning him back, teeth gnashing and eyes flaring. Nurse Joanne Samuels stood there, eyes glazed, cradling her arm to her chest as Harry Yazer, doctor resident at Farrington Rehabilitation Centre shot Charlie with a more than hefty dose of valium.

As his subconscious was subdued Charlie became vaguely aware as Nurse Samuels gently collapsed to the floor. The sun dimmed.

There was a knock on Doctor Beaumont's door. It was strange in itself that he should get any kind of visitor at his private apartment's, he actively discouraged it in fact, let alone at this late hour of the night. Slowly, for age was taking its inevitable toll, he raised himself from the deep leather armchair of his library and settled the line of his waistcoat.

"This had better be vitally important." He muttered, "Or I shall not be pleased in the least."

Beep.

Eye's, in the darkness, a glint of eye's. Fear, there was fear, not in the eye's but within the beholder. It was dark, murky but full-blooded all the same, and there was a glint accompanying the rustle of long dried leaves.

Marks crouched in the gloom, his heart pounding. It would be hard to tell whether there was recognition in his mind, threat was certainly apparent on his face. A canine tweaked out from his upper lip as his face convulsed into a snarl. Anger, so much anger. They had taken his dignity, tied him down, burnt up his insides with drugs and electricity. They had dehumanised him. At least that's what the pent-up pain forcing his instinct told him in the fraction of a second before his muscles bunched and he leapt, full-force at a point a few inches below those glinting eyes.

"What is it?" Doctor Beaumont opened his door, fatigue reaching around his face. It was easy to tell that he was not impressed, he had been busy going over a great many reports. The effects of sedative on some of his favourite therapies. So far he was unsure of the next step to take, however, a likely solution would no doubt present itself.

Beep.

Blood, tearing, fingernails ripping aside skin, a panicked frenzy. Marks teeth chipped on bone, he felt a crack as they met behind the gullet, and tasted iron as blood bubbled in a desperate attempt by the body to just keep breathing. An arm flailed in a single last-ditch attempt and was slammed back to the mulch covering the dank night time soil.

He looked into eyes, blood dripping once more thickly from his chin, and watched as they dulled and deadened into nothing. No more struggle, no more to fear, for now, and for now the itch on his brain was also dulled. Although in his hindbrain he knew that it was not gone, yet.

Beaumont sat back in his armchair, not daring quite yet to breath.

"I... I had no idea he would be quite as dangerous as that, I assure you Sergeant." He at last stammered.

"I'm quite sure," replied the police officer, "however, you understand that the township will not tolerate such behaviour, be he a lunatic or no. The boy was eight sir."

"Eight!" repeated Beaumont in astonishment. "Damn Frankson, that lobotomy should have been carried out weeks ago."

"Just so sir. However, men are now gladly hunting the wretch down. I understand that he will be shot on sight if capture is deemed out of the question. Otherwise he shall be hung at the gallows by the neck. Even so sir," continued the Sergeant, "and begging your pardon, but like hell are those men waiting for the gallows. Your man's as good as dead."

Beep.

"We can't treat her here." Said Yazer, tightening the bandage around nurse Samuels wrist. "that sedative will keep him under for a while, but not indefinitely, and I really don't think it'd be good for them to wake up together."

"I'll phone for an ambulance then shall I Harry?" suggested the porter, a young man.

"Good idea, better than my car by far, especially as she doesn't seem to be coming round either. I'd hate to transport her without the proper support. Where did all that rain come from, it was full sun just five minutes ago."

"I'll get an umbrella."

Beep.

Diary of Doctor Joseph Frankson
February 14ᵗʰ (Last Entry)

Unfortunate events of late, which due to my depositioning I have only just heard of. It makes me wonder what more I might have done. Indeed, this seems to be the question on a number of lips as my lawyer contacted me late last night to inform me of my forthcoming inditement. I am a ruined man. The charge will be Gross Clinical Negligence. Suffice it to say that my career is over. No respectable establishment would consider me for a moment after such a travesty as this. The tabloids will have a field day, I have no doubt in this. What more scandal could be had?

It occurs to me whether suicide might constitute an appropriate option, however, before I address that matter properly I must put my financial matters in order, such as they are. Thankfully I have no family to speak of since my divorce, so that is one consideration I can neglect. I imagine that if I did have a family I would educate them as to honourable death. Such I wish mine.

Beep.

White sheets, clean, only slightly ruffled. There is a light blue blanket as well, it is thin but well made, not that it matters. No-one comes, there's no point, he does nothing. Nurses feed him, they clean him, they shave him.

A green light. It travels straight for a fraction, then quite unexpectedly it peaks. *Beep.* Only for a moment though, then it flattens again. *Beep.* There is nothing behind it, only darkness, like his eyes, unresponsive darkness. *Beep.* Pixilated.
The nurses talk sometimes, talk about what goes on, behind the darkness, the dull apathy of apparent dereliction. *Beep.* They conclude nothing.

A trolley wheels past outside the door, it is metal, there are three men pushing it.

One said, "She was admitted yesterday by her sister, apparently there's no waking her, and the sister doesn't have the time to be a full time carer, worked at the clinic, nice girl..." But then it's past and there are only murmurs, not that it matters.

Chapter Eleven

In their sleep they cry out. Sweat, putrid, beading, stinking sweat lies on them… them like a film. One is pain, embodying this fetid emotion through semi-blocked pores of underground humanity. They suffer unbearably through him. One seeks abominably to rid the pain, the itch that as yet still cannot be scratched. One seeks to stop the itch being scratched, although they don't know it yet.

Blood, tearing, gristle, snarling. A stream, scent, man-flesh, succulent, abominable, out-cast, man-flesh. Sating, quenching, crunching, gnawing. Indescribable as pain surges through the brain cavity. Consuming, protection, addiction, purity. Purity. Clarity. Plausibility. *Neglect.*

Charlie shook in his sleep. He had not woken since the incident, but as a precaution was kept under a steady and watchful eye. He suffered constantly from nightmares, which were obviously taking their toll on his never substantial frame. Drawing, sucking his life away like a leech, leaving him as gaunt as the day he had entered the clinic. However long ago that had been.

Doctor Yazer avoided him as much as possible, although that was fairly hard in the clinics small infirmary. Memories of exactly what had happened those six days ago were washing away, even memories of Jo Samuels, but there was an imprint of something, something not right, a brightness like the sun, glaring and full lit, and then all of a sudden dimmed and smothered. The look of concentration on Charlie's unconscious face was desperate and unforgiving.

Torches, to the side, and yelling. The crack of a rifle and a bullet thudded into a tree trunk not far from Marks. He snarled viciously in its direction before moving off at full pace through the undergrowth. Itch, in his brain, an itch, an abscess burning and blocking, waiting to burst and flood into his mind with its filthy puss. He screamed at the unseen torment, scraping violently down his face with blood and grime encrusted nails. More blood began to gush now, rivers of it down his face, blocking out what human image was left and covering it with slice upon slice from his broken fingernails.

An end to it, this was the end to it. Acceptance. Pausing not even a second longer Marks tore off towards Saint Austin's Psychiatric Institute.

Eyes open, white staring, In Thrall of Annwn, eyes wide, love, such strong love. He had kissed her and taken her with him. In Thrall. She could see perfectly, see the running man, see the Annwn, and there she was, stood in between, peaceful as the running man came towards her. Peaceful, peaceful, and calm, there was no need not to be. Beautiful comfort around her, she could feel him as strong as ever, feel that he wouldn't let her go, telling her, caressing her, even though it was costing him in his own life's energy. *Cŵn Annwn... Charlie.* But he could see it all, in his hindbrain, and she saw it all as well.

A figure on the road. Gates, a horse and carriage. Vague awareness of distance, not far now, closing in.

Anger. Hatred. Pure and unadulterated.

There was shouting in the trees behind him and figures raced, torches in hand. Closing in. Not long now. Branches whipping at his face and body, adding their insults to his fury. People were yelling louder now, much louder, trying to warn the figure by the carriage, but with every single step it could feel the itch grow, feel the abscess strain.

Doctor Beaumont tripped as his head was rammed forcibly into the carriage door. He felt his skull grinding together as he slumped to the floor, knowing that the injury was fatal. There was weight on his stomach, and then gunshots.

Rage filled its mind, its soul, its very being, and as it held the old mans head between its hands, ready to smash it open on the cobblestones, Marks opened up, and he allowed it to fill him.

There was a rush of chaos in a mind, chaos so beautiful and pure that it could fill the universe a hundred times over and still have a remainder, tiny but glorious in its solitude. It is this remainder that

264

filled her. Chaos in a mind, a mind so wide with wonder, taken over by everything inside of it.

She stood in the middle, between the two of them, keeping them apart, in Thrall of Annwn.

She stood, eyes white, in front of his bed, staring, eyes white, and there was nothing else to be done. Green flashed across the screen. *Beep.*

Fire flashed through Marks head as the abscess burst, and he slammed Beaumont's skull down hard against the stones of the road. Blood gushed from his nose and eyes, joining the mess of his face, and as bullets pulped through Simon's body he...

A woman, dressed in a hospital gown. Her feet are bare. The man on the bed opens his eyes, they look at each other. There is plenty of time.

One says, "You have hell's beast in your soul."

One says, "He raped me." There is a slight pause.

"I know who did this. I know now." Says one.

One replies, " So do I, and I am all that matters to him."

She puts her thumbs gently over his eyes.

"Sleep now." Says one.

Blood sprays onto the walls as she pushes down, deep into his brain. His body stiffens, fitting in epileptic spasm, blood gushing from his mouth in obscene amounts. His head spins from side to side tearing at her trapped hands, she makes no noise, no sound in any way, just a bland, passivity. There are loud snaps as her thumbs break at the second joint as they are jolted against the optic cavity. Someone has heard the commotion, they come running. Hands drag and pull at her, they feel as if they are tearing her in two, peeling her skin from her flesh just by their touch. It is abominable to her that they should even consider themselves worthy to touch what the Annwn holds dear. She tears her hands from the now still figure on the bed, eyes white, she is listening, but there is no sound in the room, no-one can speak words in witness of what they have just seen. She is sad, a tear drops from her sight, and with her mutilated fingers she pushes into the soft tissue of her own eyes, that in doing this she might one day learn to see as clearly as they do.

Hands regain control now, they pull at her, wrenching her away. She fights, struggles frantically, and in the panic of the moment a fist crashes into her face. She is unconscious now, she is enveloped in the love, it surrounds her and cushions her fall. *It* is coming to her, coming to *her*, to show her the path that she must take, because any other would be heresy. She prepares, there is a time for all things, and at times all things must change

PART III

It begins with one.

Burning Heat, fire in the mind,

Retreat but without the foot so

Fleet in tar it lies. As it

Turns to stride through the

Minds open door, that great and powerful tor,

It stutters, it falls, and

Upon the moon it rakes its claws to

Diminish that which is

Both beginning and at the finish.

That which is hidden remains so,

That soul and truth for the

Beast are uncouth and puts

Fighters toe to toe.

One so near, so far to fling

Ideas that make him king when

He feels the burn, the sting, that sweet

Opiate that seeks to sate his

Thirst. That when quenched

Always returned.

That one that in mind

Breaks the bonds that have tied

Him. That have lied to him,

And when his mind is open

He dies, or so it seems to living eyes,

But the Sun lives on.

Fire in the soul, in the mind that

Seeks its kind. That when tied

Binds more deeply, and ignores

Entreaty of conscious thought.

Takes control in satiation of

Madness. To great Thrall in

Sadness control is gained, together

Both minds are restrained.

And out breaks the wolf.

The mind fully engulfed.

But even so, encased in

minds tormented grasp renewal,

revival, an encouragement to

survival for one that seemed

so lost. And yet now its soul is

tossed to the dogs, for fiercest

reprisals his mind tormented in

age and time as old as rock.

And as he descended so did the
People into panic and pain, as
the rain fell on a city ruled
by need, by greed
of one they fled into the corners and...

Chapter One

A radio crackles in the dark. The sound is stark, but someone is apparently tuning it. You can almost feel them enthusing upon it their need, the entreaty to their own greed that would speed them on their way to knowledge that as yet they may not understand. And although this at first may seem well and grand to Sergeant Morris whose job, nay duty it was to remain well-informed, far from intellectually scorned, it was difficult for him to see that the wavering bandwidth would mean so little. That the force was spread so thin and brittle that his spittle held more worth. Especially on this turf.

Things may have changed he knew that. In what seemed like no time at all something had gained control of *his* city. His home that although not pretty had been his guardian for so long a time. So long a time that no rhyme or reason would separate his blood from the stones should it come to him living or just leaving his bones. This was his worth, but something had changed. Within days of Marks death, that tormented mess that had greeted his eyes, although for some reason here he let instinct dictate not to his surprise was the D.I. prostrate and decaying on the table...

He felt like he was in some sort of evil tale or fable, because not one or two but hundreds of dead were now piling high, and the causes of death were frankly pie in the sky as far as he was concerned. And so Morris was determined. Determined not to leave the city, that entity of sanctity that he considered home, left to roam alone in something little understood. But as an officer of the law, every window and door should be open to him, open within this barricade that had been built.

It hadn't taken long at all for the government to see that things weren't quite as they assumed or were meant to be within the great state. A great state that was firm and situated on a ground of it's own. That was home to so many cultures and frames of mind. But now there was a new kind. One that couldn't be seen. And because of this at first it had been deemed that there was no way in hell that *any* nook or shadowed knell held more to fear than the average lecherous sneer of a rapist, or murderous intent of whichever human was hell bent on the destruction of life. But through this the strife continued, and though lock and key were thrown at many and often as well books a-plenty there came a time, a time when all had the same in mind. That something was out of *its* time. Something unseen and evil, something that may have seemed so simple at first took on a new dimension and through theoretical expansion the council found that they were fast losing ground to a peril from within. Not man nor woman but something else, a creature of sin. And there stood the truth, at least such as was held by the people who didn't leave, couldn't, who stood their ground. Not that there were many of them now.

An armoured car rumbled by, eyes to the floor, the sides, the sky and he knew that although they might look they'd never see, if something came for them it would be quick, it would be tight, and besides all this it wouldn't come by night. It would come by day when surrounded by friends. And suddenly what their eyes thought they saw ends, and then one that was there is gone. Life isn't fair mused Morris, he knew as much, he also knew that all it took was a touch, not that you could see, not that believing made any difference. But in deference he knew that despite the cannons and the razor wire, none if any had been slew. Not that he or anyone knew what they were or what they looked like, but in spite of this they took you away in plain sight of day and further to this no-one could say when the one they loved went. But then they were back, their life all but spent.

Below all of this, another the other *Annwn* sits enthroned together not smothered, both this and that from hell sits behind and mortals to fore and inside can be seen the most ancient of lore. There's something occurring quite out of sight, and ultimately life can but not at the same, see that deep in the vein there's something not right.

And through all of this pours a mind and a truth that though ruthless to self and selfless to none but his own he atoned and now understands that what he sees and he feels is not quite Elysian sands.

Further and deeper, a journey of sorts but without the close comrades he collected at ports so long and so far and so deep in the

272

mind, he heads towards something that feels kin and kind but he knows that he had from the earliest start a fraction of knowledge. Like a tree in potentia he grew from his mark and his name stands firm like the roots in the ground, that before he might rest on that Elysian sand he must be imparted with faith in the life that he hands down to the next. But when and which that might be, ultimately comes down to the man, the ghost from his past that took him by hands and helped him cross glass. And with that inertia his potential was freed, but by woman we know he was brought to his knees. And in this Marks himself sees that before minds were freed he fell deep in between.

So between worlds he heads, neither mortal nor dead, and through thought he passes the wolf in his stead. But dogs to the fore to welcome him home for in *Annwn* sits his master grandly enthroned and he knows that he's seen him in dreams not long gone. In which his mind floated like a duck on a pond. But further to this the man that he was is there and both gone, is exploded not lost. And not the wolf but the dog emerges at last and through *acceptance* was how he came to terms with his past.

A shadow in the night, a table, but for a second day took fright. Not through dark do we see but in stark light of day, it will and it may quite easily be the shadows own fault that the light that was gay did perish, could not revolt but returned a second later, and revealed the once live and animate eater.

273

Ten minutes earlier, a house on a hill, nothing too drastic nothing to fill the gaps in the mind where the dark things might lie. But instead a room of four that behind that closed door sat and said grace without the faintest of smiles, the faintest in sight. But their plight, their plight was yet to come.

At the beginning of trials, of plagues in this city when none were aware we set this entreaty, and further although the word may progress at this point in time we seek to address that which occurs behind those closed doors because despite gore and grief it speaks deep and true of relief of the facts that none thought could be true.

So back to the table, and that which was once just tale and fable jumps to the fore, and that which was there, the mother of two and wife of a lover was split clean in two while seeming to hover just feet above a slowly dampening floor. And worse than this because those three sat beside and eating in peace didn't see any gore until they'd finished their feast. Both quietly and quickly at evening it struck, and even the lover although older he was, was blind to the fact of what happened above. And quite halfway through a mouthful half chewed he did see and could feel there was something not right, that someone perhaps had blinked out of his sight. But try as he might he could see not who, until she came back, almost in two.

And for her part she screamed as she wrestled about, but nothing connected not even her doubt of what at once she knew just could never be true. And then blood and gore, the body, the

274

floor, and she knows this is it. But while calling her lover he seems to have quit both listening and caring for all that she sees is a forkful of fish and something like peas as she struggles and screams in a desperate way, the food in their mouths not escaping the spray that exudes from her flesh bright red and congealing. And already the creature is done with its stealing and they see but they dare not believe. Their mother is dead, his lover gone, and they saw nothing at all but the corpse of the one.

Then far to the right, a man out of sight, under a desk he is lying and still he is spying his colleagues, their plight and soon he takes flight. His office is gone, his colleagues dismembered and he remembers the time not so far and he trembles because deep in his soul he knows he's done wrong. That in leaving the dying, in not even trying the CPR that he knew, he may as well spit, he may as well chew on their bodies like them, whatever they were, that although still unseen had forced open the door. That had thrown him aside and left him for dead while friends all around were rendered by head and by arm and by leg they did die, as they ripped them apart inside each mans eye. For although they'd not see, it was plain and clear that to Matthew his office had become someone's dinner.

And as time progressed the city both great and now dim came distressed at its own inner fault. That somehow the people had opened a vault into hell. But as mentioned above the deep shadowed knell that these creatures whence came were not of the city's own personal shame but were brought there by one, who stalked by the sun and the moon and both same would be true. That he would destroy what he hunted at night and by day what he saw, what gave him his sight. That moon was now dead but sun was unseen and despite the demon inside the human was clean but departed, and instead was willed out another, the other, so long since it started its deep and demanding course of its standing to make and come true what it thought, what it knew. And so in they came, brought by it, by its fame by its Thrall and in respect they did tell it that its honour was tall in these matters. And as the blood spatters from army cadets, untrained as they were because as yet we can see that the army, the military did not have a clue of how to deal with you. Charlie.

So with dead piling high, on both sides to the sky but with humans unknowing how well they were doing while Marks was gone, the city fell down to its knees like the Somme. And barbed was the wire like razor it wrapped around the great city and on they capped great cannons and tanks and howitzers there, and mortars that fired at night lit by flares. And the people inside, most made it out, and most of the vans that held them about did drive through the gates of the great barricades that had been built by the council both local and dazed in nothing they thought but a few days. Despite this it seemed though that the city soon teamed with invisible foes that caused pain and woe to those trapped and left to rot and decay, though live they might be, for the moment it seemed. And some were cut off, small pockets alone, and trooped to these ghetto's the rest tried to roam. To safety they thought, to slaughter for some and their journeys of course through them we run. Some of them armed, most of them not, they travel through broken bones that rot, and the crunching they hear of gristle and bone makes them tired, makes them feel like they're quite alone. The ones that walk round, that stalk them by night, hold no more fear than their dead daylight plight.

Chapter Two

…over before he could even realise quite what was happening to him.

Vision blurs, but not petulantly. There's something more to it though, definitely something that requires attention. But past all of this the question remains in the fallen mans eye, was he going up or down.

What very much was the case in fact equated to neither, but perhaps... There are myths about this place, of the *Annwn*, the otherworld, ruled over by the king of the Fey, *Gwynn Ap Nudd*. The place that lies between worlds, neither living nor dead but unalive. Guardians of the last space, the leaders of souls, guides to the recently deceased. But not judges themselves.

Although they might be at the *lead* of the hunt it isn't them that instigates the matter. As far as all are concerned. But even so, when they ride out tidings are far from positive. In their wake lies war and plague and famine. But it isn't them that brings it, they foreshadow it certainly but they don't bring it themselves. As far as all are concerned. But there are things at the centre, things between that make no sense, that need not make sense, that are a matter of perspective.

There are two grains of sand in Marks eye. He blinks, once, twice. A tear breaks the rim and pulls them down his cheek. There's not much more to be done really.

"Hello... Simon." He looks up. Confusion quickly enters his face followed closely by... The figure starts to walk away into... into what? But this is irrelevant at the moment.

"Hey," Marks raises his voice, "Do I... I know you don't I?" The figure stops. Unseen on its face it smiles. "Why do I... why do I know you?" Questions tumble inside his head but for some reason he can't focus, he drags his fingers across his eye and down his cheek. The figure doesn't move.

"I'm known to many, those on the brink, on the edges." There's a brief ejection of air, Marks surmises a chuckle.

"Why can't I... why.. can't I concentrate?" Panic entering his voice.

The figure replies; "It is your punishment."

Run! Faster than you think, faster than you know, faster than you feel when behind your fear will... Stop think, fast a dozen, bakers choice, right hand turn head down palms moist with sweat as your heart beats hard. As his heart beats hard. Deep within, his mind apart from what he thinks he knows, he must...

And then it's over. A snap as brittle and battles done. Another gone, one less to run.

"Am I in hell?" asked Marks meekly.

"Do you want to be?"

"What kind of question is that? Answer mine first!"

"In that case you are not in hell."

"Where am I?"

"You haven't answered my question, I thought that was the deal?" Replied the figure.

"No. I don't want to be in hell. Can you face me when I talk to you?"

"Yes." A brief pause.

"Will *you face me when I talk to you?*"

"Yes. But I have answered a question already, before I turn you must answer one of mine."

"Yes." Replied Marks.

"Good."

There is silence. It's unnerving, although the same could be said for the whole situation. What could also be said is that despite his unnerved state Marks was still teasing with what he had left.

"Well?"

"Well what?"

"What did you want to ask me?"

"I didn't say I would ask this instant."

Marks was frustrated now, "But you refuse to show me your face until you've had another answer from me."

280

But the figure was gone. Had never been there, was still there in some respect although what or which it was incredibly hard to tell. A simpler concept to navigate would be the noise emanating from about him. A deep guttural sound just on the lower range of human perception. Well, perception at the very least.

A voice is heard. It is the same familiar voice. "The Moon is dead, the Sun is tainted, they are beyond repair."

"I don't under…"

"You don't need to! *It was never your place to. The seed was planted within you, instinct drew you to the man, to the Moon and still* Ulfhednar *escapes,* Vargr-wulf! The Viking!"

"What do you mean. I can't concentrate… please. The man, the Moon, what do you mean?"

"The man of ambition, vanity. The one that you took print from until you broke.* Cochrum. *And then to deplete me with drawing you back only to have death upon you… this Otherworld is sacred. Is your* prison *not* Salvation!"

As he spat the last word the noise stopped. The rumble, the growl that had been barely on the edge of perception now somehow stole the air from apparent lips.

"Hello?"

Each bound to a soul through lineage trapped, through blood they're imprisoned for they cannot adapt to the pace of our change. They remain estranged from the world, to save those about from the sin they unfurled. Dogs to the sides, the floor. Tearing ripping dripping with gore that would otherwise maim. Not wolves nor monsters nor creatures deep but Dogs of this Otherworld, Black, fired plain.

On one they set their paw, their maul, their long splintered fangs ripping skin, making raw. From masters call they sound their salute, one howl, seven dogs but one more astute than the others. For unlike them he's his mothers' son, strong willed and not liking to be undone he rolls his sleeves, his shirt torn down, his leg seems to bleed as he's pinned to the ground but he *fights*. And with it earns certain rights. Because its one thing to do as the Master says, but another to yield when he holds the key to your days.

Marks stood up. And with him stood the *Cŵn*. The dogs, the hounds, they surround what he sees what he feels what is conventionally grounds for defeat. But for him no retreat as he knows now, that how and why and wherefore would he, he was there and the dog in his soul knew it to be.

He pants as the last of the beasts drags itself away. He calls out in despair.

"Why are you punishing me? I know… I know they were my own kind! Why are you punishing me?"

"You fight well."

"I know what I am, I've seen what lies inside my heart. I know the animal inside me. Now answer my question!"

"First you answer mine." Marks slumps to his knees.

"Yes."

"You are different?"

"Yes."

"How?"

"That's two questions!"

"How are you different?"

"I know myself. The dog and the man. I am me. While I was mad, in the house I saw, in the woods I knew. I had to accept the wolf, had to accept my anger. But the desert. I had to know the man. From them came the Dog."

"Ah." A shadow moves forwards in the distance but its still too dark to see. After a while Marks tired eyes see the vestiges of expression starting to outline themselves.

"You."

"Hello... Simon. How are you feeling?"

"No, you can't..." wailed Marks, backing away. "You're not real."

"The same could be said for a great many things..." Replied Frankson.

There is less food now, for the living. For the thriving there is plenty but for this one bounty remains empty, nonexistent non-extent without the cause, without intent there is the potential to kill. And at will this may consume the mildest mannered. For in survival morals stammer and fall. And the longest to drop is for those that are tall, that are consumed with themselves, with their own contribution, reputation. And with preparation Matthew sharpened his blade, or so he thought, but in truth it made no difference. In deference his prey absconded, left him hungry, but despite this the thought had been there. Had rattled under his fair hair. None would know, would see or tell if he took something precious in that shadowed knell. And to deepen his thoughts he wasn't alone, not that he knew, not that he would atone but they saw and they left, despite his cold heart because deep in his soul they saw not evil but art.

Time is beginning. There are no explosions, no fanfares or flaming swords, but time has begun. Within time exists nothing, and from this nothing comes everything. Not quite yet but... now! And as the physical nature of things begins to take toll we kow-tow, we bow down in descent. Nascent decent of man into madness. But not quite yet.

When time began, when beast walked with man things were different. Both heaven and hell were closer than twins, disregard of course too the original sin but we see come what may what was not meant to be, but within the dark ally's they broke into three. From what was both true and vital a cause, a third was created a space, a pause between living and dead. A place for those *vargr* all too well fed on the bones of their allies unknown.

Dogs are mans friend and the wolves are their twin, but when they committed *their* original sin they were broken. Entombed. Torn from a world they enthused their attention upon. And given to a king, a man, the one. *Gwynn Ap Nudd.* King of the Fae. Both cruel and gay to be trained in all else but the destruction of man, when wolf bit mans hand, when wolf opened the vein a power much greater found it hard to restrain his anger.

And so not dead not alive not undead unalive they are now. In *Annwn* sit entombed, forced to grovel to bow to *Ap Nudd.* But they still hunger for evil, for good they are not. And between heaven and hell in *Annwn* they still rot but one breaks free. Adapts to the change, forces the human to open his chains. Smashes the door so weakened and old. That the boy Charlie had not a chance and was destined to fold. And he draws first two then three then hundreds more kin to his kind, that between them they find their promised land. Break and build their promised land from what they take from mans other hand.

And YOU *were meant to stop him!*
Marks shuddered at the quality in Frankson's voice. It was something other, not choral certainly but something other, something that he couldn't place.

"Gwynn Ap Nudd, what does it mean?"

"It doesn't bare regard, I have many names. My duty you should attend to."

"Then what is your duty?"
285

"I guide the souls of the dead. I imprison those who seek to disrupt this process. I hold the wolves in the sky."

"The wolves?"

"In the beginning man and beast walked side by side, and demon beside them, angel too, we fae. Psychopompos all."

"Yes."

"And the first to disrupt *our* world *our* peace *was not man, not angel or fae or beast but* Demon! *And so a third space was created, was baited to hold them. This space, our space. And in it we placed the* Cŵn, *and all else within were of broken sort, not subtle but gruesome and hard of heart. And we* Fae *guard the entrance. And* Vargr Ulfhednar... *Charlie broke free. To break the bond between the sky and he. To destroy both Moon and Sun above and absolve those singles from their tough and addled morals. To cause quarrels and death and when both were dead, the First breaks free, the one that bit then refused to flee. The one wolf left, not dog, not he. But you. You're different.*

The demon and the man in you have given you strength. You are White. As Charlie was destined to fall, although never before has the opportunity arisen, so too were you destined to chase. You're human nature dictates such, the wolf in you forces the issue."

Family of four family of three, not knowing how or where they should flee. Run through the torrid streets around, falls to your knees, picked up from the ground by your father the other the man who loved mum, who unfeasibly stared at her body with peas in his mouth that were sprayed with her blood. That despite him not being our *real* dad is *good*. Who'd not leave.

But where to go, where to hide, the city penned in, wire on all sides. Where to go, where to drop, where to sleep, where to scoff the food you can see. Any tins left, meat going green but you try, try, try as you might because you know that the mortars still fire at night. You hear them away but you can't make it out, you hear the gunfire, the screams and the shouts as they get torn apart. Those brave men and women in armoured cars.

But to go to the edge is death for sure, stay in the city, the middles secure. At the edge fire the guns, teeth that tear, blow the bombs, but here in the middle its fair to assume that the devils steer clear. That there's possibly, although not definitely, less to fear.

And although combat takes place so far from this now, there still stalks in between roads an endless dark frown of creatures come back, drawn forth from *Annwn,* guided of course by the *Vargr, Ulfhednar* that steers their course. That aims for the sun, the city his course. Safe haven for none, his kindred his kind, Demons to one whose presence of mind could save mans demise from what happens inside those ghettos about. At one our poor family will end up no doubt.

"You've forgotten much it seems."

"I have."

"You were released for a reason, placed inside the casing of Marks, but now you are both, the human doesn't restrain but the demon doesn't fight. You are symbiotic it seems. The Ulfhednar, *the warrior, berserker. He has gone* Vargr, *rogue or wild. He seeks to free the First, Lupus, placed in the sky and bound by the Hundred, Centaurus. You failed to save the moon, lost yourself inside the man and lost the trail. If you would now save the sun it may be too late. She was your demise, in Thrall to the other, and now he owns the body."*

"What do you mean by that?"

"That which was Charlie is dead, something dark now lives in its stead. It haunts the streets, its power unfolds, it knows the depths of the worlds secrets untold even to them of the wyching way. Only in myth are we known to those living today. But he's amassing another, the other, the side from dark mothers who fight light of day."

"How... how is he doing this?"

"The life remains within, within you, the demon inside can call out to those can set them aside. But without the presence of mind such as you, this Vargr, *this rogue takes the city. The few that remain will be food for his hoards, that come to his fame. Don't you understand, you could've* stopped *this."*

"Show me, show me what he's done, what he's doing, Show Me!*"*

"No. I have answered three questions in turn. This *was* not the deal. *Now you must answer me three questions, and with each you will prove to me your capacity to fix this. With your knowledge restored you might stand a chance.* Let the Dog chase down the Wolf, let the pack restrained set loose the one that knows right from wrong. And stops the end of a world in song. *Three reminders I have to form this new dance into time. And for rhyme and reason I don't know how, with my attention on dogs that I must make bow, on your own you must stop the sun going down.*

For Charlie she yearns, the fire in her chest, it rages, it burns out her mind, her soul you might find is diamond encrusted and precious as gems.

But without proof for faith I can't allow you back there. To the mortal world."

"Then ask me your damn questions." Whispered Marks quietly. Gwynn Ap Nudd, nee Frankson readied himself, clouding his eyes for a moment. Mist hung heavy in the air.

Morris fired into the dark night time air, his taser was jammed, he thought, if he cared. But the ghost was now up, his blood seeped around and his cup, his cup was empty. The plenty that had sustained, that he had trained himself to rely on, to resolve and replenish at each and every finish was nearly gone. But he smelled burnt hair. He'd hit *something* at least.

Broken leg, through the skin, hit on the head and bleeding. Without mercy he'd fired, his bullets run out. The Kevlar he wore his only shout at living. Last line of defence, mustard gas gone, his taser two charges one left and one gone. Mist hung in the air, an omen to someone not dimwitted or fair, but dark and intelligent, resilient and striking, from *Anwnn* they came through, seeking the Viking. The one that at heart they knew was their sire, they broke through so fast the gaoler tired, and they got out… and *in*.

But Morris knew none of this. And as he closed his eyes, made a fist. Then in crashed the door, splintering wood, and three soldiers did pause at the sight of his blood. But they bandaged and swabbed, brought morphine to vein, and propped up the man who'd battled in vain with an enemy still unseen. But still as he flew, despite the help, the few that remained, Morris still knew that they'd move out of range. Or else all that stuff that he'd seen that night would happen to them, although not by light. They'd be unseen, their bodies left still, so he'd talk to the squaddies, tender the bill.

Gwynn Ap Nudd speaks, his voice is of an unearthly tone and yet at the same time it is all of earth itself.

"In Poems he sits, he thinks and he knows, in war he strides fore foes die at his blows. Not Tyr nor Loki, Fenrir he's not.

With eight legs in the sea he's no minion of Lyr but he runs like the water under that name, and no less is his regard his joy his fame." His eyes are white, he stares at the Dog, the Dog stares back. Illumination seeks his face. His face is found.

Chapter Three

The word is faint, unfamiliar. It feels almost wrong, insincere...

The tanks have already been, they've seen they've heard, they've sounded their call. They lie, they spoil just meters from the initial barricade. Now deserted. The rank stench of decay pervades the air, broken jaws gape, open eyes stare at what was never seen, heard, believed. And yet in they teamed brought by the Viking, *Ulfhednar-Vagr*. He stands at the centre of it all, tall in his greatness, that the lateness of the hour is so far for what he thought or deemed the fate of the one he adores, who spawned and provoked him, guarded by the hundred, tied to the sky, bound thrice in chains so great a brace of stars to him taught. And yet not broken. A link in the chain not severed, the beginning not begun, the hound still caught, still hung in the sky for all to bare witness. For him to pay penance for the first bite, first betrayal, the *First*...

And with all of his power, a single tower, a great unbreakable tower that once was Charlie cannot fathom why the eternity that has plagued so much upon his sanity is not yet come to close. And so in deaths throes, in tears of painful steptoes he sneaks through to the conscious minds of many. Calling them forth, his kin his kind, so that he might use, might fight, might find the Sun so full and lustrous so vexing with life. Will bring a knife to the rope, will slacken and snap and crack with power unleashed. But while sun shines on earth and moon soon forgot, not a jar not a jot will be brought down. And so the onslaught continues. Man after child may fall at these throes as he tries... tries to find the lullabies that will bring her to her sleep. That will begin the world anew, will snap the chains in two and set the captive free, will break not one not two but three. And man will walk with beast and angel and fae... and demon will take what is his by right.

...but there is a part that recognises, deep in the soul a part that knows, can see the goal ahead. Can feel what lies what lives what dies at what was once a mighty stead. King of war of poems true enough writ for none but you to see, and rides on steed so fast it meets the sea. Not Tyr nor Loki, nor Fenrir, and with legs eight... the hand of fate.

    "Sleipnir!"

    "What makes you say that?"

    "It feels right... feels safe."

    "Safe?"

    "The correct and comfortable vestige."

    "This seems more appropriate."

    "Yes?"

    "Yes... Simon." There is a pause, however brief.

    "That isn't my name."

A name is a thing is it not? A call to arms, to canter, to trot… to stop? But what when a thing has no name is the name of the thing that had name placed upon it. Is it not still judicious to give it frame, is it not the same. But when name covers name, when same covers that name then when and where do discussions… stop. Trot. Canter. Stop. Who or what answers the call, draws themselves tall and steps in place. But a trace… a trace of a mind remains, covered by fame of others, by glory and subconscious division of circumstance, of happenstance, of cerebral power. Some glower and contrive, this is foreseen, but to cover that which they may consider malign is to stupefy, to circumvent that which is deemed right for the individuals survival. And because of this a rival is formed, is grown and turned aside from the rest. So meek in comparison as to instil derision within the whole, to rebel. And then only acceptance will fill *this* shadowed knell. But when not one, or th'other takes dominant part, what is the name, where is the heart, where is the hand, where is the trick.

"You will be neither man nor beast, you shall hunt the lone warrior, hunter, survivor. The last relic of time immemorial. The first gladiator, the tutor of murals. He hunts and you shall hunt him, with spirit both human and demon of which none other possess… You are Amaguq of spirit and in survival of this relic, the trickster, the stalker, the prey and the previous."

At last Marks speaks. He hears, he understands. There are wings, meters across. Mist hangs heavy in the air.

"I am Amaguq."

"That which is right you will know."

"Why do I feel lighter?"

"You're penance is done, you are acceptable. You may return to the world at any point once you have filled your new name with that which you already knew."

"You speak complete shit you know?"

"Thank you Simon." There is a slight pause before Ap Nudd speaks again.

"Not evil himself and fallen he's not, but the ear of the one he has won't forget that he does his duty. And would never refute the claim of his name that one of death not of life may have opened the grave. Rolled the stone so far away."

Marks face contorted in inexpressible ways, knowledge was there after a fashion. And it was knowledge, it was just... different. As if it was his and yet someone else's at the same time.

"It's the blending of consciousness." Interjected Ap Nudd. Marks stammered slightly.

"How did you..."

"I have seen many things."

"What do you mean blending of consciousness. I'm a little unsteady on my feet here you may have noticed."

"Your minds are merging, accepting one another. A symbiosis that has never nor never will again be achieved."

"I feel a... a separation."

"Your soul is making way for the demon, it will be over momentarily. Focus on the question. Answer the question."

"I don't know the ans..." But he did know the answer. It was as plain as it could have ever possibly been. And there was a connection as well, of sorts. *"Azrael."*

"What makes you say that?"

"He's an angel, rolling the stone from Jesus tomb, not a fallen angel but one of death, of duty to the dead. Not evil."

"Yes."

The sun shines. Hidden away, but it shines. To some it shines brightly, although to those that may be able to bare witness to this grandeur, this splendour their vision is blurred, the prophecy spurned by a state of backwater... of bridgeless waste. A ground to taste but not to dwell on. And so they turn, they run they hide, they whisper their snide little comments about a world afire but without the energy to produce flame. That they first must tame the inner world, quell the darkness *he* unfurled, this does not bare conscious derision.

But to the sun, to that world that springs forth life, is a prison so dark and captive fed that to be chained to a bed, to smoulder and darken, blacken and burn no more is all that it can stand, and hungrily waits to be led

Moving by night and by day, whenever away, whenever not still, they snake their laden way around industrial tools. Like fools in a playground but without any mirth, instead with ineptitude they run across turf. Unaccustomed as two when carrying one more, to judge by capacity how far to the door. To safety. From unseen eyes to unseen tongues their progress is tracked is watched with keen and knowing glances. And with dances, those commentors, those judges that sniff, and turn to whiff the human sweat, that courses from four mens dread. It is they that instil the fear of mistake, they that stay stiff and still like a snake ready for its kill. And as such those three and one other, as quiet as mice, make their way through what lies abandoned and still. But unpopulated less, at least a lot more than would relieve stress. And so they *do* trip and fall, lose breath and spoil themselves in the dirt. Because they're scared, they're in fear, they don't want death to hurt.

"Move faster." Whispered Morris, " I think…"

"You heard him Ste, stop stamping around."

"He's bloody heavy though Corp. Swap for a bit."

"Watch your language."

"Sorry Sarge. But you aren't 'alf a fat twat."

"I said watch your fucking language. Now shut the hell up and get to the buildings, we're wide open here."

"Yeah, you wanna end up like Swab?"

"Why aren't you helping though?"

"'Cause I'm the only one with a goddamn rocket launcher!"

The remaining two squaddies muscled their way to the verge of the estate, tall tower blocks ringed with giant concrete blocks. A bastion at one point. Perhaps only a few days ago. Now blood blackened on the steps and the smell of acrid flesh hung heavy in the air from the remaining pyres.

Corporal James Squared his shoulders and turned, planting himself solidly in a covering stance. His body armour had been taken from front line, he still hadn't said what had happened to the rest of his unit. Shock troops. Ste pulled out his hand pistol once Morris was safely behind them.

"Well?" Hissed the Sergeant.

"I can't see sod all."

"Wait… Did you…?"

"Don't talk shit. You're talking shit again!"

"Will you *shut up*. We're in the clear Sarge, any signs of life your end."

"I've not got a hardon if that's what you mean but I don't think my legs gonna be the same again."

"Shit Sarge, there's bits poking out of it."

"*Don't* touch it... Ste." Morris sighed as once again he swatted the squaddies hand from the gore of his leg. "But if you've got any more morphine that'd certainly be a help."

"Sarge you've already had more than you should really have..."

"Fine, then piss off and check James, I'm sure he's got a shrapnel wound, check his gut."

Ste scuttled off, his red armband lost in the blood that covered his gear. He also hadn't said anything about his unit. Nor had Morris gone into too much detail about his own situation. They were together, that was a fact and a matter, but they would never be together in those moments. In those moments they would always be on their own. A gun rattled to the side, Morris jerks his head away from the noise, feeling the pressure so close to him. There is mist heavy in the air, out of the gloom resolves the figure of Corporal James, Ste is close on his tail.

"*Sarge*... I nearly shot the sodding twat!"

"Did you?"

"Not yet."

"Fuck you. He had an inch long piece of metal in him, nearly shot me when I took it out."

"It *hurt.*"

"Wuss."

"Shut the hell up both of you. We've got to keep moving. As far as we know they're tracking us right now, or they're already

299

here, who knows. Movings better than not moving. There's no-one here, it's gone, let's move on."

"...seeking a clearer understanding it's plain to see."
The mist is incredibly thick now, viscous and wet, but not chocking, there is still oxygen. "There is a final question that you must answer me."
"And then you'll let me return."
"To a point at which you deem acceptable, yes."
"Could this…"
"I believe I have answered enough of your questions, here is mine: Am I poetic in fury, or words of the seer, when man worked with iron I replaced Tyr. For a hand he had lost and I like all my limbs. Shapechanger, healer, winner of sins. I brought man victorious, in prophecy spoke and for those unbelievers with magic I smote."

The words appeared slowly in the haze, seeming to people the air with figures and images that were so intrinsic in their very essentiality. And something deep deep within Marks spoke. An old voice that was both his and not his and his all the same. It spoke an old tongue, laced with the affluence that centuries of wisdom have given. They say: "Wōþuz. Prophet of the ancients, the Guardian of the First in replacement of Tyr after the loss of his hand. You are the keeper of the First. You are the answer."

Gwynn Ap Nudd smiled, it was annoyingly knowing. "I was always the answer, in some manner. Where will you go?"

"Take me to the Sun." answered Marks.

Chapter Four

Let me speak of Aubade, of that which accompanies and all
encloses light. Let me speak of the Sun. That… one.
Let me speak…

When beast walked with man and angel and fae, when day turned to night and night turned to day there were and always have been those not so accustomed to the way that things seem. In ages gone by, when mist did spread further than either leg or eye could travel. When morning came with dew and flutter, the stutter of life in its beginnings. In this time things were different, that we bare deference in all acquiescence is obscene, uncalled for if now serene in its endeavour. What was has been and shall be forever… Even so, amongst the down, amongst the feathers that history spreads over deeds like lead there is one small, who in his own right will become tall. After a fashion.

His whiskers twitch, he smells the air, hind leg to flinch and off he goes. Over hills, his home the meadows. But not so soon, not so late, when hours are early he hesitates, he holds his ground for what is neither depression nor mound. But in front of him sits, or lies that's to say, a mark on the ground at the start of the day. That he is the first to rise, the first to wash, the first to tie his bow upon his back means surprise for a rabbit who's not alone for all that.

And when wisdom he seeks from those older and wiser he's slapped down in his seat chastised and derided. But earlier he wakes, day on and day off, and each time as he leaves he sees dark marks in his trough. Like some footprints he's left, not an hour ago, but the size of a man and before he could glower with his presence. And so the pretence goes on, rabbit on the run, trying to catch the shadows.

Shadows are all around this place, they evade capture, they dance and mutter. And outside the mist pulls in. It foams and whirls, forever changing, cascading. Light pushes through and hope is here. That as yet it has not been subdued is resourceful to say the least. Is astonishing in actuality. But in its sensuality it remains lethal. In Thrall of Annwn. Not of one, not of other, but of the essence belonging to both.

There are giant grey blocks in this place. There are tops of reinforced masonry, girdered with steel, and in amongst them one remains. Tied to a bed, restrained. Considered deranged by all who had contact. But this place, this Space *is now deserted save for the pervading moisture. Vapourous water that gets everywhere. That rusts iron bars and sets captives free, that if followed shows the way by tracing river or taking tea. Water is essential. The mist is thick but not cloying, almost as if toying with the life that was*

303

present... at one point. This is agreed by all. But one remains, bound by chains. Not chains of the sky, she's far, far too shy to be condemned in such a way. But to be bitten by the first, to thirst for satiation of his madness and to kill. There was no thrill, but instead is left behind the shell of a woman, forever bound, forever tied to that which she as yet doesn't understand. And even to compound this issue there is consciousness left within living tissue to know, understand, regret.

At a time that is discussable, a disused receptacle, unknown and unknowing our rabbit takes flight. Over the hills to check on his plight. The thing that has caused him so much concern... but as he approaches he feels the burn. The snare that he set, to catch the beast, to turn and churn all of his anger toward is too bright. That he might fight, fight fight for his place, for his space of existence. As the fastest, the sharpest, the earliest of risers... but home he tears, with tears of fear in his eyes, that he leaves in place his woodland spies is to be expected.

"Fuck you arseholes!" Yelled James as his empty cartridge clicked into the mug. Quickly he grabbed onto Morris' shoulder and bodily threw him onto his back. "Ste! Ste where the crap are you, I can't see shit... Ste... Ste I think they're here."
Suddenly to his right a figure pulled itself out of the mist.
"Fss! This way, keep down, there's cover."

"Ste is that you?"

"No it's the fucking RSPB, who else would it be. Come the hell on."

James silently muscled himself and the recumbent Morris over toward the figure. *"Look, we've got a second, here let me stop his bleeding, it's cracked right open again."*

"Where the shit did they come from? Thank God for this mist that's all I can say or we'd be..."

"What do you mean? Last I saw you were two paces behind me, then you'd gone. Next thing there were bullets an' yelling an' all this shit. What the hell?"

"The mist moved... There wasn't... I couldn't see anything but I could feel..."

"Quiet, I can hear something." Ste paused for a moment, listening intently.

"Sorry."

"What?"

"Grinding my teeth."

"Why?"

"Just 'cause, now shut up, I gotta think."

"What about that building, half a K Sou' West."

"Secure, lets head out, there's no point staying here."

There is shouting, well, not quite shouting but raised whispers certainly. Jo puts an ear to the mattress so that she can better

305

understand the mumbles and mutters. Just outside the door. There's someone just outside the door. Two people. Two people carrying a heavy load. This is disturbing to both Jo's inner self and her exterior Thrall. This cannot be tolerated.

"Jesus Christ what the hells that." The screaming and snarling continued unabated. Clattering and banging coming from within, and without James quickly readied his handgun. Click.
   "Alright Ste don't worry son I've go this covered." Ste was hastily fitting a new cartridge to his own weapon and pulling his Kevlar closer. James mimes numbers: Three. Two...

The door crashes in, there are men, two, both are holding weapons of a sort. Not the weapons that Thrall, that Aubade would recognise, but certainly one that Jo Samuels recognises. Senses.
   "No, Please, don't shoot!"

The creature so lost, so caught in the snare, has nowhere to hide, no-way to tear itself free from this restraint. Its complaint as such is that night follows day, day follows night and its anger is that it must give up this fight. It burns more instead to the world it is tied, it burns at its heart, its mind and its eyes and it *hurts.*

But what of the rabbit that sets the heat free, what of the rabbit that runs in its lea. That Sun is the heat and rabbit is gone, but what of another so far from home. That this rabbit and that are not one and the same, deepens the heart, cuts through with shame. *He* cuts the chord, sets light and life free but for penance the Sun pays with one final deed.

Outside the ground moves, shifting ever so slightly against the breeze. There has been a lot of killing in this place. That one survived the slaughter shows a bond to the others, that they would not kill their own kind. Blood has soaked into the mud, minuscule fragments of flesh and bone trodden into the sodden earth by stampeding feet. There are empty shell casing here and there too, the odd item of torn clothing mashed with blood. But the ground moves… slightly. Pulling together. And from this ground seeps the substance of life. The biological fragrance that holds the structure to sentience. Like mercury it tugs in, pooling and stretching, and slowly congealing, pulling in and upwards like a great stalagmite. Soon fragments of bone and gristle are being pulled from the dereliction round about, seemingly carried on the ever-shifting earth. Blood and flesh fusing, realigning, coalescing into a whole. It pulls its body out and makes to scream but as yet vocal chords haven't formed. As a mild steam begins to cover the outside of the carcass great welts of scarred skin begin to appear, they callous and fuse, spreading across the tormented mass like fungi. And then finally all is done. Marks stands, his form settling slowly into smoother features, his gristle eroded by motes in the tempest. But these features are not entirely familiar to him. His teeth are set wider and sharper than they had been, and his hair which had always been dark is now a grey-white. His nails too are different, sturdier, shooting straight from the bone, and sharp as well, sharp as razors. This Marks was new, this Marks was complete, neither one nor the other. Created from many, with the strength bestowed upon him by their constituent weight. That he was blind was a minor inconvenience. That his eyes had been taken from both him and the animal in their death, moments before consciousness ceased, created a unique template upon which to build. Not that Marks could see per se, but certainly he could sense, he could feel the outline of things by the very space that they took up in this material universe. Matter was his centre of sense and he could feel its echo through the honey-miasma of distance. In these ways Marks could see every profanity of the world.

Footsteps move down a darkened hallway. Lights flicker, not because of him, but despite him. He is neither wolf nor man, he is the Dog of Ap Nudd. She senses his presence, prescience to consciousness present on her mind. Guns ready, aim steady, but when he enters there is no gunfire. Only one consciousness recognises him. With subconscious dreams it is possible to say that Morris may have bore some recognition to the apparition in the doorway.

"You are the sun." says one.

"Yes."

"I feel you. Do you feel me?"

"Yes."

"There is darkness clouding your vision. Let me pull you forward." Marks brow wrinkles in concentration. There is a faint light coming from somewhere but the experience is odd enough that all present are far too preoccupied to notice. The light grows, it seems to focus around Marks hands. "Let your hands meet mine." Jo puts her hands on top of his. Suddenly she is transported. Her soul is touched by another, by another so much stronger that hers is willed to the surface. She feels light, that she can breathe the air again, that she can feel her chest expanding and her blood racing again. Blood pumping again. A flush to her cheeks, she gasps and staggers back. No longer is she lost in the fog surrounding her mind, now the case stands more the opposite. Now her mind surrounds the fog, has access to and may manipulate, has potential. Now she feels comfort in the place of fear, and to Marks she is part Thrall part not.

"You poor creature. I took your eyes." Marks growls in response, a gentle growl but animal in origin all the same. "You took your own as well it seems."

"I still see after a fashion. Although things have changed now that I'm me again."

"I also see after a fashion it seems. The outlines…"

"… the spaces left by things."

That the tail is gone is of no great loss, that the body lands light like falling on moss, that it's caught as it tumbles is better than not, and to the barricades leave at a canter not a trot.

Chapter Five

"Who're you talking to?" Ste turned quickly, nervously, *"Who's she talking to Sir?"*

"Tell us, who you're talking to miss?"

"They don't see me."

"Why?"

"Wha'd'ya mean why? Is there someone else in this room?"

"What... yes, can't you see him?"

"They don't expect to see me, and therefore they don't see me."

"No we can't bloody see him. Miss... is... is your life in danger?" Jo shakes her head.

"Shall I get the launcher?"

"No, I think... shit, I dunno. You'd blow us all to shit Ste!"

"It... it's alright, I know him."

"Private, where is this place?"

"Institute for the criminally insane sir."

"Right."

"No...no you don't understand... just put down your weapons, he says he's going to do something."

All at once a brilliant light filled the room, brighter than either of Morris' small patrol had seen before in their lives, not

311

that they could see. The glow was so intense, so shatteringly hot that for a moment, just for a moment their conscious minds ceased to exist. And in that split second they were reborn as if new, all previous perception gone.

"Who the hell are you…What the…" Pull back as James reaches for his gun. Focus. Freeze the instance, the second of occurrence. This is the focal point, as they say once bitten twice shy, but can man forgive the original sin.

"Don't Shoot." Jo's voice was urgent, desperate as of that of a lover.

"They won't shoot." Murmured Marks.

"Why does my head…Corp?... Aagh!"

"Stop that, what are you doing?"

"Forming acceptance. Don't worry, it'll be over… momentarily."

Corporal James vision shifted slightly, briefly but enough for it to catch and run.

"I…I thought that you were dead sir… we all thought that you were dead. There was a…"

"…Memorial, was it nice?"

"Sorry, bit shit really, went out for a piss an' a fag half way through."

"Hm, shame."

Pan out further, see the streets surrounding the hospital. There is nothing. That is to say that there is a lot of *stuff* as such, it's just that all of it is shit! This is of course a technical term coined by Corporal James on their ingress to the buildings. In matter of fact what it *does* consist of is less inclined toward the human waste that James would have us perceive but more instead towards *remnants!* Relics of a long forgotten past, perhaps not quite yet forgotten but then *something* is definitely gaining a foothold. This is obvious towards even the least militarily inclined. Pan out further, and further still, feel the air whip beneath your feet. Wait, don't retreat, here see, look deep and peer through crystal eyes *Ulfhednar-Vargr* and all his spies. Looking searching, through alleys and tracks, but some still steer clear, hide in their cracks and move *past* the Bastion. The last of it's kind, of crude make and build but steadfast design. Made with blood sweat and tears through more than their fears, through hope of a kind, dead guidance realised.

A clatter in the dark... a tumble and it's stark to all that may have once occupied this bumbling metropolis this temple that people once again eat at their empty table.

A father it seems, two sons behind trail, all armed set to flee but too terrified too fail. Set forward and through. And when one comes to greet, call him by name, calls him so sweet recompense for their trouble *Matthew.* That same office worker who troubled by death, through stress of his own life took flight, ignored their plight claimed leadership. And without chip to bear they signed to it. In blood to all intents though not known to any not known to one.

Chapter Six

Matthew muttered behind closed doors, Matthew stuttered through half unknown prayers, prayers that weren't directed to any*thing* conventional. This behaviour was half intentional half guided by another, feelings integrated, thoughts osmosifying through his skin, permeating the man within. That Matthew was corrupt, was foul and usurped in soul, this remains evident. That his eyes darken within, face pallid, skin taught against his bone might simply bemoan the effort of his survival. That in reprisal, in protest to the scorn of *his* city, that he might show pity was *seen* was heard and believed that he did *not!* And quick as a shot they moved in, they took his soul his mind his all.

"Dad says he found some more containers."

"About time." Replied Matthew, "Put them on the roof with the others, the more rainwater we can collect the better."

"But Dad says that it won't keep that long, it'll go bad."

"We can *boil* it can't we, stupid boy. *Do what I say*."

The pre-teen young man scurried off, nervous at his adoptive fathers annoyance rather than the tone of their supposed leaders voice. Although that tone *was* worrying in its own right. There was a quality behind it that wasn't entirely all there. That none of the three could quite place, and yet it definitely existed. It made them uncomfortable. Craig was pretty sure that this was why their Dad had handed over the gun. Matthew had taken it calmly, gently, but now he always carried it on him at all times. He might even *sleep* with it. Which was a bit shit really considering Dad found that gun. It was his. Bastard! There was an unsteady nervousness in Craig's mind, he knew that this was as safe as they could get without any help but he wasn't sure that their *'leader'* could provide it.

"He says we can boil it Dad."

"*Right!* Well I'm still not convinced, there's a lot of stuff from the sky falling into it, God knows what's in those clouds… See here…" Malcolm pointed, Craig looked. There were little bits of black gristly stuff floating on the top, occasionally they twitched or seemingly took a quick breath.

"They look alive, what is it?"

"No idea… *Peter*," he called, "chuck all of those down the drain, there's some ant powder in the cupboard, chuck that down as well, that'll kill the buggers." He grinned to his youngest, "We'll find cleaner water than this, there's a bit left in the bottle if you're thirsty."

Craig took a swig of cool refreshing water. Even though he'd filled it himself it still tasted a bit funny.

Marks looked up from his sleep. Not that it was sleep. Not that he was tired. *Shit* this was odd. He'd had his eyes closed at least and had also been bored for the past four hours. That was *kinda* like sleep! Jo was snuggled tightly into his side, her forehead resting lightly on his shoulder. She was breathing heavily, sleeping. Carefully the demon disentangled itself from the sleeping woman, beautiful though she was and made his way over to the high grated window. This seemed familiar to him, to a part of him that Marks had begun to recognise as the separation, the *other*, the wolf. He remembered rusted iron bars and doctors, fire burning in his mind and an overwhelming desire to sate his long subdued anger. There was something falling outside the window, thick like tar. No, not falling, drifting in the breeze. One hits the high pane, it appears to wriggle against the glass before being caught up once more and carried off.

"What the hell was that." Breathed the beast, Amaguq.

"What the hell was what?"

"Nothing, go back to sleep."

"I wasn't asleep anyway, can't seem to these days." There was a slight pause.

"When did all of this start James?"

"Reckon it must've been round about when you died Sir."

"How long ago was that?"

"'Bout six months I reckon." Marks suddenly turned round.

"*Six months,* I was only down there for a few hours at most."

"Hard to say Sir, how long'd it take to grow a face like that." There was a chuckle over by the door.

317

"Jesus Christ… Ste, is that you? I nearly shat myself, I thought you were the fucking bogey man."

"Sorry Sir, just thinking about mutton chops over there."

"What do you mean mutton…" Marks hand automatically went to his face and to the thick covering of hair that now adorned it. It was sleek, silver, and made the prominence of his teeth even more terrifying.

"What's the black shit outside then Herman?"

"Herman?"

"Come on Ste, keep up… *Munster!*"

"It's nothing," Marks paused, considering what information to give and what to withhold. "The water's tarnished. What you have in your flasks, that's all we've got. Drink that stuff out there and you'll rot from the inside out."

"*What!*" James looked dismayed, "Why's that happening then? It doesn't make sense."

Marks thought. After a moment he spoke very quietly, "They're trying to flush us out, make us search for drinkable water, they're trying to force us into the open. Well…" He turned and looked pointedly at Jo.

"What… you mean, you think they want… why?"

"She is the Sun, the life giver and the life taker. She forms part of the chains that bind the First in the sky."

Corporal James answered very slowly. "Right. So… what do we do?"

"Until I find the one at the centre of all this… we run, we hide, we protect her at all costs, do you hear me."

"Yessir."

"Good."

"Sir?"

"Yes?"

"The Sarge.'"

Marks walked quietly over to the prone Sergeant and knelt down beside him. He was sweaty and pallid and there was the smell of illness surrounding him.

"The breaks infected, the leg'll have to go or he's going to die."

"How're *we* going to do *that*." Said the Corporal.

"We're in a hospital aren't we… look, you're the ideas man!"

Rain fell on a city. Polluted. A unity of disgrace that seeks to wash away the very fabric of existence. Water. That water can seem or can be malicious in any refrain seeks disdain, but that water was this and *that* and the splish and slash of raindrops gradually turned into the heavy *splat* of dark black on black. A city turned, felled and spurned, the army fled, not fled but rent in two by buildings through which entered the unknown carnage. Focus down, surround your perception by what is contained within, the sin of one man Matthew at the moment of inception. That he is burned within and empty, a receptacle of welcome for the new occupant. That he is vacant yet strong, drawn out, mind long and steady with the thoughts that he knows. That upon those that he owns, those contained within the great spire that is The Bastion he bestows his gift. A gentle taint, a rift within their minds, turning them, changing them, setting them aside so that once again those banished before might place flesh and blood upon the floor. Might occupy those bodies there, might capture them within their snare. As it stands without mortal case, these base and evil things can't live. Can't stay long within this darkened realm, must return to their shadowed knell and recharge, recuperate, regenerate.

Only with *Vargr* as a beacon, with him radiating life, can the darkened force remain and cause us all more strife. But to break away, to move so far, to find an open vessel, so full of life and fear and hate remains still irresistible. Then once freedom's tasted, revelled, enjoyed, prepare the way, invite the boys.

"What do you mean he's coming round, he's been out of it for like, a day and a sodding half."

"It must be the pain Corporal, see his face."

"Well shoot him up with something then."

"The fat bastard already had it all, I've got none left."

"Grit your teeth gentlemen, I'm about to cut an artery… I *think*." Interjected Marks.

"Hang on, let me tighten that clamp." There was a click, "There, done."

"What next?" asked James.

"Bone."

The Corporal blanched but held his nerve, this was worse than anything he'd seen or done before in his life *ever*! Carefully he applied suction to the weeping muscle. He was glad he had the easy job. At least it was below the knee, he thought.

"… think it looks pretty sharp." Ste was saying. "If you can hold the leg Detective Inspector. Corp, can you grab the shoulders in case he jerks about."

James readied himself and closed his eyes tightly. Almost immediately he could feel the weight of Morris' torso going backwards and forwards ever so slightly. The sound of bone splintering sounded quite wet he thought, unexpected, not like wood being cut at all. When he opened his eyes again the offending leg had been gently dropped down beside the table, tugging slightly at the drip feed as it went. Ste was focussing very carefully on stitching and as James focussed on *not* throwing up Marks headed out to look for a pharmaceuticals room. *This* would definitely be one to tell the kids.

A group of men and one woman move out into the darkened sky. The dry humour of the moment as Sun steps out into a moonless night. Along with them there is a slumped figure in a wheelchair, he has a blanket across his knees and a gun concealed beside his stump. He pulls in and out of consciousness, vaguely aware that there is an entity with them that he both knows of old and has never met before. He feels weak, drained but at the same time the nausea has gone and he's starting to regain an appetite.

"What happened to the Moon?" Asked Jo suddenly. They were currently half hidden moving through the wrecks of burnt out cars and concrete blocks that surrounded the hospital.

"Cochrum."

"Excuse me?"

"No… sorry. A man that I knew, he was lured by the thing at the centre of all this and destroyed. His vanity was his death. And my stubbornness."

"What do you mean?"

Marks continued, "I'd forgotten who I was, why I was put on this planet. I followed the correct course but my mind couldn't accept the correct reasons and so I came up with my own. And Cochrum… He was stupid. Vain. Foolhardy. Thought he could do it all himself."

"Then how did…"

"I pushed him to it. We all did. We were forcing him out but instead we pushed him too far."

Ste rushed over from where he'd been talking with James. "Corp says there might be a stronghold. Says he heard of some civvies who started a wall. Might be our best bet."

"Sounds good to me, how far, which way."

"Well you see, that's the thing… we *think* it's *that* way."

"Okay."

"But it might also be *that* way."

Marks rolled his eyes. Just like being on the force again. "Which section of the city is it in Ste?"

"'ang on. *James*, where the crap was it."

"Near the civic quarter." James called back.

"Well we're in the civic quarter now," Marks muttered. "So lets work out our pattern."

"Not a good idea to split up."

"No."

"But if we do I bags the rocket launcher!"

Marks thought pattern was momentarily derailed. Ste cracked a grin. "Anti-clockwise spiral, spreading outwards. It'll take time but we're guaranteed to hit it eventually."

"Sounds like a plan to me Steve." Ste scowled.

"Don't call me Steve." He retorted and scampered off back to the Corporal.

Night is darker than day. *This* night is darker than day. That they swim in the murk, roll in the hay. They hover and drift, flit and sift through sleeping minds. Called there by *Matthew* under rule of the First. In deference to Charlie but to sate its great thirst took mortal flesh against his issue. But he wills his thoughts to control their tissue. That they might become his ears his eyes, his woodland spies is to be expected. And so into receptacles dive and consume, into the father, two sons all entombed in their skin.

Now also with demons within.

Chapter Seven

Charlie sat in thought. Or rather he sat while thought happened around him. The creature surrounding his mind was strong, this was certain to him. It had eradicated every semblance of his being. Charlie no longer sat in thought. Now *Ulfhednar-Vargr* sat in his place, in this space and considered his next move. The Sun had protection, this was seen through eyes not his own but between worlds like his all the same. And like pets they were tame to him. They were all tame to him, chained to him in some respect through power assumed. Charlie's mind was attuned to each and every one.

Survival of the fittest the fastest and strongest, survival of the First, whose thirst upon the Earth although not quite enough to drain it dry would certainly surpass eye for an eye and so *preparation*. Dissemination of information through the massed hoard, that of all the tawdry and dry comments *the Sun must go out* was the constant lament.

But through origin of this world, though still of *otherworld* too. They sit and stare and stand so grand but cannot bare to do naught but *search*. Whether by leg or eye, from house to church they seek to spy.

And as they twirl and sing through the air, through the sky, through the hair of those that let them go by, only by olfactory sense can they see the tense and desperate form of Jo, on her protected yet slow progress across the civic-quarter. And with their vision full yet minds in amazement those protectors that stand still and defend send those viewers to their slaughter. By gun and by knife, taking scratches and all but trifling with death they see their enemy, they see him flee to report. And on Amaguq's orders the creatures' lives they abort.

"Through the *eye* dammit Ste!" James levelled his own handgun and pulled the trigger twice. "You gotta *think*." He said sharply, "That thing nearly had you!"

"Where in all thats sweet *was* it's eye!" retorted Ste in consternation as they walked back to the others. "Seriously Corp, you saw it, that thing had way more nobbles than the one you 'ad."

"Stop making excuses."

"Look, I'm a goddamn medic, I've only 'ad basic."

"I'm a policeman in the riot corp, so what. *Look at them.* What training prepares you for *that*." James pointed, ten meters away something black like tar was bubbling where the cadaver had so recently lain.

"Is there an issue gentlemen?" Interjected Marks.

"No Sir, just Nancy here can't point a gun."

"Piss off."

"Alright you three, Christ it's like working in the clinic again." Jo sat down sharply on a burnt out tyre, she leant back and arched her spine against her ache.

"You okay?" Asked Marks quietly.

"Just tired. Are we getting close? How many rounds left boys?"

"Six mags between us, thirty pops per mag. Not bad. Still got the launcher. Bodygear took a bit of a bashing on that one though, you didn't tell me the pincers came out of *there!* A guys just not ready for *that!*." He tugged at the crotch of his Kevlar in uncomfortable recollection.

"Stop making excuses." Muttered Ste under his breath, a small smile on his face. James turned and playfully bashed him on the shoulder. "Sod off." He joked.

The high spirits continued for some time. In fact they didn't stop for around a mile and half. The first sign that things weren't as they seemed or indeed could be was a change in the texture of the air. At first only Marks was aware, but soon all those in the little posse could sense that there was something *otherly* ahead.

"My skin feels disgusting." Jo rubbed her arms, she was still in the hospital gown that they'd found her in but now at least maintained some dignity with a spare pair of coverall waterproof trousers. That the men had looked, although tried not to had been obvious. But Marks maintained a quiet sincerity and dignity about his attentions. He made her feel safe. And the disquiet in her own mind about her shifts in perception were reflected in the unsureness of his own tone. Sometimes, one of those times when he said something that was unfamiliar to the human, he seemed to

327

utter hidden questions in his pitch. As if he knew the fact but couldn't pin ever having known the knowledge. It was endearing. He was a puppy. She had heard Ste and James commenting occasionally on his appearance. He was different in her eyes. In her eyes he smelled warm, of musty strength. And the space he seemed to leave... the way she saw him, an outline, glowing tracery of detail making up his features. Tiny effervescent wisps of light, forever moving upwards in a gentle yellow. This was the space left by Marks. She walked over to him and put her arm through his. He looked down, she smiled lightly.

"So you're going to impose your disgustingness on me?" He smiled too and patted her hand.

"We can be disgusting together." Marks chuckled at her comment.

"For Gods sake, its like the blind leading the blind 'round here." James purposefully moved past at a faster than necessary pace.

"Do you think he was talking about us?" Jo giggled girlishly and began to run after him. Grinning as he glanced behind, James quickened his pace.

"No, we've got to stay in a..." Marks broke into a sprint, unnaturally powerful and Ste staggered behind still pushing the now jostling frame of Morris. He's got a little more colour in his cheeks now.

A group of silhouettes stop on the horizon. One draws a pistol automatically and raises it. Another puts his hand on the firsts shoulder. The first lowers his gun.

Pan up and around, across the ceiling of the very sky itself, see with the eyes of the tamed wolf. Black as tar and dark as night, through the skies drift with delight. Alight. And fight in tiny droplets of black to a place, to a form, to counter-attack. With feet made no waste and with haste to the chase they did move, from all round about coalescing congealing with something to prove. And great welts in the land came to ground, and burrowed down deep to the *otherworlds* sand and let them come through the ghosts and the ghouls. And like fools they came, drawn by the life, drawn by the light but condemned to fight for the First, by *Ulfhednar-Vargr* and his assassin of course, that one they named *Matthew* moves his power to course through to these pools. And out come the fools, coated in mess, and imprisoned to one they cannot help but impress leadership upon, the one. *Ulfhednar-Vargr.*

"What are they doing just lying there like that?"

"Drying out." Replied Marks, "They're forming some sort of shell as they come up…"

"That's why you gotta hit 'em in the eyes, that black shit."

"But it was coming down from the sky."

"*Vargr* is growing stronger." Said Marks quietly.

"Is that something we should worry about?" asked Jo, equally subdued.

"He's the one that made you. You tell me?" Marks moved off abruptly to see more closely the pool. "Sorry, that was uncalled for. It's nothing we should worry about for now." Jo's face had fallen, he smiled warmly at her and gave her a brief wink. "James, any of you boys smokers?"

"He's got a rocket launcher!" put in Ste quickly.

"What you wanna smoke now for?" Asked James reaching for his packet.

"No, not the cigarette, never touch them, the lighter, matches, whatever!" James fumbled about his Jacket and trousers, eventually finding his lighter. It was a cheap silver metal one. Looked nice. Plain. Simple. Marks flicked the top open with a ping and spun the wheel. The flint cracked. The spark caught the fumes. The wick burnt.

"Hey… what you doing? I need that!"

The burning lighter trailed through the air, seeming to slow in the thick atmosphere. Then suddenly *Whumph!* A few feet above the tar pool the fumes caught.

Struggling with the tar coating still sticky on their bodies those of the *otherworld* drying in the sun were immediately set alight, burning with a beautiful blue green flame and sounding the air with terrifying shrieks of agony. Those closer to the epicentre were fragmented, dissolute in the mass of burning gas and ick.

The screaming was intense even within The Bastion. A testament of intent upon the dying signalling the alive. To drive force between their gums, to have them ready to level their guns. There was *danger* on the way. That they would not this time roll in the hay didn't *matter*, but the stutter of energy that persisted with that great tower of strength, that dark force within The Bastion entrenched in bodies man and boy, to look and toy with their lives was *vital* to survival. In *their* arrival saw the herald for more, that perhaps *Ulfhednar-Vargr* could widen the door just a little bit more. Then by taking these forms, these frames left behind, these open eyes staring, disembodied, untied could remain. And retain their place by mans side. That they could then laugh and deride.

But anticipate this, that *Matthew* so far from his usual stride, might sense his own kind before they arrived. With foresight he saw that they'd open a door, head in and hide. For a time. That was sure. That in *Charlie's* own intellect *Matthew* did see what was obvious, plain and free from challenge. Take The Bastion. Hold The Bastion. The Sun *will* arrive. That she is accompanied by his own *kind* changes matters somewhat. That he is a new breed, unknown and fresh makes it hard, adds to the test. But there are four and four and one unconscious beside, so who wins the battle, who stems the tide.

"They're creepin' all 'round the place." Whispered James, "How'd we know they're not inside as well?"

"They don't look to have penetrated the walls... Can you see any signs of a break?"

"There's the entranceway, but I would've thought that'd be pretty well fortified... If there's anyone left!"

"All right Corporal," Marks voice was an intent hiss, "Lets not get moribund quite yet shall we?"

"Right sir." Replied James stoically.

The little party had by now moved around the pool, taking their time and avoiding as many of the dying creatures as they could. As it was James had expended half a cartridge and Ste had lost his satchel of medical supplies. This hindered things somewhat but luckily he still held onto the antibiotics for Morris. The Sergeant was more awake now than unconscious but less than lucid at the best of times. When he did appear to make coherent sense there was an air of the feverish to what he described. Colours, sounds, the taste of words.

"He's describing the *Annwn*." Stated Marks.

"What's that?" Ste had asked.

"Where I come from." Marks had replied.

On a rooftop a man looks out. He has a rifle. A big one. Something is climbing towards him up the side of the great Bastion. Malcolm , father of two, pauses, his eyes skip and an inhuman hiss emanates from the base of his neck. There are small tears, like gills but lower, they seem to crawl with black tendrils just beneath the surface. The creature on the wall exudes an appearance of surprise as the bullet thuds through its head. This ruse must be complete. There must be no sign of infestation within. Within the *Sun* and everyone besides could be penned, could be trapped to their slaughter. Brought to order by the *true king* of the *Annwn. Ulfhednar-Vargr.* Their cage, The Bastion, might prove a welcome reprieve from the struggles outside. The very thought that Marks power might turn the tide of those within and purify their every sin was not contemplated.

"We could use the rocket…"

"Look, I've only got one head for it so just stop… *think!*" James shoved Ste out of the way and crept slowly over to where Marks was crouching. They were tucked neatly down a back-ally about half a mile from the entranceway. The burning pool of tar sat on a hill half a mile in the other direction.

"Well we don't have enough ammo for that and hold out, unless there's anything in there. We *could* in theory use the launcher, but that might damage the wall, I mean look at it. It just turned over lorries and cars."

"What's the building behind it? And the tall thing?"

"That's a crane miss, they were renovatin' the old Opera House. Bloody sturdy building. Look, it even took a howitzer blast

333

on the 'O,' half of it's missing. Must've used the cranes to build the wall."

"Yeah, lorries don't normally stack so neatly three stories high!"

"What about the rooftops?" Said Marks suddenly. "We could get over the wall using the rooftops." The looks of dismay about him led him to further explanation. "Look at these. These are industrial wooden beams, used for roofing. They're a bit heavy but they'd easily cross the gaps between these houses. We could just walk across."

"You mean crawl!" Said Ste sardonically.

"Yeah, you're used to being on your hands and knee's aren'tch'a medic?"

"Piss off."

"What about the Sergeant? We can't just leave him."

"Certainly not, I'll carry him." Said Marks simply.

Chapter Eight

Figures on the rooftops, black outlines against the sky. The city seems to glow the deep red of fire beneath them. Above them the sky is darkened by cloud. The time of day is irrelevant. The last of the group summits the building, coming out onto the roof through what must be assumed is a fire exit or maintenance door. The figure bares a heavy load on their shoulder, occasionally it stirs.

"Come on then James, get the bloody plank over."

"Sorry sir, it's a bit of a tight one, there's only gonna be a couple of inches on either end. Here Ste, foot this will yuh." Ste planted his foot firmly on the plank. "Right, well I guess I'll be…"

"No," interjected Marks, "Let me." There was a pause. He had that look about him, that look of unsureness.

"No fear mate, all yours." Began James, but Marks had already mounted the parapet, had already seemingly placed foot upon plank, had his lank frame halfway between and then done, his foot ready to brace, the trial begun.

"It's safe, it's well held, just keep your balance. James, you next, then I'll come back over there and get the Sergeant okay?"

"How the hell did he do that so fast," muttered James to Ste, his first foot on the plank.

"Sheer willpower Corporal," called Marks to James surprise, "Now come on."

335

"And how did he hear me." James looked down. In the darkness below he was sure he caught a glimpse of something looking up, but he couldn't be sure. Okay, relax, endure the vertigo, the noiseless nausea, foot before foot, hand before hand. The plank shakes, shifts, moves, drifts but he doesn't fall. Doesn't want to, doesn't dare. Finishes with magnificent flare, slips on the wood, dangles through the air but up and *over*, safety now, sigh of relief, wipe the brow then Marks is gone, over and above. And sends Jo forwards light as a dove she moves, she crosses, she proves her own steadfastness, doesn't care, doesn't rush.

Marks holds for Ste, Ste crosses fast, Marks shoulders Morris, who grunts at the task in hand and he stirs, once again against his murmurs. And then all are across, one building gone and lost. But to the fore scream the streets, twenty-seven in neat, neat rows. And so on their torment goes, moving forward, very slow, going carefully, row by row. And down below as James had feared they *were* watched. They were steered.

Jo wobbles, falls, is caught by unknown hands. She feels something, something that she's felt before, something akin to love but she knows that it isn't. It tries to push its way out from the captivity within her mind. She holds on to the arms supporting her, slumps to the floor, still conscious. She hears voices, she focuses. She is in control. The Annwn does not cover her anymore! With a pendulum of effort, forcing and giving, forcing and giving she pushes the wool aside, forces it back within its prison. She looks up into concerned eyes. At least, the space left by them. There are tiny motes of light, the warmth moving forever upward. Marks. Comfort.

"*He's close.*" *She says.*

"*How?*"

"*I don't know but he's growing stronger inside my mind, I know that he's close.*"

"*Do you know which way?*"

"*No.*"

She's gathered up in arms. There is movement around her while bodies are switched. Corporal James is carrying her now, he smells of cigarettes but that's okay.

"Shit Corp, look at 'em. They *really* wanna get to us!"

"Shut up Ste and keep popping the top ones off. *MARKS* you *bastard... MOVE!*"

Marks tore across their faithful bridge just as another black armoured demon clawed its way to the top of the parapet. James fired, his cartridge clicking empty. They're so close now, just one more bridge and they'd be on the face of the wall, and then *up* and to safety! Ste's handgun clicked out and as the serrated creature levelled its head to charge at James a single shot rang out. Fragments of eye and ichor oozed from the beast and it staggered to the side, all depth perception lost. More claws were tearing into the sides of the building now. Corporal James made a dash for the bridge, but was *just* too slow. The injured demon staggered over the edge, taking the beam with it.

"Goddammit!" he screamed, more shots rang out. The posse turned to face the direction of their saviour as bullets flew through the air, pinging across shell and shattering brain.

"Who is it?" Yelled Ste.

"Never mind, we'll see soon enough," said Marks levelly, "James, stand back."

His muscles bunched, crouched he sniffed the air, tongue to his lip to taste the direction. Instinct takes over. He jumps. A single static leap. He lands exactly where James had previously been standing, tiles crack beneath his feet. He grins wolfishly and in a single movement sweeps up the startled Corporal and leaps for the other side.

The jump is misjudged. He feels the difference in weight midair and knows that he has to do something. He bunches his weight, centred at his core. Grabs James stoutly about the leg and shoulder, spins and *throws!*

James hits the flat concrete of the other side and rolls. Marks direction isn't so true. He smacks into the wall opposite, demons gnashing underneath him he scrabbles for purchase. There is none. He feels his weight shift, he's beginning to fall. Quickly instinct takes over once more, his punches his bodyweight forward,

338

ramming his fingertips hard into the masonry. He feels the shock all the way up his arm to his shoulder, but he holds on.

The razors protruding from his finger bones scrape and claw their way to the top, like so many of the beasts below. That this demons intent is pure opens many, many new doors.

And then quicker still, with creature to back to fore and sides, scratching for handholds, roaring their derides. And for a moment Marks is lost. Cannot see the end. Cannot redeem the cost. But with darkness around and the fires for sound and the roars to the ground and the claws and their *sound Marks accepted his anger once again.*

He grabs the regained corporal. "You ready to go again." He growls. James grins evilly.

"Have I got a choice?" He glances to the wall, to the screams below. Marks tenses, grabs by leg and shoulder, and before he releases gives one final bellow.

James flies through the air, and as he hits the side of a double-decker bus, despite the shock he finds a grip and climbs across. There's a creature on the roof with them now, no two. Quickly Marks grabs Jo and Morris and hurls them with all of his strength, they tumble through the air, Morris crashing through a window and Jo following behind. Ste is also sailing through the air now, and Marks is on the floor, claws crashing around him. He punches upwards, fingers pointed, through the carapace. Find the stinking heart, rip it out and drink it's blood! As he does so more shots ring out. The gunmen at the top of The Bastion continue in their barrage, and as the team move through the machinery of the great wall, dragging, being dragging, climbing... and as Marks leaps, his silver beard dripping with congealing black mess he knows that the horrors outside will be equally matched on the inside. No matter how many gunmen fire from the top.

Chapter Nine

A group of people creeps through a mass of machinery on machinery. This wall, this testament to human ingenuity and persistence is a place of peace compared to the snarling outside. Claws scratch and scrape at windows and chassis, but they lack the suppleness of skin that would allow them to easily pass through.

Built by the cranes surrounding and restoring the city's great Opera House each and every open street or path is walled by fifty-foot high blockades of derelict burn outs. Lorries, busses, cars, masonry. The remainder consist of buildings, entrances blocked by whatever means necessary. The Opera House itself, the centre for the activity is a Victorianesqu masterpiece. A catacomb of rooms and corridors ornately carved and painted in the most glorious spectrum of reds, greens and golds. The outside is sandstone and so easily eroded. It has taken some damage in the fight for the city. Pitched battles have raged here, but that was some time ago. Or at least may have been. A mist covers everything, days seem like months, months feel like years. The miasma of sleep adds confusion to the situation, distorts time frame and place.

The rain is thick, congeals into black messy pools that steam. They seem to appear from all around, come up from the ground. But from the sky they came, from the mist for the fame.

From the moisture in the air, to live their lives, to get their fair share. And so with the *otherworlds* mist they come, dancing on webs like something unspun and they form. They gain *their* norm, a pool to the sands like *Ellysia*, to *Annwn*, to invite others through to begin their lives. And in symbiosis they thrive, they cling to the creatures hides as they emerge. They purge the mind of the one they assume, they mate with the mind, digest and consume and become. So brittle, sharp tongued. And the pools on the road, on the path, with their load to bare bring fruit in mist, in form of fog, to the glory of one, to distaste of the dog.

"Wait..." James holts their progress through the crush of dereliction, "I think there's a passage up ahead."

"What do you mean... a passage?" Growled Marks from behind, still feeling his aggression, although allowing it to subside once more.

"Well, there's a..." The Corporal kicked a metal plate sharply, "...bloody passage." James continued. To the right something creaked in a metallic way and the plate spun quickly back into an opening. A void, dark as it was. Marks manipulated himself to the front of the group, leaving Morris behind slightly, and wriggled up to face James. He was a sight, gore congealing on his chin and fast healing rake marks across his face. His fingers were dirty, and the once polished razor claws that tipped his fingers were now distinctly more ragged and evil looking.

"I think I should possibly go first... don't you corporal?" James backed off slightly, unnerved by the silence in Marks voice, it certainly hadn't been present when they'd first met.

"Is there something wrong sir? Why are you speaking so quietly?" There was a short pause, eye met eye. Marks turned and looked at Jo. There was a sweat of concentration on her brow and she was breathing much quicker than normal, although she had recovered much of her faculty during their progress through the wall.

"We can feel something inside." Marks gaze levelled with the policeman once more. "Therefore... I think I should...?"

"...possibly go first." James finally caught up with the dog. Marks began to wriggle past toward the passageway ahead. Before he ducked inside, he paused and took a breath.

"I only saw one shooter sir." Whispered James with a sickly smile.

In the darkness... in the darkness a stark dust settles on Matthew. His mind is bent, askew and his intent is to hide. To confide only in his brothers but to shield them from the smothering gaze of those touched. Marks, the trickster, Amaguq, who has fooled mens minds, allowed them to see his own kind must be tricked. Must be clouded, his vision licked by glamour. A shower of beauty instead of fear, a tear, an unknown tear rolls down his cheek. His mind has no reason why. That this shell, this carapace might rebel took the

343

demon by surprise, and for an instant looked out through human eyes. That shed tears. That despite cowardice hears the cries. But cannot help.

And so deep beneath the final testament of this fair city, beneath the Bastion, its silent treaty is spawned and the Demon Matthew allows Ulfhednar-Vargr to take his life, his soul pawned for the power it bestows. And so on it goes, with Vargr's will and Matthews place, with senses dulled begins the chase. That Matthew chanted, focussed mind, blocked out each and all of his kind from those now inside. And waited for the time to spring, to ride the unquelled tide of Ulfhednar-Vargr to glorious rise. To release the First, to let go the tide. But time must bide, the right place to strike, to rule the land, to take the fight only when commanded. As Firsts only channel demanded. That turning was better, possessing the best, to takes the dogs soul and give him no rest by torment. That he might lament the day that Vargr he chased, that his bones be broken and cast into space like the First. And that instead of sitting in stars his atoms disperse. This was the promise.

Amaguq, the dog Marks jumps into a rough corridor. It's panelled with whatever spare scraps were left lying around, wood, metal, car doors. The floor is made from wooden packing pallets. There appear to be some stairs leading up into the wall proper, to a gantry, a room, a rampart. There is a shadow approaching down the stairs, as it rounds the corner it is seen to be carrying a long rifle.

Marks tenses and pushes himself further into the shadows. His posture is low, strong, alert. He is hidden but despite that should not be seen. The *beast* in him fades into the shadows. There is something not right at all, like the taste of the air around the approaching shadow is trying to alter its very self. The figure resolves itself fully. It's a man, about the same height as Marks but with dark hair. Dark like Marks hair used to be. He levels his gun at the dog, his aim is true and without hesitation despite Marks hiding place. Marks focuses, draws on his understanding, extends his mind to the other, touches, extends, touches, probes. The space is null. There *was* something. Had *been* something but it's gone, clouded from him. Like and as if the person in front of him is shielding his true nature. Marks back foot shifts to spring, there are voices on the stairs behind the man, casually he pulls his shirt closed over what appear to be deep scars near the base of his neck, he turns his head slightly. Despite the shirt there is a hint of dark black snaking up his neck. It could be a tattoo.

"Peter... Craig stay back." A young man comes forward, a boy. Marks gently softens his stance, reduces the threat he poses. Of course this man has something to hide. Something to protect. That didn't account for *everything*, but it certainly made sense of the void that his understanding had found within the man. A man that had built walls of protection had found protection in his mind. And yet how could they see the dog, how could they see Marks? But there was no time for an answer. All of this happened in an instant, the boy Peter rounded the corner, his gun was already levelled. Marks braced for the impacts just as his body had softened in misplaced understanding. Suddenly there is a commotion to the hole in the wall. Jo bursts out, the spaces where her eyes had been raining tears of fear.

"*No, please no!* He's one of us," the words poured out of her like the last woman to the last man in their last supper moments. "...I *know* he doesn't look like us, I *know* okay..." and gradually the men lowered their weapons. Jo was weeping on the floor, tears of desperation turned to tears of relief. Marks took another quick glance to the men to see that the danger was past and moved quickly on all fours to where Jo was. He put his arms around her and held her as tight as he could. That she had saved his life was no mean feat. That perhaps next time he wouldn't be able to return from the *otherworld* did strike Marks and he spared a toothy snarl for the older of the men.

This room is dark, is stark and open and yet doesn't contain a great deal. No final meal, no enthusiast or free for all ticket sale. The Opera house remains quiet in resplendent magnificence, yet it's essence is changing, being deranged, deranging those about. And at the centre of this shout sits Vargr's power pool, Matthew, the tool. The implement of decay, distraction, misdirection. That he might fool those within, cradle them, infect with sin then be done, move on.

346

There was an uneasy silence around the campfire. Although without doubt Malcolm was a taciturn man, he did stare at the fire in a *very* odd manner. Ste was off in a room somewhere close by caring for Morris and Malcolm's two boys Craig and Peter were in the gantry on the wall. The wall, it truly was a magnificent thing.

"So you were here when they were building this thing right."

"No," replied Malcolm, "We came... after." James wasn't put off despite the other mans obvious disinterest.

"How did you get in then? What was here, there anything else useful?"

"You've seen what we've got." Malcolm got up abruptly and stalked off to the other side of the fire, he watched it even more intently.

"Don't upset the man." Jo whispered sleepily. She had her head resting on Marks lap and was covered with a thick blanket. It looked like some kind of wool. Marks stroked her cheek with his hand, he caught a glimpse of a claw and moved to pull away but Jo took it gently, very gently. "And anyway, can't it wait until morning?"

"Yes," Agreed Marks uneasily, "It's been quite a full day, perhaps we should all sleep."

"Yes, sleep." Malcolm moved as if to walk away.

"You won't want the campfire?" asked the dog slyly, "There's a chill in the air for the time of year."

"Fire. True. And sleep will be better." Replied the other man. James watched the back and forth, eyes ticking and tocking but poker faced all the same. Marks was unsure about something and that was definite. And if Quasimodo didn't like something then James had learnt very fast that things wouldn't be as they seemed. He put his head down and closed his eyes, unclipped his gun holster and quietly moved his handgun to his ration pack.

Ste sleeps deeply. Tendrils of blue-black vapour drift past his nose. The remnants of... Ste sleeps deeply.

There is a figure by the bed of Sergeant Morris. It's Matthew. He chants softly as he takes a blade and very carefully slices into the stump of Morris' leg. Blood oozes from the wound, fresh but thick, almost healthy. Gently Matthew reaches inside the black hooded greatcoat that he's wearing and pinches. Carefully he pulls out a very fine, very small needle. It looks organic. On the end there is a clump of white material, Matthew pushes this inside the open stump, forcing the ball of white matter firmly up against the break of the bone. Another ball of white matter he pulls again from the greatcoat, this time he winces. This ball is delicately placed just under the skin by the spine at the base of the skull. As Matthew withdraws his fingers from the wound tendrils of white, like little roots begin to spring from the disgusting lumps in Morris

348

flesh. Like taproots searching, they dig into the folds of raw meat and pull it shut, fusing with an odd web-like scar.

Suddenly the door bursts in, hearts are racing, James looks around pointing his tin gun pop toy, that would save from harm and seek to destroy. Matthews form shudders inhumanly, his shriek is high and slices through the air. Marks ears prick, despair, he knows he's right and off at a tear but...

Malcolm collided with him hard, slamming him to the ground. He heard the sound of a gun, a crash, tremendous, and falling masonry. A car crashes to the ground, it's already crumpled bonnet bending completely under the jolt. Something *jumps out onto the gantry. It doesn't look human and yet at the same time has a definite semblance of humanity. It shudders inhumanly and something on its back rustles, cracks and spreads.*

The black greatcoat ripped at the shoulder, revealing the wisp-like dragonfly wings of Matthew. Under the control of Charlie, Ulfhednar-Vargr, the one who would kill the sun and set the First free from the sky commands retreat. The deed is done, the task complete. Now just to wait and the time will fleet by. The sun will die at a comrades hand and the sands of time will retreat, unfreezing the First, bowing their feet.

There is an amazing droning. Wings beat against the ground, Hard. A knife is at Marks throat. He growls. He can feel the tip of the blade. He focuses, builds, touches his soul, both one and two and one together.

Light seared through the eyes of all. Malcolm screamed in agony. Falling down the stairs of the gantry Craig and Peter too were both brought to their knees. White cascades burnt all around them. The demons within them blanched at the power of the trickster, the dog Amaguq.

Gentle fumes trickled from Malcolm's eyes, disappearing quickly even though the breeze was gentle. Jo tore across the courtyard to the two children. Peter was already beginning to stir.

"It's just the steam from their tear ducks, they'll have sore eyes for a while I'd imagine." Panting to catch his breath Marks still managed to push out a chuckle. It was either that or admit to the distinct feeling that he was completely out of his depth. He rolled the other man off of him. Jo was kneeling over Craig now. He hadn't moved. She turned and looked at the dog, tears on her cheeks.

"The demon was too strong?" Whispered Marks.

"I don't know," replied Jo, "Was the demon too strong? More to the point..." She paused and took a breath, "...I can still feel him, even this far away, he keeps trying to panic me, make me reveal myself."

Marks said nothing. Jo took a step closer, she reached out with her hand but he didn't take it, much as he longed to. Eventually she spoke.

"Is the demon too strong for us Simon?"

Chapter Ten

The pressure of the massed machinery on top of James told him fairly fast that his prospects weren't good. He was wedged fairly tightly between the wheel arch of an estate and a large slab of masonry. More to the point his left arm was starting to go numb and he could feel a wetness dripping from his fingertip. There was a grunt from the metalwork to his right and James shakily raised his handgun.

"Stop, no it's me you stupid shit!" Morris dragged himself along the floor from beneath the car. "He's gone I think, or it, whatever it was… Through the roof. Ste's dead, I found his arm."

"You okay Sarge," whispered James, "How… we didn't think you was gonna make it sir."

"Well sod you very much too Corporal, now what the *hells* going on?"

James recounted their tale to date, as best as he could, but with each utterance he could feel his blood slipping from his veins, "… Sarge… I don't feel too good…" His face was pale now, pallid, his eyes sunken. That there was frenzied activity on the other side of the crush was unknown amongst the mass of mechanical noise. Screeching and screaming and weight re-shifted for hours. That Marks lifted more than any man could would be astonishing if it wasn't for the fire-like digging of those around him. For this group of counterparts, playing pieces had become a family... now contained a family albeit smaller than it had been. Each had lost something, this was also stirring and relevant, this bound them tighter and stronger. Craig had passed and there was little sign of Ste save for a mash of gore extending from the place he had occupied, the epicentre of the cave in. He was dead. Craig was dead. They all knew and shared. But that some might survive, some might not perish was hopeful, spoke full of the way they thought and felt, the way their minds worked, deals dealt. And through and past all of this, to the last, to change history, herstory, itstory we find two broken wrecks, one with surprising life and one with surprising little.

"Fetch me a *fucking needle!*" Jo screamed in Malcolm's direction. Still overcome by his own grief and his own actions of late Malcolm eventually snapped to. James lay bleeding on the ground by the remains of the campfire, his bicep torn laterally and deeply, there was bone visible. Marks stalked about Sergeant Morris, proprietal over his injured pack. Malcolm soon returned and Jo began to stitch the ragged edges of James arm back together.

"He was lucky, it looks like it's missed anything important. He's gonna need years of physio..." she trailed off. Marks looked over to where she was, he walked over and put his arms on her shoulders as she worked. "You're doing fine," his voice was gentle, low and comforting, "He's alive because of you…"

"No he's not!" Jo snapped suddenly. "He needs blood, lots of it and there's no telling when we'll be near a hospital." Her voice turned to an urgent hiss, *"He's going to die Simon!"*

The dog looked down at the man, his friend, his skin was so pale it was turning blue at the lips. "We need him." He pauses, considers a time, hesitates then finally, ultimately speaks. "My blood will be fine." he says and his sharp incisors slash out a section of his palm. He winces in pain.

"What are you…"

"Quiet!" Snaps Amaguq. The blood has turned almost black, congealed to a glistening tar. The dogs' soul is different to the man. He breathes heavily as he smothers the mass over the raw wound of James arm. It bubbles and spits, growing and pushing, oozing inwards. James writhes against it for a moment until he feels it hit his skull, it covers and calms, warms and bubbles. Colour begins to return to his cheeks, his lips return to a healthy pink. The dog Amaguq is pale, his eyes are sunken and his gums are white and drawn. "He will be fine now, no more death… not from my hands." He pauses, "Do you hear anything?" Asks the dog.

"No!" Whispers Jo, unable to look away, a tear on her cheek. "Are you okay?" The dog doesn't answer for a moment. He considers the question, his eyes flashing in the firelight. At last he speaks once more.

"Not at the moment no… I must rest."

"Why did you ask?"

"There's no noise, they've left. They want us to follow. I say we follow."

"A trap?"

"Screw their trap!"

Ulfhednar-Vargr in human form Charlie raises his head, sniffs the air and without a care in the world sits and bides his time. He feels the presence, the one, the trickster, controller of minds. Amaguq. Although he bares no trait his soul shakes at the chance that is taken, that he took. Mind against matter, the pen and the sword, Vargr sees none, his power void in these matters. He will send many against few in order that the insider, the confider of his secrets might have the chance to bare fruit, hatch and recruit by infestation. That the gestation of those inside might coincide with unfortunate circumstance to those waltzing this dance. Vargr may begin his rule with the mind at his side and the sun at his fore ready to do his foul consent, to lament their lives and thus bring rise to the First, pinned in the sky and held by the hundred Centaurus. Lupus must be freed. The one who bit the hand held to feed.

The free mind might suspect, might reject the trap laid, might be deranged internally by the infernal lee of minds very parasite, the erudite Ulfhednar-Vargr. Instead they choose life, choose to cut end and curtail their strife and set forward. That Marks mind, the dog Amaguq only knows that something is amiss is a mistake, and one that will lead to a sticky fate for all involved. That he does it through fear, as one man to another might shed a tear when in mortal combat so does he, and in his pain forever must live beneath that shadowy tree. But they rush on, and on, to battle, to rattle the cage of the Viking sage, the Viking page in time whose time is long done, must be unspun. And at the cajoling of Amaguq, the trickster, the dog Marks they creep their way to seek their vengeance in canine hope that they would provide distraction enough to Charlie before whatever it was took control of Morris.

The scent is in the air, the trap exposed, revealed, laid bare. Each outsmarts the other, perfect counterpart uncovered and so to head on head battle deranged. One body bag for certain will need to be arranged.

Morris hobbles over to the destruction, something has caught his eye, his makeshift crutch rattles on the mud-caked gravel. He bends and picks up something bulky, shoulders it.

"Put it down!" Yells James sitting up, "We've only got one round"

Chapter Eleven

Silence.

Or at least the semblance of silence. Something equal yet opposite. Patience. Lupus watches, patient. The First forever trapped in the sky, guarded by the hundred. The moon is dead, its decaying orbit drags it ever fractionally closer to the planet below, to its demise, this is inevitable. The ground will shatter and from it will erupt destruction. Time will stop. Time will stop and wait for Time to begin again. *Gwynn Ap Nudd* focuses and pulls. The sun must be reborn, the prophecy will be fulfilled, time will begin again and the First will be free. *Ap Nudd*, nee Frankson knew it would be his demise, that his death would mirror the death of the earth to which he was tied, that he stood in Gethsemane one more time. But in the suns rebirth there was *hope*. That this hope was torn between Thrall of Marks and Thrall of Charlie meant danger. That the sun be reborn with a black soul, that it would burn darkness instead of light and cast darkness upon the world below it. Or that the sun be reborn with light in its heart.

The ground trembles and Frankson stumbles, he turns about to look at the cages behind him. Each and every dog sits still. Doesn't flinch or twitch. What must be a face looks upwards, all follow. Suddenly there is a cataclysm of sound. The howl goes up, goes on, layer upon layer of noise, harmonic, disharmonious, a noxious brawl of sound that brings Azrael to his knees.

Marks stumbles on the side of the road, there is a whistling in his ear, pulling. He tries to carry on forwards but the sound is too much. He falls to his knees. Jo is at his side, he looks up into her eyes, trying not to show his fear. But there *is* great fear. Her eyes are clouding. The eyes that were, that have left empty spaces. Every step they take closer to the wolf they grow whiter and her comments become fewer and lighter.

"Don't you hear it?"

"Hear what?"

"That whistling, it's driving me insane!" Suddenly there is a pop beside them. Morris cries out in pain. Blood seeps from his stump, and the base of his neck is swollen and bulbous. He screams the high-pitched scream of a man in absolute agony. Peter hides behind Malcolm who raises his gun.

"Don't shoot!" Yells James, raising his own weapon. "He's our own!"

As James is speaking great rents began to appear in the taught flesh around Morris' neck, his screams grow more and more high pitched until finally the skin bursts.

His face sagged almost immediately, and his hands reached up behind his head. Jo vomited quietly behind Marks as that which was Sergeant Morris peeled the skin away from his new face. His eyes appeared to look at the flesh in his hands, it looked at James, and at Marks. Finally its eyes found Jo. Legs erupted from Morris' stomach, insectile like the face, heavily armoured. Guns fired, two, bullets erupting and flashing through the air. The creature sprang toward Jo and seized her, vomiting, making sure the mucus entered her mouth. Immediately she fell still. Marks tried in vain to crawl toward the beast, pellets thudding into the slowly cracking and chipping exoskeleton.

"*No,* you'll hit Jo!" The bullets continued. Marks eyes closed in pain. Every nerve in his body was now screaming in agony. The noise felt as though it were permeating his soul. A calling that was tearing his in two. There was a tremendous snapping sound and the large plate that was covering Morris new back span off toward Malcolm. He quickly jumped out of the way but even so, as it flew past it just touched the edge of his cheek. The flesh immediately shrank back as he cried out in pain. It tightened as though dying, necrofying before its time. The searing spread, slowly at first and then faster, pulling and paling, drying and stretching. Peter wailed in anguish but James grabbed him firmly by the arm as his father reached out his hand. The boy struggled against the corporals grip but the older man knew more sense. He tugged Peter into his chest and as Malcolm's eyes glazed and shrivelled he made a silent promise. The boy would not be fatherless.

The creature Morris beat the air with his wings, forcing the dying father onto his knees. Jo screams as she is hoisted by pricking claws. As the silence spreads once more through Marks mind he sees the dim shape of his one love flying toward the one he should kill.

In the darkness the demon Charlie smiles. Even when in his human self there are strong elements of the demon about him. A pointed ear or tooth, the curl of a lip and toughness of the skin. His grin stretches slyly halfway across his face, his sharp and jagged teeth a match for the evil barbs of his fingertips. Not just the very end but fully half the length of the finger was a serrated blade. As though demon should never touch softly, as though there were no tender moments or moments of joy. That there *should* not be. Slowly he draws his index finger across his eye. Blood immediately fills the space and he draws a breath quickly. As he removes his finger he feels the rush of healing adrenaline, his eye fuses over and whitens, hardens before paling and dispersing to its original visage. It feels *good*. He feels the opportunity. That the sun be born anew has always been inevitable. That the sun be born of demon, that it shine the light that the First craves will be appropriate supplication for the last aeon. Let them live beneath the demons eye. The dark star that will bring balance back to the land. The demon Charlie pulls a smirk and a guttural chuckle can be heard. The demon

Charlie willed the moon closer and called to the one held so long in his thrall. *The Sun.*

Chapter Twelve

Marks roared in rage, the primal demon inside him taking control just that little bit more. Marks allowing it. As he rent his wrath at the sky and the ground James stammered to the fleshy remains of Sergeant Morris.

"What the *hell* Simon?" there were tears in his eyes, he had lost the second of his original companions. "What the *HELL?*" He threw himself at the dog, both of them feeling the loss of all involved. Peter now stood by himself weeping. Shamelessly he buried his head in his hands and wept. For his father, for his brother, for his mother, for himself.

James similarly now was crying, but on Marks shoulder, and as the soldier wept and the child mourned, his form resettled. His rage had taken his heart, his soul was now in the battle one and all. That *Ulfhednar-Vargr* would even consider taking from right under his nose... More than that though, that he had suspected and yet hadn't said a word to anybody. Had thought to flush out the ambush and deal with it at the time it came. He hadn't banked on an incapacity on his part and he berated himself over and over inside, building the rage that he knew was not only possessed of the demon bound to his soul, but was also now within his human half. Tendons tightened and muscles bunched, his back cracked and his trapezius spread. Through all of this he remained silent, calm. White hair grew thick over his body and a bright white spark filled his eyes, as bright as the sun and yet the colour light *should* be, the light that angels bring. The dog Amaguq's hindquarters broadened and cracked, Marks winced slightly as he was forced down onto all fours. His fingers spread and bunched forming thick paws, at least a full foot long. His back stretched and as he twisted his neck to better settle it in place he felt the pull as his jaw stretched forward into a muzzle. His torso and waist thickened exponentially with muscle, layer upon layer, building, growing. Finally, as his ankles travelled further up his legs and his toes strengthened his trousers ripped and a magnificent white tail shot out behind him. He flicked an ear, testing his audio reflex. Good. His mind was sharp.

"Climb on my back." Growled the silver wolf, "The man and me are safe, he is inside, for now Amaguq controls this body." His head reached to the sky and growled into a howl that made the very buildings around them vibrate with energy. Somewhere in the distance a brick tumbles to the ground.

"He knows I'm coming. Hopefully this will give us time before he acts. He will want to dispose of any… *distractions* before the rebirth of the sun."

"I don't understand?" Said James slowly as Amaguq stood, "If Jo's the sun and she has to be reborn, that means a baby. And as she's a woman, well… wouldn't she have to be pregnant?" Amaguq roared one more time and violently leapt down the road.

Screeches ring out all around, the tactile shriek of insectile chittering. A rumour spins forth through the hoard. That the sun has been captured and that the trickster is free prey.

Claws pound the dirt. The tarmac roads are covered in dust now, debris from the carnage of brickwork. It flies up in great sheets behind the Grey one as he tears across the broken landscape. Pan up and out, take a steady look. There are trails following him, three of them, two on one side and one larger on the other. Gunfire rings out from Amaguq's passengers, heavily armed since the departure of their comrades. The larger of the dust clouds stumbles suddenly, sprawls to a halt. All that can be seen is a bubbling mass of tar steaming into the darkened sky. Rain begins to pour, faster and faster, clitter-clattering on rooftops and spattering down what remains of drains. Pan out further, see the panorama spread before you, the city in ruins, great gashes in the landscape where fire and howitzer have taken their toll. Through it all pounds the dog, the Trickster in control, toward *Ulfhednar-Vargr*, the rogue possessed within that which was Charlie. The call has been sounded, the ground set. From the Opera house a direct line is drawn to the city square, along this and toward the town hall Amaguq tears, to the centre of his feeling, to the place that his soul knows Jo Samuels has been taken.

Wings disturb the fragile air within the great, pillared building. Beating, lacing the ground with turbulence, screaming can be heard and the Sun is thrown to the floor. She falls heavily and lies weeping. The human semblance of the beast turns. As it approaches it roars its transformation into life, splitting skin and cracking gristle. The man becomes the beast, and as the shadows pass over its torn face it grunts toward the woman.

"How are you able to fear me?" his voice is less a growl and more a rumble. "You adore me!"

"A part of me does yes, I can feel it deep within my mind, clouding me and calling me to you."

"Then why do you fear me?" Charlie's growl was curious but insistent and with that instigation Jo reached out her mind. There was nothing. Nearly nothing. On the fringes of perception she felt the man she knew as Simon, she felt him reach back, felt that he was coming.

"My soul is elsewhere."

More wings beat the air. The scratching and chattering outside had been building for some time. Suddenly the vacant space that had been Matthew smashed through the window. He thudded hard into the wall opposite and from his mandibles shot a yellow-green ichor. His chest was split and oozed gently, as he fell to the floor he lifted a hand to the wound... *The door smashes open, flying to the direct centre to the room. Jo stands in stunned silence, Charlie reacts faster. His roar can be heard for seven miles around. The door flattens the insect Matthew, spreading his intestines across the floor and walls. Gunfire is heard, semi-automatic, single shot rounds. The screech and scream of demonic life as lead slams through hard chitin. Dust settles as the last rays of light stream through the opened entranceway and Amaguq paces forwards. To either side of him are Peter and James, firing off shells with no notion of the fight back out again. A sharp claw slashes across James' thigh and he responds by snapping the brittle appendage to stab the beast in its face. The battle is not pretty. Percussion firepower is their only real advantage, but even so they fight tooth and nail. Time slows, and as the moon crashes headlong into the Earths equatorial rim all movement freezes bar the Rogue Charlie and the Trickster Marks.*

Charlie's head slammed onto the hard tiled floor, blood spraying from his serrated maul. His claws scraped along the marble, carving great grooves as he stood. A stop-start miasma surrounded them as Jo was turning to flee. James and Peter were covered in ichor, slugs cascading in never ending showers from their guns. James hand reaches slowly, every so slowly toward his jackknife, and as the dust moves fractionally in the air the edge of a blue-black silvered blade can be seen in its slow but sharp jab outward.

Vargr grunts himself back to his feet and hurls himself at the Trickster. Caught on all fours Marks goes bowling off to the side, a great gash fast healing across his midriff. In seconds he's back on the dark wolf, biting, snapping, gouging, ripping. Flesh is pulled from bone time and time again as light and dark both focus their energies. Charlie pushes with his mind, forming an edge, sharp as any claw or tooth, his mind is focussed as he gives his attentions not to the physical battle but to his long-term survival. Marks the trickster slashes and tears, ribs being laid bare he smashes his claw-tips through the dark wolfs intercostas. *A movement from behind.* The dog is thrown to the ground by something from above, there is the heavy beat of wings in the air and the smell of thick fug and tar, like an impenetrable mist. He focuses on the human part, thus laying *himself* bare to *Charlie's* onslaught, although despite the dimming of the wolf in him and Marks physical form resettling once more Charlie had sustained so much damage in the previous bout that his energies were currently on healing himself. The trickster exploded with light, searing through the eyes of all around…

Time returned with a snap. Not that time can do this as such but this time in fact is displaced. The world, the planet itself ceased to spin in this moment, ceased to crack and explode with energy as the moon pummelled into it. But the time, the instant in which time should reset instead became transfixed. No longer did the contents of the land abide by its wishes, now they moved freely. Instead the earth and the moon hang caught in that cataclysmic instant.

Bullets rain out of James' revolver. His last loaded gun. Wings beat over his head and suddenly he's lifted bodily from the ground. Before he can tell what's going on Peter too has been lifted. A familiar sense comes over the corporal as he and the teenager are sent flying with bodily strength toward the second floor gallery, to comparative safety. As he's sent sailing the weight on James' shoulder lightens, heavy artillery losing its place.

Jo runs for the side of the room, shelter at least from the chaos around her, she looks up to see what was Morris sending James and the boy flying through the air. The creature snatches the rocket launcher before Charlie slams heavily into him from the side. The question hung, had Morris regained control? Did the man command the monster? Demons swarm over Marks, pulling him down, tearing at his too slow to heal flesh. They're killing him, inch by inch. Amaguq roars in pain and tries to force himself free but the weight is getting too great for him. Jo sees the launcher. Sees the smouldering remains of what was Morris. He lies right by the entranceway. Painfully he points at the doorway, point blank range, no care for the direction the flare will take. The hoard pressing to enter try to push back, but the weight behind is too great. They struggle in the doorway, wide as it is, but cumbersome as they are they can't move fast enough.

The explosion wracks the room to its foundation, and as the wall caves in on itself several demon-kin are trapped beneath the falling masonry. The back blast from the launcher punches a fist sized hole through Morris and slams him into the wall opposite. There's no hope for the once Sergeants life, but forgiveness has been earned eternally. Jo whimpers in grief as fire engulfs his body and drags its way up curtains and across the remains of furniture. Marks snaps to his side, crushing the heads of two demon in his massive jaws. Charlie's serrated maw is at his throat now but Amaguq has the chance he needs, a moment of distraction. Patience is a virtue. He reaches, touches with his soul, seeks Charlie's inner being. There is very little left, a few tendrils of the man that was. And even as that man was so little there was still enough. Amaguq's eyes flared the brightest white, and with them flared the shreds of Charlie's true soul. The demon screamed in anger and anguish, pain tearing through the mana of his being, the rent in his centre so unexpected and weakening. Marks is thrown to the side, his energy spent and his body weak and ragged. As his physical form pulls back to reveal a more bianthropic semblance Jo rushes over to him. She kisses him deeply and he looks fondly into her eyes. Demon, both alive and dying attempt to crawl for any exit available, the chittering outside also vanishing into the distance. There is a deep strain on the beast Charlie's face, an inner battle of massive proportions. Suddenly there is a horrendous cracking, and as the dog watches the wolfs face crumbles and cracks, one side crunching inwards as if the human inside sought to regain its own life once more. Charlie fought. For the first time in his life, he fought. Fractions of rib and skull pull inwards, tearing

369

pain through the creature as human fights demon in internal yet physical struggle. Fire stretched up to the ceiling on all sides, forgotten behind and around the battle. A burning roof timber crashed to the floor just feet from Marks and his eyes flicked to his companions. He was so close to ending all of this, that the beast was not dead concerned him. That he might lose his love again and to fire terrified him.

"We need to go, quickly." Snapped Marks as Peter and James pelted down the stairs, recovered from the aerial rescue. "Follow me." As they left Jo caught his hand and pulled him into her, she smiled and kissed him gently. The fire from the rogue wolfs eyes seemed to frame them for an instant, and as he finally fell to his knees Jo's soul was no-one but the dogs.

Epilogue

In the dim light of dawn Charlie's face contorted. It was raining hard, and had been for a number of hours. In his minds eye a wolf pads through the undergrowth, the weather is similarly not good here, but somehow the sky is a deep burnt umber rather than purple or grey as would be expected. There is a girl in the distance, a woman. It is an inconsistency, it can't be upheld.

Suddenly there is a flash of lightning, followed by a roll of thunder. The wolf howls. The woman drops dead, her eyes white. The Sun may not be reborn dark, but who's to say that the sun will be reborn.

Pan out and up, look and see the panorama of space, the place that seems to be both in-between and present at the same time. Look and climb and feel the freedom as sun that was, has been, will never be ceases to exist. To have ever existed. That mist hugs the air and darkness steals the mind is evident. Earth hangs in the instant of death and rebirth, the moon frozen in collision with the African continent and surrounding seas. Great slabs of rock remain like islands frozen in the air, water cascading from their tree lined edges as a tidal wave of epic proportion folds in upon itself and hangs mid-between time and irremembrance. The earth itself forces one last attempt to hold onto that which was. The people now mill about with demons in the air, and although there is no sun in the sky, the remnants of light lie frozen in the

371

atmosphere, spreading an incandescent glow across the entire planet. There is no longer day, there is no longer night. There is *The Planet That Was*, frozen in the instant, forever still. And the people contained thereon condemned to remain alive. After a fashion.

Printed in Great Britain
by Amazon.co.uk, Ltd.,
Marston Gate.